Fortune Reigns

Clay Warrior Stories
Book #6

J. Clifton Slater

This is a work of fiction. Any resemblance to persons living or dead is purely coincidental. I am not a historian, although I do extensive research. For those who have studied the classical era and those with exceptional knowledge of the times, I apologize in advance for any errors.

The large events in this tale are from history, while the dialogue and action sequences are my inventions. Some of the elements in the command and control of the Legions are from reverse engineering the requirements necessary to carry a command from the General to a Legionary on the end of an assault line, fighting for his life. Hopefully, you'll see the logic to my methods.

I need to thank Hollis Jones who kept the story on track with her red pen. Without her, the project would have wondered far from my plan.

J. Clifton Slater
E-Mail: GalacticCouncilRealm@gmail.com
Website: www.JCliftonSlater.com

Fortune Reigns

Act 1

Fortune Reigns takes place when two Legions crossed the Strait and arrived in Messina. It marked the start of The First Punic War and the first time a Legion crossed a major body of water to fight. And it was almost a tragedy for the blossoming Roman Republic.

Welcome to 264 B.C.

Chapter 1 - Outside Messina's East Wall

The last blade rapped against the last shield sending a final sharp sound over the Legion positions. It carried beyond them and, a bowshot away, a detachment of Syracuse cavalrymen heard the report. The horsemen nodded in approval at the vicious strike.

"Step back. Set to re-engage. Keep it tight and make it hard," ordered the weapons instructor. "In case King Hiero the Second's men are deaf."

"We already know they're blind and stupid," the first shield holder observed as he braced. "Fine. I'm set."

"Don't discount Tyche's blessing," chided the Legionary standing in front of him.

"The Goddess is with us," the next man in the half squad suggested. "She may be Greek but, so far, her smile has brought us luck."

The five facing pairs of Legionnaires all nodded at the statement.

"Squad, about face. On my command, left pivot wheel right to face the enemy. Right pivot forward ten paces," Alerio Sisera ordered. "Execute!"

The left side swung around, the pivot watching out of the corner of his eye to be sure the shields were tight and the line straight. As their line circled, the right pivot directed his half of the squad forward. Within a few steps, the Syracuse horsemen could see the five Legionaries wheeling left would end up diagonally facing the other five. Smiling at the out of sync drill, they waited for the Legionaries to break ranks in order to run to get into position to engage.

Alerio waited until the left pivot's line was three steps from slamming into the back of the man on the end of the right pivot's line.

"Right pivot. About face, wheel left and advance," Alerio shouted. "Execute!"

The five turned about. As their line swung to face the converging line, they slammed gladii into the shields of the left pivot's line. As if a drum roll, the sounds of cascading strikes rolled down the five shields as the right pivot's Legionaries came online and met shield to shield with their adversaries.

"Left pivot. Advance," weapons instructor Sisera ordered.

After taking the hits, the left pivot's line shoved with their shields and, while drawing them back, hammered at the opposing shields. It was payback to their squad mates for the heavy initial strikes.

The horseman's joy at the busted drill vanished as they witnessed the precision of the Legionaries' field maneuvering.

"Step back two paces," Alerio called out. He marched between the lines of Legionaries and turned to face the third man on his left. "Do you owe him coins?"

Alerio jerked his thumb over his shoulder indicating the man behind the weapons instructor.

"No, Lance Corporal," the Legionary replied.

"Are you sweet on him?"

"No."

"Then why did you give him a love tap with your shield?" demanded Alerio.

2

"This is theater for the Syracusans," exclaimed the Legionary. "I didn't think it would matter."

Lance Corporal Sisera turned around and took the big infantry shield from the man behind him.

"Brace!" he ordered as he spun around to face the offending Legionary.

Without pausing, the weapons instructor slammed the borrowed shield forward. Driving with his legs, Alerio forced the Legionary back until the man tripped and fell. The shield rose and pounded the downed Legionary's shield three times. With each hit, the man's shield bounced off his chest, driving air from his lungs while his back crushed into the dirt and rocks. Although protected by his armor, the emotion of hopelessness from the overwhelming violence, the inability to catch his breath and the claustrophobic feeling of being smothered by his own shield, caused the Legionary to panic. He raised his gladius.

Alerio swiped the blade aside with the shield and delivered a fourth blow. This time, he tilted the shield so the reinforced metal band at the top cracked on the Legionary's helmet. Dazed, the Legionary dropped his gladius and lay still.

"You may be playing a part," Alerio said standing and handing the shield back to its owner. "But going soft on the man in front of you cheats him out of realistic training. Do you think the seven thousand Syracusans camped by the river will go easy on him? Or gently tap his shield in battle? No, they will not. You train like you fight. Hard. Is that clear to everyone?"

While the nine erect Legionaries and the prone one all nodded their understanding, over the Legion lines, the cavalrymen broke out in laughter. It wasn't the sight of a Republic Legionary being treated cruelly and publicly debased causing the humorous response. It was relief at not being on the receiving end of the abuse.

"Get him up and form two ranks," Alerio instructed.

Before the squad had fully formed up, a runner came through the city gates heading directly for them.

"Lance Corporal Sisera. Tribune Gaius Claudius requests your presence post haste," the messenger announced as he slid to a stop. "He's at the Citadel."

"Orders received," Alerio assured the runner before facing the Legionaries. "I thank you for allowing me to drill you today. Squad Leader, the training session is complete and the unit is yours. Nice job everyone."

"Squad, attention to orders," the squad leader directed as he stepped from the ranks. The Legionaries stood in two rows facing him. "Right face. Forward march."

Alerio fell in behind the unit as it moved towards Messina. Once through the gate and out of sight of the Syracusan cavalrymen, the squad broke ranks and ran for the city's wall. There, hidden behind the rock and clay structure, they rested for a moment around water buckets. After drinking, the Legionaries picked up javelins, reformed with different sized Legionaries at the front, and marched back through the gates.

To the enemy horsemen, it appeared to be a different squad coming from the city of Messina. As the Legion detachment did during the day, they rotated squads off the defensive line for training or to rest in the city. It happened so often, the Syracusans couldn't get an accurate count of the city's defenders. As the Legionary had observed, the Goddess Tyche was indeed smiling on the outnumbered forces of the Republic.

***

"Tribune Claudius. You wanted to see me, sir?" asked Alerio as he jogged to the crest of the hill. He removed his helmet and tucked it under his arm before rendering a cross chest salute with the other.

The Tribune and commander of the small contingent of Legionaries stood with a rolled-up tube of leather held up to his

4

eye gazing off to his right. Behind him, the Citadel blocked the view of the foothills north of Messina.

"Lance Corporal Sisera. With all the training you're doing and the number of times you train the same squads, I'll soon have an exhausted weapons instructor on my hands. Or the best-trained units in all the Republic," Gaius Claudius stated. He hadn't taken the tube from his eye. "Over the last three days, I've observed an odd behavior."

Thinking the behavior was his, Alerio squared his shoulders.

"Sir, if I am doing something unprofessional, please advise me," he offered. "I'll correct my behavior immediately."

Gaius Claudius lowered the tube and looked at the Lance Corporal. Although his face was lined from the stress of endless training and caked with dust and sweat, Alerio's eyes sparkled. It was the young weapons instructor's idea to add drills to the constant rotation of the same squads. So far, the ruse worked, it kept Hiero ignorant of the Republic's strength and leery of sending his troops against Messina.

"Have you done something unprofessional?" quizzed the Tribune.

"Not that I'm aware of, sir," replied Alerio.

"Then don't. Here. Take a look at the King's tent. It's the one with the streamers," Gaius said as he handed the leather tube to the Lance Corporal.

Everyone knew Tribune Claudius was beloved by the Goddess Theia and could see details in the distance. Alerio took the tube and looked at the enemy's camp. It took several heartbeats before a blurry image of the King's tent centered in the tube.

"I see it but it's fuzzy, sir," reported Alerio.

"To the left are five horses. Can you see them?" asked Gaius. "There's an officer with the horses."

Alerio saw a blotch that possibly could be horses.

"Sorry, sir. I can't make them out," he admitted. "Can I ask what's so odd about horses at the King's tent?"

"They come and, troops go in. This one troop always leaves an officer with the horses," explained the Tribune. "He never goes in the tent. Tribune Velius told me you were in Syracuse recently. I wondered if you had any idea what they're doing."

"Does the officer slump against the horses as if he drank too much wine last night?" inquired Alerio as he thought back to his mission in Syracuse for the old spymaster.

"You think they're hiding a drunken officer from King Hiero?" Gaius offered. He took the tube and raised it to his eye. "It's the same man and he is leaning against the flank of a horse. So, the King frowns on intoxicated officers. Interesting. I wonder if we could bribe him with wine and the others to make them desert?"

"Not him, sir. He is a cavalry officer and a messenger for the Syracusan signal corps," described Alerio.

"Ah, the mounted troops are carrying the King's orders," Gaius said breaking in before the Lance Corporal could finish. "At least I know what they are. But you said him, although you can't see the man or the horses. And you somehow recognized the signal corps. Explain yourself, Lance Corporal."

"It's not the seeing, sir. It's them leaving him outside the tent. The man is Macario Hicetus, a cavalry officer assigned to the signal corps. His father was a tyrant of Syracuse," Alerio informed the Tribune. Claudius lowered the tube and focused on the Lance Corporal. "Even though he was born after his father was replaced by Hiero, the King's advisers will not allow Macario in the King's presence. They fear he would assassinate the King, call men loyal to his father to his side and claim the title."

"Would he do that?" questioned Tribune Claudius. "Could he become the King of Syracuse?"

"No, sir. All he wants is enough glory so his mother is accepted in wealthy social circles," explained Alerio. "Macario Hicetus prefers drinking and gambling to politics."

"Not an unheard-of trait for noble sons," Gaius stated. "How is your militia doing on the docks?"

"I believe I've convinced the Sons of Mars of the benefit of staying awake while on duty, sir," reported Alerio.

"I bet you have based on your training techniques," Gaius said with a chuckle. "If you have nothing to add, you are dismissed Lance Corporal Sisera."

"Thank you, sir. I should have another squad pulled off the line for training," Alerio replied. He saluted before turning and jogging down the hill.

Tribune Claudius watched until Alerio vanished behind a building. Then he began to lift the leather tube and continue his surveillance of King Hiero's encampment. But the rapid clip, clop of a horse coming around a building drew his attention to the streets below.

One of the skirmishers who survived the fighting to capture Messina came into view. He reined in a sweat covered horse and jumped from the exhausted animal's back. At an all-out sprint, he dashed up the hill.

"Sir. To the north, we've sighted a force advancing on Messina," the man blew out air before inhaling deeply. "Looks to be Qart Hadasht mercenaries."

"How far out?" demanded the Tribune.

"Half a day's march, sir," the Legionary replied. "My Corporal figures they'll camp on the other side of the ridges."

Gaius tapped the leather tube against his thigh and glanced at the clear sky.

"Rest your animal, then get back to your unit," instructed the Tribune. "Give my compliments to your Velites. Dismissed."

"Yes, sir," the skirmisher replied. He saluted, turned about and trudged back down the hill.

Gaius didn't watch the man, the city or look to the west. He lifted his head and watched clouds move across the sky as he pondered the situation. With two armies flanking Messina, the Tribune was out of tricks. After a short battle, either army could take the city. If they attacked at the same time, it wouldn't even be a battle, but more of a slaughter of his remaining five hundred heavy and light infantrymen. Defeat would result in the loss of the Republic's tenuous foothold on Sicilia and the safe landing site for Consul Appease Clodus Caudex's Legions.

Taking Messina from the Qart Hadasht garrison had required street to street fighting. Holding it against the advance force from Syracuse, involved combat along flexing battle lines. Both engagements offered annihilation or thin victories. Thankfully, his detachment, with help from the Sons of Mars, proved victorious.

When he finally lowered his head, he peered across the city to the harbor and beyond to the blue waters of the Messina Strait.

"Where are you Consul Caudex?" he whispered to himself. "We've bled for this ugly piece of real estate but have little left to shed. Come claim your success. Or remember us in tales told during feasts at Villas around the Capital."

Shaking off the bleak thoughts, the Tribune twisted his torso and raised an arm towards the Citadel. Three fingers popped from his fist and in response, three Legionaries ran from the shade of the building.

One was a quartermaster Lance Corporal, another a scribe, and the third a medic. All were initially assigned to Gaius' headquarter staff but, due to the shortage of men, had been pressed into messenger duty.

"I need Senior Centurion Valerian, First Sergeant Brictius, and First Sergeant Gerontius here, now," Senior Tribune Gaius Claudius instructed the three runners. "I don't care if they're in the middle of the best merda of their life, I want them here. Go."

It came as a shock to hear the very proper Tribune swear like a common citizen. At the bottom of Citadel Hill, two charged into Messina while the third ran for the east wall. All three were chuckling at the language as they raced to find the command staff of the detachment.

Chapter 2 - Preparing for the Slaughter

Not surprising, Gaius Claudius' command staff arrived by age. His First Sergeant Brictius appeared first followed by Senior Centurion Valerian. Last to climb the hill was the Southern Legion's First Sergeant Gerontius. The tough old campaigner wasn't even breathing hard although he hobbled a little after the jog up the incline.

"We have a force of Qart Hadasht mercenaries coming from the west and from over there," Gaius announced pointing to the Syracusan army to the east. "We'll split our heavy infantry. First Optio Gerontius, coordinate with the Centurions at the eastern defensives. I believe you have two left alive. Are they going to be a problem or should I have Senior Centurion Valerian speak to them?"

"They're good line officers. Young and no longer inexperienced," Gerontius replied. "I've been working with them and we get along fine, sir."

"First Sergeant Brictius. You'll have the other two officers," Gaius stated. "Any issues?"

"No, sir. We may be down to four Centurions and six and a half Centuries but our Legionaries are tough, well trained, and the surviving officers are battle tested. We'll hold the east and the west, sir."

"I'm going to ask Captain Creon for units of Sons to fill out our lines," explained the Senior Tribune. "As we learned, they're good in a melee but aren't disciplined. Disperse them as you see fit."

9

The three men acknowledged the Tribune's directions with salutes.

"Our strategy from here on is violence at points of contact," Gaius directed. "Those mounted troops to the east, I want them pushed back. Any probe must be dealt with by overwhelming force. I want both armies to suffer when they try to feel us out. It may only be a bloody nose but it'll make them think before committing. Preferably, any of their patrols will vanish."

The three smiled at the orders. Usually, they settled for chasing off enemy patrols, not being willing to weaken their defensive line by releasing squads to battle small enemy units.

"What about me, sir?" inquired Valerian.

"You, Senior Centurion, are moving our command post and the medical treatment area to the center of town," Gaius informed him. "Being up here is useless. There are no reserves to direct and not enough Centuries to adjust."

"Sorry you'll have to give up your observation post," Valerian expressed the feelings of the three commanders. "I'll have the staff move your field desk and bed to the new command post."

"Don't bother, I won't need them where I'll be," Gaius said.

"Where will you be, sir?" the Senior Centurion inquired.

"At dusk, I'm going to have a look at the Qart Hadasht force," advised the Tribune. "You are in command while I'm gone."

"Let me assign you two heavy infantry squads," offered Valerian.

"No. We don't have two spare squads to protect a foolhardy Tribune," Gaius explained. "I'll take two Legionaries as escorts. I may be crazy but I'm not stupid."

"I'd recommend Lance Corporal Sisera, sir," suggested First Sergeant Gerontius.

"No. I need him herding the Sons of Mars guarding the harbor," replied the Tribune. "Two Legionaries should be enough. I'm thinking skirmishers. They are quieter than infantrymen."

"How close are you planning to get, sir?" questioned First Sergeant Brictius.

"Close enough to smell the Qart Hadasht cookfires and count the fleas on the men assigned to sentry duty."

***

Gaius Claudius caught up to Ferox Creon as the leader of the Sons of Mars was preparing to board his bireme.

"Captain. A word?" Gaius called out.

"Senior Tribune. What brings you to the harbor?" inquired Ferox. He walked from the ramp, crossed the sand and joined Gaius on the wooden dock. "As you can see, I have business elsewhere."

"Pirate business, I would guess," Gaius stated.

"Not today. I'm going to conference with some of the eastern leaders along the Republic's coast."

"Looking for sanctuary?" the Tribune suggested. "Before you go. I need some of your Sons on our defensive lines."

"Sanctuary, yes. For the Sons of Mars if the situation gets any more challenging," Ferox remarked. "So, again you need us to protect your Legionaries. What's in it for the Sons."

"If I survive, a quarter of your weight in coins and precious metals," promised Gaius.

"And if you don't survive the Qart Hadasht and the Syracuse armies?" question Ferox.

"You bury your dead along with my body," replied Gaius. "At least I won't be asking for any more favors."

"That alone might be worth a few Sons," Ferox teased. Then the pirate Captain waved another man over. Milon Frigian in his easy gait strolled from a group of Sons to his Captain. "Milon. Find Gallus Silenus and have him assign two boat crews to the northern defensives. Our protectors seem to need bodyguards."

Gaius jerked at the description but held his tongue.

"I'll take my crew to the east," volunteered Milon. "I'd like another shot at King Hiero's lads."

"No. I want you here guarding the docks and keeping them open," explained Ferox as he gazed at Gaius. "If the Legion breaks, you're to get as many Sons and their wives out as possible. I'm depending on you for that."

"I understand, Captain Creon," Milon said before sauntering away.

"Does that meet your requirements, Tribune?" Ferox inquired.

"Yes, it does," Gaius answered. "Have a safe voyage, Captain Creon."

"I know you don't mean it, but thank you," Ferox added. Then he smacked a hand to his forehead. "That reminds me. I need extra blocks of cheese."

"For trading?" asked Gaius.

"No Tribune. To get my weight up," Ferox stated with a laugh.

***

While the leader of the Sons and the Senior Tribune talked, First Sergeants Gerontius and Brictius walked the defensive line. They stopped at each squad and spoke briefly to the Legionaries. At the positions with Centurions, they stayed a little longer before moving to the next squad. At the last defensive position, they found Lance Corporal Sisera sharing in the squad's afternoon meal.

"I thought you'd be tired of the weapons instructor's company by now," Brictius suggested.

"Alerio's not a bad Legionary when not being a cūlus," the squad leader replied.

"And when is that?" inquired Gerontius.

"When he's not beating one of us with his gladius or a shield," a squad member answered.

"And making us better fighters," another said with pride.

Alerio Sisera was leaning hard against a pile of dirt that seemed to be holding him up. The exhausted weapons instructor didn't say anything. All of his concentration was on a bowl of Legion stew he was wolfing down.

"We have Qart Hadasht units moving in from the north," Brictius explained. "Every squad is pulling back through the gates. Only half will come back through. Hopefully, the Syracusans will lose count. The other half is moving beyond the north wall to dig in."

"Oh, and Tribune Claudius wants those cavalrymen pushed back during the maneuver," added Gerontius.

Alerio brightened up. He finished the stew quickly, wiped the bowl and slid it into a pouch.

"For three days, the horsemen have enjoyed our drilling like it's entertainment. They laugh, drink wine, and make comments while we sweat and hurt," the Lance Corporal said. Around him, the squad grumbled their agreement. "I'd like the opportunity to bring a little pain and panic to them for a change."

"Squad leader, you want some of this?" asked Gerontius.

"My leg still hurts from Sisera correcting my stance," the Lance Corporal related. His squad members all nodded at the memory. "But what hurt worse was those donkey riders laughing. Want some of that? In short, First Sergeant, yes!"

"Sounds like you have a squad. What else do you need?" Brictius asked the weapons instructor.

"When the squads start moving, have them drop extra javelins and five bows strung with open bundles of arrows in the center position," Alerio requested. Then he glanced around the squad. "What say we run some shield and swords drills to get warmed up."

13

A collective groan came from the Legionaries but they were also grinning.

***

Four squads backed out of their defensive positions and marched along the back side of the detachment's defensive line. At the center, before turning towards the gates, they dropped bows and javelins. As they turned for the gates, the squads called out barbs at the squad being drilled by the weapons instructor.

Two more squads followed the routine and dropped arrows and javelins. One squad also left a Legionary behind the mound of dirt. While his squad mates jested with the squad drilling, he strung the bows and placed javelins in neat stacks of seven. Then he rolled onto his back, put his hands behind his helmet and watched the shields smash together while Lance Corporal Sisera screamed out corrections.

Across the open ground, five Syracusan cavalrymen threw one leg across their horse's necks and lifted wineskins. To their pleasure, the afternoon circus was beginning.

Eight squads pulled back, converged on the center and, in messy columns, the eighty Legionaries began marching to the gates.

"Sheath your gladii and drop your shields," instructed Sisera. "Stay low and work your way to the weapons."

In the mass of infantry shields, armor, and bobbing helmets, Alerio and the ten-man squad filtered unseen to the center position.

"Fifteen paces and release," he instructed. "Once you're done, get back to the line. There are more cavalrymen on the flanks and you don't want to be caught in the open without your shield."

The horsemen lost sight of the drilling squad in the crowd. Sitting taller on their mounts, they attempted to peer beyond the helmets and retreating backs. Then they caught sight of ten

14

infantry shields laying on the ground. Before the question of where did the Legionaries go could be voiced, they had the answer.

The squad ducked behind the defensive mound and began selecting their weapons. Most got a chuckle when the weapons instructor shoved six javelins in his sword belt and snatched up two more, one in each hand.

"Attack, attack," Alerio yelled as he placed a foot on top of the mound and vaulted to the top.

With him leading the charge, the rest of the squad and the extra Legionary jumped up and followed. While they picked targets, Lance Corporal Sisera continued to run. At fifteen paces, he launched both javelins at the same time. Before the bowmen notched and let fly, Alerio had two more javelins in his hands. By the time the others released, Alerio's shafts jutted from two of the horsemen. They toppled to the ground as did another rider with three arrows in his chest.

The last two cavalrymen reined their horses around causing one of Alerio's javelins to go wide. With so many arrows and shafts in the air, no one knew who took down the fifth horsemen.

"Back. Back to the line," shouted the squad leader.

Alerio glanced from side to side checking on the Legionaries. Then he looked beyond them and saw cavalry troops bearing down on their location.

"Run," he ordered as he turned and began to trot after the retreating Legionaries.

But two Legionaries spun in the same direction and collided. Struggling to untangle their javelins, they tripped and fell. With nine of the assault force almost back to the defensive line, Alerio cut at an angle and raced back to the fallen men.

He pulled two javelins and stood over them while they scrambled to their feet.

"Go," he ordered as four galloping horses converged on the weapons instructor.

The squads coming back through the gates let out a roar. The ones still heading towards the wall turned their heads to see what was causing the commotion.

The weapons instructor, they all knew intimately from knots and bruises, stood as a target for Syracusan cavalrymen. His sacrifice allowed the two clumsy Legionaries time to make it safely out of range of the lances.

Alerio stood with his arms raised and his hands gripping javelins. Hooves thundered as the sharp points of lances came at him from the sides. With the iron tips three heartbeats from his flanks, Alerio launched his javelins to the left and right. Without waiting to see if they hit the targets, he hopped back, drew two more and tripped, falling onto his back. A pair of riderless horses crossed in front of him.

He jumped to his feet, saw two more riders coming at him and, flipped back and over landing on his face. Alerio raised up searching for the lance tips of the last two horsemen. But they never reached him. The cavalrymen were riding away being chased by flights of arrows from five angry Legionaries with bows.

One of the archers stopped beside Alerio. While still notching and firing arrows, he said out of the side of his mouth.

"A weapons instructor once told me never stand between charging cavalrymen," the Legionary exclaimed.

"Oh, and who was that?" asked Alerio as he pushed off the ground and began brushing the dirt off his armor.

"You, Lance Corporal Sisera," he responded. "It was you on the first day of drills. Just before you hit me with the flat of your blade."

"Did it hurt?" inquired Alerio.

"It did hurt but, I remembered the lesson."

"Good," Alerio commented as he walked towards the defensive line.

***

One hundred of the Legionaries destined for the north wall made another circuit to the east defenses before marching back into the city. In the center of Messina, they lined up at a supply wagon and drew rations for their squads. At another wagon, they were handed shovels and picks.

"The infantryman's best friend," someone stated as he slung the shovel onto a shoulder.

"I thought it was his shield?" another ventured.

"No, it's his gladius," another added.

"What do you say, weapons instructor," the first man asked.

Alerio handed out another shovel and yawned. After the charge that put the cavalry in disarray and prevented the Syracusans from getting a clear picture of what the Legion was doing, First Sergeant Gerontius ordered Alerio to the supply depot.

"Your best friend is the Legionary on your right covering your boney backside with his shield," suggested Alerio. "Now, move along so another man can have a girlfriend."

"Did you hear that?" asked a Legionary. "Lance Corporal Sisera said the shovel is your new girlfriend."

"It fits," another replied. "It works me as hard as my wife does back home on the farm."

"Your wife works you hard so you're too dēfutūta to chase her around the bedroom," another called out.

"Say, do you know my wife?"

"No, but I know pick and shovel work," commented another. "And just like a wife with a scroll filled with chores, it'll leave you wanting nothing but a peaceful night's rest at the end of a hard day."

"You can discuss women while you dig," shouted First Sergeant Brictius as he stormed from a tent. "I need a trench and fortifications dug before nightfall. Now move along or I won't be around to tuck you in tonight."

"Promises, promises," the last Legionary in line mumbled as Alerio handed him a shovel.

"Lance Corporal Sisera. I know you've got the harbor detail and the Sons of Mars to contend with," advised the First Sergeant. "But try to get some sleep. That stunt with the horsemen had all the markings of being planned by a sleep-deprived Tribune."

"Did someone call me?" Gaius Claudius asked as he came out of the tent.

"No sir, the First Sergeant and I were just discussing your need to keep the guards at the harbor alert," Alerio lied.

"Absolutely. Now First Sergeant, let's go review our defenses," Senior Tribune Claudius ordered. "And I need to speak with the skirmisher Sergeant."

"Yes sir," Brictius replied. "After you, Tribune."

Alerio leaned against the wagon's side and yawned again before pushing back and heading for Messina harbor. He didn't remember the trip, but suddenly he was standing in front of Milon Frigian.

"Whoa there, Legionary," Milon said taking Alerio by the shoulders and leading him across the boulevard from the barricade. "I think you, Captain Sisera, need to make a sacrifice to Hypnos and plead for his blessing."

"Sleep yes, but I need to clean my gear first," Alerio replied. They circled an extra wagon that wasn't needed to create the barrier between the harbor and Messina.

"There's one of my tunics hanging on the wall," Milton pointed out. "It's freshly washed and should be dry by now. You're just across from the warehouses if we need you."

"Thank you. Set the guards," Alerio ordered as he began tugging off his gladius belt and armor. "Have someone wake me for the last watch, or..."

"Or if things get hot, I know. Now sleep Captain Sisera," Milton advised using Alerio's honorary title. The Sons of Mars had made him a Captain for his fighting and leadership in defending Messina and preventing the massacre of the Sons by Hiero's advance force.

Once the armor and helmet were cleaned and the blade sharpened, weapons instructor, Lance Corporal Alerio Sisera fell onto the stack of blankets. He didn't fall directly under Hypnos' spell but lay awake. For three days, from dawn to dusk, he was challenged and had challenged infantrymen to be their best. As with anyone who has been in combat for an extended period, his muscles jerked as if unsure if the battle had ended and his body allowed to relax. Eventually, the exhaustion won and he fell asleep.

***

As the sun settled over the mountains and darkness fell, Senior Tribune Gaius Claudius followed two skirmishers along the Legion trench. At the end where an unclimbable rise blocked the way, they crossed the footfall trench and slid down the slope into a crop of trees. From there, they circled to a notch in the next rise and dropped down a slight incline. The land flattened and became mushy. They traveled long enough for the moon to rise.

The Tribune at first was confused by the dark shapes of marsh grasses and trees with roots making the footing difficult. At one point, he veered off into waist deep water. But the Veles, who seemed to be able to see in the dark, reached out and placed his hand on one of their shoulders. After that mishap, he was guided across the muddy but firm ground. They slogged further into the night. He was damp, tired and confused by the sameness of the marsh grass clumps. It came as a surprise when

19

the skirmisher's shoulder lowered and Gaius allowed himself to sink down onto one knee.

"To your right, sir," one of them whispered. "You can see their cookfires."

"How many?" inquired the Tribune.

"Don't know, sir," the skirmisher admitted. "I can't count beyond my fingers and toes."

"How many sets of fingers and toes?" coached Gaius.

"What?" the man asked.

"Abstract mathematical concept, forget it," the Senior Tribune mumbled. "Get me close enough to get a count."

"We'll need to crawl, sir," the Legionary informed him. "And stay silent. Their sentries are just at the edge of the marsh."

"I understand. Let's go," urged Gaius.

They moved slowly between clumps of marsh grass and small trees until the skirmishers dropped to their bellies. Then they eased forward on the wet ground. At the edge of the marsh, the land firmed and opened as if a flat black sea. Moonlight reflected off a short defensive wall that extended from the swamp to the waters of Messina Strait. From behind a thick shrub, Tribune Claudius raised up, looked over the wall and began counting the flickering fires.

Gaius Claudius reached five hundred sixty fires and estimated at least five thousand six hundred Qart Hadasht troops. With more rows still to be counted, one of the Velites put both hands on his shoulders and forced him to the damp earth.

"I was…" the Tribune started to say when a hand clamped over his mouth.

"Listen," the man whispered in Gaius' ear.

From among the fires, the rattle of armor and the clink of weapons shifting around bodies carried to the brush. Then, the voice of a commander called out in a language the Tribune didn't understand. He didn't need to know what the man said because the tone was no different than a Centurion ordering his Century to fall into formation. Soon another voice in a different language, but with the same tone, called out.

Boots and sandals crushing tall grass and weeds marched by and a skirmisher pressed on Gaius' back. He understood and laid still. Once the units passed, he expected to crawl away from the brush and the enemy camp. But more voices approached. These speaking Greek in a conversational tone.

"It's just a probe by a couple of our companies," a voice whined. "There's no need for you, General, to be out here in the night. Besides, King Hiero's note stated he would send a royal messenger to announce his attack."

"And because of a King, I'm to sit in my tent, sipping wine and talking philosophy?" the General demanded. "While my men throw their lives away on the swords of the Republic's Legionaries? You can go. I don't believe there will be much call for a diplomat tonight. Unless you'd like the Captain to lend you his sword and you can follow our men into combat."

"General. I certainly didn't mean to infer that your presence didn't bolster the men's morale," nasally voice insisted. "I am, after all, a member of the expedition's command staff. And, as is right and just, I'll stay with you."

"Fine but keep your comments pertinent to the mission," scolded the General. "We will test the strength of the Legion for ourselves before lounging around awaiting word from Hiero."

Tribune Claudius counted six more besides the General and the diplomat. Plus, other men had kicked brush out of the way as they entered the marsh to his right and left. Possibly the General's security force. With no way to escape, the Tribune and his two light infantrymen rested on the damp grass and listened to the Greek part of the conversation. The other members of the Qart Hadasht staff spoke in the Phoenician and Gaius could only guess at the meaning of their words.

Chapter 3 – First Blood of the First Punic War

The dark shapes of five large Corbita freighters rowed into Messina harbor. Before the Sons on sentry duty could sound an alert, three triremes scratched along the pier and deposited armored men on the dock. On the half-moon sands of the harbor, the transports beached and more men in armor leaped over the sides, dropped to the sand and raced for the town.

As Captain Sisera had directed, the last guards off the docks paused between the warehouses, snatched scoops of charcoal from fire amphorae and lit lanterns. This served two purposes. It put light on the assaulters while keeping the Sons at the barricades in shadows. It makes you less of a target for spears and arrows, Captain Sisera explained. And, the lanterns served to alert the commanders of each alleyway to the danger.

"Defend the barricades," Captain Milon Frigian said to the oarsmen close to him. He walked among his sleeping crew and kicked those not moving into motion. "Wake up. We've invaders on the docks."

Almost silently, the one hundred and twenty oarsmen of his bireme grabbed spears, swords, and shields. Soon the overturned wagons at each warehouse passageway bristled with iron points. No one remembered to wake Alerio Sisera.

"What is this?" demanded a voice from behind the ranks of Legionaries standing between the walls of the warehouse.

"It's a blockade as any fool can see," Milon Frigian shouted back.

"And who are you?" inquired the voice with a sharp tone.

From the docks behind the man, the rattle of shields rapping against armor announced the arrival of the Legionaries from the transports.

"Captain Milon Frigian, commander of the docks," Milton boasted. "Defender of the harbor, proud Son of Mars, and the key to the city of Messina."

"If you don't lay down your arms and open the barriers," threatened the voice. "I'm going to smash it down and put all of you up on the wood."

"That's not a very enticing proposition. I don't fancy my crew or me being crucified for doing our duty," replied Milon. "So, I can inform my harbor captain, who should I say has come knocking at our door?"

"I am Tribune Maris Eutropius of Caudex Legion," the voice replied. "Now, surrender your arms and open the barricade in the name of Consul General Appease Clodus Caudex, the Senate and the citizens of the Republic."

"Why didn't you say that in the first place," Milon stated. "Hold your mentula while I have the lads untie the ropes."

"No more delays, move the wagons," commanded Tribune Eutropius. "Pass the word. First ranks, forward. Remove the obstacles."

Heavy hemp ropes bound the wagons together and crewmen began to unknot the ends. The lines were valuable and there was no way the sailors would cut the hemp. Just as the Legion's leading rank reached the wagons, the last knot came free.

"Sons of Mars, back up and let the cūlus Tribune and his lads do the work," directed Milon.

The Legionaries shoved the wagons forward and once in the center of the boulevard, they angled them off to the sides. With a final shove, they flipped the wagons over. Alerio woke at the crash of sideboards smashing on the road. He was groggy but accustomed to the Sons' noisy ways. Stretching his back, the Legionary remained in a half dream state until a voice shouted.

"Frigian, show yourself. Hold that man."

Then the unmistakable sound of a gladius being drawn reached Alerio. When Milon Frigian cried out in pain, Lance Corporal Sisera went directly from sleep to battle mode. In one motion, he grabbed his gladius and vaulted the wagon. In the shadows of the moonlight and a few lanterns, everyone was a silhouette. But he could make out two men holding a sagging Milon Frigian.

"Who is the fool now, pirate?" a tall man holding a gladius sneered.

Alerio sprinted across the boulevard and slammed his shoulder into the tall man's back. The man bent backward and the Legionary used him as a battering ram to shove aside one of the men holding Milon. Releasing the two men, he jumped across the sagging Sons' Captain and kicked the other man off Frigian.

"Get the Captain behind our lines," Alerio shouted as he spun in an arc holding out the gladius to defend Milon. "Form ranks."

Five sailors ran to their captain and pulled him into the crowd of Sons. Alerio followed. The entire episode lasted five heartbeats and none of the newly arrived Legionaries had a chance to respond. Then the raggedly dressed and scruffy pirates snapped into ordered ranks, raised and locked shields. Every shield had a spear or javelin thrust over the top edge with the iron tip held solid and ready for an attack.

Over half the Legion was composed of new recruits. Recruiters from Caudex Legion drew them from farms and small towns around the Republic. After a shortened version of training to test for strength, fitness, and special talents, they were issued equipment and weapons. On the long march from the Capital to the docks at Gioia Tauro, the experienced Legionaries drilled the new men in squad tactics and shield work. While they had improved, they were untested and unbloodied. The display by the Sons of Mars shocked the new and the experienced Legionaries.

If the nine hundred sixty infantrymen of the first maniple had been at the boulevard, Alerio and the Sons probably would be corpses on the street. But the Centurions for the twelve most experienced Centuries, after seeing no resistance beyond the initial confusion, marched their Centuries into Messina. Most of the Centuries from the second and third maniples crossed at the other end of the boulevard and far away from the standoff.

The only experienced unit in the area was the squad assigned to protect Tribune Maris Eutropius during the march and the sea voyage. Two of them had held Milon Frigian. The other eight had their backs to the Tribune making a half circle to keep the flow of arriving Legionaries back, giving the Tribune room to discipline the pirate. Out of position, they turned in time to see the staff officer they were assigned to protect launched into their squad leader. The man assaulting the Tribune and the wounded pirate disappeared behind a solid wall of shields.

"Attack," Eutropius screamed as he picked himself off the ground. "Attack. Show no mercy."

In a battle, there were many people shouting orders. The new Legionaries, through rough lessons, learned to respond only to their Centurion, NCOs, squad leaders and pivot men. Plus, the Legion was shuffling from the beach, between the warehouses and moving into the dark city. None of the Centuries' Centurions, Optios, Tesserarii or squad leaders were paying attention as they passed. This left only one unit to respond to the order. Tribune Eutropius' protection squad formed in two ranks, drew their gladii and waited for their squad leader's directions.

Ten heavy infantrymen facing off against a wall of twenty-five shields four ranks deep gave the squad leader pause. Luckily, it drew the attention of one passing NCO.

The Tesserarius noticed the standoff and tapped the arm of his Sergeant.

"Optio, should we be involved with another of Tribune Eutropius' merda storms?" he asked.

The NCO turned his head and eyed the ten Legionaries across from the shield wall.

"I'm not sure, Corporal," then the Century's senior NCO called to his Centurion. "Sir, is that any of our business?"

"It shouldn't be," the officer said in exasperation. "But I guess it is. Sergeant, form the Century." Then the line officer glanced at the private walking beside him and ordered. "Roll out the colors."

As the officer and the private, who balanced a pole on his shoulder while reaching into a pouch, pushed through the lines of moving Legionaries, the Sergeant and the Corporal separated and began shouting.

"Caudex Legion, Requiem Division, Second Maniple, Tenth Century," they bellowed calling out the Century's designation. "Form on the colors."

Repeating the call, the NCO's pushed into the Legionaries coming from between the warehouses and crossing the boulevard. Soon, groups of Legionaries began assembling around their Centurion and the Century's colors.

"First Squad of the Tenth, set the assemble point facing the Sons of Mars," the officer ordered then added. "I hate fighting in the dark."

"Sir, should we wait on your Century?" asked the squad leader from Maris Eutropius' protection detail. "The Tribune wants us to go in now."

"Lance Corporal. Keep five of your squad on the Tribune for security," instructed the Centurion. "Assemble the other five at the back of my Century. When we advance, pull them out and go watch his back."

"Centurion. I ordered an attack," growled Tribune Eutropius as he stomped up to the line officer. "I expect results. Instant results."

"Nice stomp, Tribune," the Centurion remarked. "But the Legion stomps only with their right foot. You might try working on that."

"What are you talking about?"

"Tell you what, Senior Tribune. You have my permission to lead Tenth Century in the advance," the line officer offered. Then he turned to the protection squad leader. "I gave you orders. Follow them."

"Yes, sir and thank you," the Lance Corporal said before going back to his formation.

The Sergeant marched up with ten Legionaries in tow. They each carried two lanterns.

"Where do you want the light, sir?" inquired the Sergeant.

"Put the men with the lanterns at the head of our formation," the officer directed.

During the time the Centurion was orchestrating the elements, his eighty heavy infantrymen arrived, dropped their personal gear, pulled on helmets, removed leather covers from their shields and leaned javelins across their shoulders.

"Tesserarius, you have the First through Fourth squads on the left. Keep them tight," ordered the Centurion. "Sergeant, Five and up on the right."

"What about the lanterns?" inquired the Sergeant.

"The oil lamps?" asked the Centurion as if he had forgotten about them. "We're going to throw them at the pirates. Let's see how well they hold with the center of their formation burned out."

"Very good, Centurion. Tenth Century, standby," shouted the Sergeant.

Eighty hobnailed boots rose and thundered as they stomped the boulevard.

"Standing by, Sergeant," the Century replied.

"Sir, Tenth Century, Second Maniple is assembled and ready," the NCO stated.

Before the order came for the Tenth to advance came, a voice called from between the warehouses.

"Legion attention," the deep voice ordered. "General Appease Clodus Caudex, sitting Consul of the Republic and worthy citizen approaches."

Then the leading rank of Headquarters, First Century marched onto the boulevard and Legionaries not fast enough to move, or those blocked by others who delayed their movement were shoved out of the way.

In the center of a moving square strolled General Caudex. First Century was oversized with one hundred forty of the Legion's most experienced infantrymen. Its Centurion, Optio, and Tesserarius roamed the square keeping it parade ground tight.

"What is going on here, Tribune Eutropius?" demanded the General. When he stopped, First Century stopped as if it was a part of the Consul. "Have you located Tribune Claudius? Or have you been playing punishment Sergeant again?"

"General. This herd of ruffians failed to open the barricade," reported Maris Eutropius. "I was just about to teach them respect for you and the Legion."

Caudex ran his eyes over the Tenth Century and their officer.

"Centurion. Do they need a lesson in respect?" the General inquired.

"Sir. I wouldn't know," the officer replied. "But Tribune Eutropius ordered ten infantrymen to go against a formation of fixed shields and spears. I figured the squad could use some help."

A commotion at the center of the Sons of Mars' line drew everyone's attention. From between two shields, a man with a bloody bandage around his middle was helped into view by another man.

"A nice way to treat your harbor defense," Milon Frigian wheezed. "Next time, I'll let the Qart Hadasht have Messina."

"Harbor defense?" question General Caudex. "Where are the Legionaries?"

"North wall and south wall," reported Milon. "What's left of them. That is except for our harbor captain."

"And who is the harbor captain?" inquired the general.

Before Milon replied Maris Eutropius bobbed up and down and pointed at Alerio.

"That's the brigand who attacked me," Senior Tribune Eutropius blurted out while pointing at the man supporting Milon. "I want him whipped to death for assaulting me."

"Him?" asked Milon indicating Alerio with his hand. "That's our harbor captain. And the only Legion representative at the harbor."

"And who are you?" the General asked.

"Sir, Lance Corporal Alerio Sisera of the Southern Legion, Planning and Strategies section, Headquarters staff," Alerio reported. "And Captain in charge of harbor defenses."

"That's ridiculous," Maris Eutropius exploded. "No one would put a Lance Corporal in charge of anything. Imagine a common Legionary in charge of an important harbor like Messina. I propose that this man is a deserter and is hiding here shirking his responsibilities."

Tenth Century's Centurion held out a hand behind his back and raised a finger. He pointed it at Eutropius' security squad. They got the message and each put out a hand and steadied their squad leader. The Lance Corporal had jerked when Eutropius made the comment and the Centurion was afraid a fine young NCO would ruin his career by reminding the Tribune that a Lance Corporal was in charge of guarding the staff officer's life.

"Sir, I've worked with the Sons of Mars before. Tribune Claudius and Senior Centurion Valerian thought I should continue," Alerio said in his defense.

"Nevertheless, this man attacked me," accused Eutropius. "And he is out of uniform and asleep at his post. For those infractions, despite his claims, he deserves at least twenty lashes."

General Caudex stepped towards the Tenth Century and the First Century stepped with him. As they came forward, the two Centuries almost collided.

Getting ahead of the confirmation, the Centurion ordered, "Second Maniple, Tenth Century, left step five paces."

The Tenth moved away as an edge of the First took its place.

"Centurion. Put two lanterns next to the Lance Corporal," directed the General. When Alerio's face was lit, Appease Caudex let out an evil chuckle. "You're one of Spurius Maximus' protégés. I was going to let your infractions go unpunished. But seeing as Senator Maximus, who I believe needs a good whipping, isn't here, I'll let you stand in for him. Ten lashes to be delivered when the sun tops the eastern mountain. Be sure every Legionary, not on duty, witnesses the punishment."

"I'll see to it personally, General," promised Maris Eutropius.

"No, Senior Tribune. We have a punishment Sergeant for that," the General informed him. "Come with me. We need to find Tribune Claudius and see what other insanity he's allowed in Messina."

As the First Century and the General moved away, a Centurion of average height but with wide shoulders walked to Alerio.

"Lance Corporal Sisera. You are to be held until sunrise at which point the punishment will be administered," advised the

Centurion. "Will you come along or, do things need to get bloody."

"I'll come with you, sir," Alerio replied. He handed Milon Frigian's weight off to another of the Sons and requested. "Take care of my armor for me." ˌ

"I'll take care of it for you, Captain Sisera," the pirate assured him.

The Tenth Century was dismissed as the Sons of Mars broke formation.

"Who trained those pirates?" asked the Centurion as he and Alerio marched into Messina. "Their formation was excellent."

"And they can hold it against a phalanx," bragged Alerio. "At least until they get overwhelmed by the Hoplites."

"Hoplites can do that to inexperienced warriors," offered the officer. "Who trained them?"

"I did, sir," Alerio admitted.

"You?" the Centurion asked. "What's your name, again?"

"Alerio Sisera," the Lance Corporal replied. "And who are you, sir?"

"Sanctus Carnifex. I'm the weapons training officer for Caudex Legion," the Centurion answered.

Act 2

Chapter 4 – An Inauspicious Beginning

Senior Centurion Valerian paced around the supply wagons at the command post. Sometime after moonrise, two medics arrived with a wounded Legionary, passed the man off to the doctor and reported contact along the northern defensive line. Then, they sprinted back to First Sergeant Brictius. Since the message, Valerian had no further updates so, he paced.

From the east, a line of Legionaries marched up from the direction of the harbor. Valerian couldn't tell the unit as no flag hung from the polished flag pole. Helmets bounced at their sides, packs hung from their shoulders and covers protected their shields.

"Report," called out the Senior Centurion.

"Centurion Valerian. First Maniple, Requiem Division, Caudex Legion reporting in," a Centurion responded. "What's the situation?"

"We're in contact to the north," Valerian explained, waving the leading rank to an open field. "Stage your personal gear and form up in columns."

The first maniple's twelve Centurions smoothly directed the nine hundred sixty battle tested infantrymen into ranks on the field. After orders were passed, they dropped packs, leather bags, and covers fell to the ground in stacks. Then, the first maniple marched for the north wall.

Valerian stood with his hands on his hips staring into the dark street. Even after the units' standards vanished and the last rank disappeared in the black shadows, he maintained the pose. Relying on his years of experience, he strategized where to place the rest of the Legion as the units arrived. He no longer paced uselessly.

***

First Sergeant Brictius raced from one end of his position to the other side. There, runners from the young Centurion reported contact coming from that side. Then he pounded ground to the other side and received the same report from the other inexperienced line officer.

The Qart Hadasht's probes, so far, had been on the flanks. The center, where the First Sergeant expected an attack to be focused, remained quiet. With squads spread out and Sons of Mars' oarsmen filling in the gaps between the two hundred or so remaining Legionaries, he'd managed to cover the defensive line with two ranks. But two ranks could be breached in the night. His personal laps between placements were his attempt to find the breakthrough before it got out of control. As he ran back to the other side, he heard a familiar sound and stopped.

The unmistakable stomp of hobnailed boots came from the northern gates. Soon, ranks of men appeared in the moonlight.

"A Century to the left," First Sergeant Brictius ordered. Once the last rank of the eighty Legionaries came through the gates, he shouted again. "Next Century to the right."

Brictius' forces had just doubled with the arrival of the unknown Legion units. As more Centuries came through the gates, he realized his Centuries actually had been relieved.

"What's your unit?" he asked when a third Century came through the gates and a Centurion approached him.

"First Maniple, Third Century," the officer replied. "I hope you've left a few Qart Hadasht for the lads, First Sergeant."

"I'm going to pull my Centuries back," offered Brictius realizing the new units were the most hardened veterans in the Legion. And the veterans didn't play well with less experienced units. "My two Centurions are young and might not appreciate first maniple's gentle manner."

"You do that. We've got this under control," the Centurion assured him. "Give me a rundown on your defenses."

As they talked, two more Centuries came through the gates and split left and right followed by the rest of first maniple. Once the gates cleared, stretcher-bearers carried bloody Legionaries to the doctors at the command post. The first blood of the First Punic War poured onto the ground from wounded Legionaries.

***

"Where is Gaius Claudius?" Appease Caudex demanded. "I thought he'd have the courtesy to meet me on the dock."

The First Century of Legion HQ surrounded the command post except for three of its members. Two of them bracketed General Caudex while the third Legionary stood at his back.

"General. Senior Tribune Claudius left at dark to do a reconnaissance of the Qart Hadasht forces," explained Valerian.

"Why would a staff officer be doing the job of our scouts and raiders?" asked Caudex. By his tone, everyone knew it was a rhetorical question. "Just what is going on here? Pirates under the command of a Lance Corporal guarding the harbor. My Senior Tribune running around beyond Legion lines in the middle of the night. And an unguarded command post in the middle of a city. Where are your reserves?"

"This is unprofessional," added Tribune Maris Eutropius. "Clearly there is a lack of leadership from the command staff."

Senior Centurion Valerian bristled, snapped around and started to reply to the accusations. But the sounds of hobnailed boots shuffling on the street caused him to turn away.

First Sergeant Brictius came into view surrounded by walking wounded. Behind him, two bloody Centurions marched beside exhausted and dirty Legionaries.

"First Centurion. Move your line and let my Centuries through to the medical tent," growled Brictius. "We've just come from killing Qart Hadasht soldiers in the dark. I imagine my lads will have an easier time killing in this lantern light."

A ripple ran through the Legionaries behind the First Sergeant. Although half of them were injured, they responded to his words by picking up their feet and marching with their backs' straighter.

"Half-moon formation," ordered the officer and one side of the First Century shuffled inward opening a path to the medical tent.

"And what is my First Sergeant doing, commanding Centuries in battle?" complained the General.

"Sir, if we could move to the Citadel, I can give you a full report," suggested Valerian.

"An excellent idea," replied Caudex as he glanced at the supply wagons, the medical tent and the dark streets surrounding the command post. "And someone find Claudius and have him join us."

As the General and his entourage marched westward, Valerian hesitated.

"Nicephrus' Division of Caudex Legion has yet to make the night crossing," he explained to Brictius. "The rest of Requiem Division are staged two blocks from here. Get them dispersed to our defensive lines. Leave two of our Centurions here to coordinate. You and First Sergeant Gerontius take the other two Centurions and get a handle on the dock. Secure a warehouse and stow the Legions' supplies. And be sure our lads coming off the lines have extra rations and get prime campsites."

"Yes, sir," said Brictius. "It's good to have fresh heavy infantrymen."

"That it is, First Sergeant," replied Valerian before turning and jogging after the General.

But the second Legion never arrived at Messina Harbor.

***

Colonel Palaemon Nicephrus, after consulting with Tribune Velius of Southern Legion's Planning and Strategies, decided to take his Legion directly into the fight. Despite Velius' objection, Nicephrus Division of Caudex Legion sailed from Rhégion to a narrow strip of beach between the south wall of Messina and the forces of King Hiero II.

Thinking to catch the Syracusans while they slept, Colonel Nicephrus landed two Centuries for security. Then, he jumped to the waters, splashed ashore and stood watching as the specialized transports rowed in. Three hundred horses and cavalrymen hit the beach and, once sorted into troops, were ordered to attack King Hiero's camp. While the horsemen galloped off to begin a shock and awe campaign, the rest of Nicephrus Division began the tedious task of landing. Its four thousand men came in wave after wave of ships grinding onto the shore. If the beach had been wider and, the transports unloaded faster, the infantry might have been able to support the cavalry.

***

Syracusan patrols missed the beaching of the first couple of horse transports. By the time the Legion cavalrymen gathered, messengers were racing to warn Hiero's soldiers and horsemen.

The mounted Legionaries split apart and approached the campfires in a three-pronged attack. Their horses trotted over unfamiliar ground and the mounted Legionaries lowered lances. Then their formations flexed and broke apart as Syracuse cavalry charged into their flanks. In the dark, the Syracusans burst through in mass, circled and charged from all sides. After three passes, the integrity of the Legion cavalry disintegrated and the officers ordered a retreat.

However, the hasty decision to attack without first allowing the infantry to set their lines left the horseman with

36

two choices. Ride for Messina's defensive line or fight their way back to the beach.

Many of those trying for the campfires at the city wall were chopped down from behind. While the mounted Legionaries had to pick routes over the ground avoiding holes and gullies, the Syracusan cavalry knew the landscape.

"Caudex Legion," shouted the first Republic horseman to reach Messina's defenses.

His arrival triggered a response from some of the second maniple, Requiem Division. By the time five more riders reached safety, the nine hundred sixty heavy infantrymen of the second maniple were up and forming a barrier of shields and javelins. In the moonlight, they opened for Nicephrus' cavalrymen before snapping their shields together daring the Syracusans horsemen to come against the iron tips of their javelins.

***

At the beach, messengers alerted Palaemon Nicephrus of the failed attack. Quickly, the Colonel ordered what Legionaries he had to form a defensive line.

While Centurions from the second and third maniples shouted for the Sergeants and Corporals to gather their Centuries, some of the veterans of first maniple marched forward and set a short defensive line. After some shuffling, they pulled the covers off shields, pulled on helmets and tossed anything unnecessary to the fight behind them.

"Step on my cover or gear and I'll gut you after I finish with the Syracusans," the veterans warned the maniple forming behind them.

By the time troops of returning cavalrymen reached Nicephrus' Division, there were three lines of shifting shields to create lanes. As the horses raced through, the shields relocked. Instead of the Legion's full maniples, the lines were half that number. The mounted Legionaries were ordered to the ends of the lines to prevent Syracusan cavalry from getting behind the formation. Meanwhile, on the beach, as Legionaries landed, they found their places and the Legion's battle lines grew in length.

In the grey false dawn, Colonel Palaemon Nicephrus ordered the last of his transports to make for Messina Harbor before the Qart Hadasht Navy found them in the Strait and sank his supplies and support staff. Then, seeing Hoplite phalanxes heading his way, he directed a retreat to the walls of Messina.

Three hundred horses landed but only one hundred seventy-five cavalrymen survived. Most of the blood spilled that night was Legionary. This among other things threw General Appease Caudex into a fit of anger.

Chapter 5 – Caught Between

"You are telling me, Senior Centurion Valerian, that I landed two Legions in a stew pot at full boil?" General Caudex summarized. He walked to a chair and sat. Glancing at the signal corps officer, he inquired. "What of Nicephrus Division?"

"He hasn't landed in the harbor," the Centurion reported. "I've men stationed there. You'll be the first to know when his ships arrive, sir."

"It seems, I will be the only one in Messina who knows anything," shouted the General. "And where is Senior Tribune Claudius? Probably as dead as my plans to sneak quietly into this backwater den of pirates. And before I could solidify my position, we already have contact with Qart Hadasht forces. All I need now is for King Hiero to wake up."

The door to the Citadel opened and a man with a slight stoop and narrow set eyes stepped into the planning room.

"Colonel Requiem. What news?" inquired Caudex. "Tell me something to please me."

"Requiem Division is settled in and all the defensive positions are manned," the Colonel stated.

"I sense more and, from the look on your face, it won't make me happy," suggested the General. "Out with it. This night can't get much worse."

Colonel Pericles Requiem crossed the room, poured a mug of wine and took a sip. He swirled the vino around in his mouth as if it was the last drink of his life.

"Colonel Nicephrus made landfall on that short stretch of beach south of here," Requiem informed the General after swallowing the wine.

"He what? We discussed landing there but discounted it," Caudex said while his hands waved in the air as if to clear the knowledge as if it was offensive smoke. "You said we couldn't get enough Legionaries on land fast enough to fend off an attack. How do you know he landed there?"

"The remnants of his busted cavalry units are filtering in through my second maniple," Requiem informed him. "I assume his infantry is near the beach. My Centurions are swapping the positions of my first and third maniples. If the Syracusans chase him, I'll have a reaction force of veterans ready."

The door opened and an out of breath Legionary rushed to the signal corps' Centurion. After a few quick words, the officer looked at Caudex.

"General, Colonel Nicephrus has landed at the beach," the Centurion informed the General. "A segment of his cavalry has reached our defensive line."

"Tell me something, anything, I don't already know," General Caudex ordered.

"Nicephrus Division is egressing from the beach and moving towards the Legion defensive line," the Centurion responded. "They are not in contact as they move."

"And how would you know that?" inquired Caudex.

"One of my Legionaries has the blessings of Theia," replied the signal corps officer. "Once he had some light, he was able to report on the movement."

"Well there's something," admitted the General. "I haven't lost any more of my heavy infantrymen."

"General Caudex. If Colonel Nicephrus is to be replaced, I stand ready to step in," offered Maris Eutropius. "And do my duty."

Consul General Caudex's mouth fell open and he had to stifle a laugh. Visions of Eutropius dispersing punishment and extra duty or reduced rations for the merest infraction during the march and while boarding the ships, sent a shiver through his body. If ever Tribune Maris Eutropius gained a command, the Legionaries under him would mutiny. And the General would probably join them. The last gave him the first laugh since the march from the Capital.

"No Maris. You are a Senior Tribune and belong at my side. I need you to direct the other Tribunes," the General informed him. "Now, let's go outside and see if Colonel Nicephrus can finish the movement without losing any more of my Legion."

The command staff followed the General out of the Citadel. A short distance from the structure, they stopped on the crest of the hill. To the south, they saw fuzzy masses drifting across the landscape. If they didn't know better, in the low light it could be herds of goats or cattle. northward provided only a view of sharp ridges and a few Legionaries walking their posts. The Messina Strait resembled a dark ribbon but they could see the outlines of transports rowing for the harbor.

"Well at least one thing is going right," General Caudex breathed out. "Nicephrus' supply ships are going to make it safely into the harbor."

But the outlines appeared to be motionless. The longer they watched, the less progress the transports made towards the harbor.

"The tide has turned and the transports can't make Messina," commented Colonel Requiem. "They had best head for Rhégion. If they miss that port, the Qart Hadasht triremes will sink them."

"Don't you ever have joyful news?" the General inquired.

Pericles Requiem believed himself to be a critical thinker. He weighed each situation and offered the wisest solutions always with the best intentions. However, joy was never a consideration. Then he glanced down the hill.

"I believe, General," he said letting a smile cross his thin lips. "We've located Senior Tribune Claudius."

At the foot of Citadel Hill, a Legionary from First Century Headquarters stopped a man covered in dirt and sand. The man's rough woolen clothing was caked with mud from his chest to his sandals. Even his hair and face displayed recent close contact with damp earth. Yet through the grime, his eyes flashed and the firm set of his jaw revealed the determination of the man underneath.

The guard held his javelin across his chest and blocked the man's path. In two heartbeats, the Legionary stepped to the side and saluted. Gaius Claudius was back from the dead and he wasn't happy.

***

"General Caudex. My apologies for not meeting you upon your arrival," Gaius stated.

"I can see you've had your hands full," Caudex replied. "A lot has developed since you went raider."

"It was worth it General. I estimate seven thousand Qart Hadasht troops to our north," reported Gaius. "They're behind a short stone wall at a choke point between the Strait and a marsh.

41

Combined with King Hiero's troops, that puts our enemies at over twelve thousand."

"Yes, that's interesting," the General said. "But the Qart Hadasht army is Colonel Requiem's concern."

"Gaius. You look exhausted," suggested Maris Eutropius. "Why don't you go clean up, have a bite to eat and get some rest. We can handle it going forward."

"That's an excellent idea," Caudex encouraged. "We'll talk later."

Claudius half turned towards the Citadel and a satisfied grin snaked across Eutropius' face. But the Tribune didn't walk away. Raising a hand, he summoned a staff servant.

"Water, a rag, wine and my viewing tube," Claudius ordered.

"Right away, Senior Tribune," the man said. Then he ran for the Citadel.

"I thought you needed to rest?" inquired the General.

"No, sir. For three weeks, every Legionary in Messina has been doing double watches and double duty," Claudius responded. "We've held this together and kept the Syracusans confused enough that they didn't attack. With only five hundred Legionaries, they could have walked into the city after a brief skirmish. But they didn't."

"How did you manage that?" asked Pericles Requiem.

"By rotating squads throughout the day and all night," Claudius bragged. "Plus, we trained the squads all day long. The same squads over and over. We had King Hiero so confused he must have thought we had three Legions posted here."

"That is an impressive ruse," acknowledged the Colonel.

The servant arrived and Claudius washed his hands, scrubbed his face and took a long squirt off the wineskin. Then he raised the leather tube to his eye and scanned the Syracusan camp.

"Someone has stirred up a hornet's nest," remarked Claudius.

"Colonel Nicephrus made a daring night raid on them," blurted out Maris Eutropius.

"And the results?" demanded Claudius.

A hand reached up and gently moved the tube so the Tribune looked southeast.

"Not very impressive, is it?" remarked Colonel Requiem.

"Their formation is a little loose," Claudius observed while watching Nicephrus Division cross the empty ground. "Although they are running over uneven ground."

"What are you looking for?" questioned the General.

"Every morning, I come out here at daybreak and, while directing the operations, I watch King Hiero's tent," explained the Senior Tribune as he shifted the tube to its initial target. "There's a rhythm to the messengers who come and go. When they plan a probe, the cavalrymen strut. So, we have more bows strung. If they're lethargic, they have nothing planned."

"Very astute of you, Tribune," Caudex complimented. "What does the rhythm tell you today?"

"That the Qart Hadasht mercenaries are about to attack," Gaius stated.

"However, can you tell that?" questioned Caudex.

"Because Lieutenant Macario Hicetus has just been invited into the King's tent," Gaius reported. Spinning around, he looked at the signal corps' Centurion. "Find Lance Corporal Alerio Sisera. I need him here, now."

"Ah, Gaius. Lance Corporal Sisera is otherwise occupied this morning," sneered Maris Eutropius as he shielded his eyes with his hand to check the location of the sun.

"I don't care what detail he has, get him up here," insisted Claudius.

"Now Gaius. Settle down. The Lance Corporal is on the punishment post this morning," General Caudex stated. "What's so important about him?"

"He attacked a staff officer and earned himself ten lashes," Maris Eutropius interrupted. Then he offered as if it was a superb jest. "The General ordered it personally."

"What's so important about this Lance Corporal?" inquired Colonel Requiem.

"Without him, the Syracusan and the Qart Hadasht will attack at the same time. Twelve thousand enemy troops will hit us," explained Claudius. "Lieutenant Macario Hicetus will deliver the royal message from Hiero to coordinate the attacks."

"Tribune. What does that have to do with Lance Corporal Sisera?" questioned General Caudex.

The lower edge of the sun rose over the eastern mountain.

"General, he is the only one who knows what Macario Hicetus looks like."

Chapter 6 – Punishment Post

Alerio marched through a room of the house and into a storage area. The squad escorting him pulled the leather curtain over the opening, leaving him in darkness and, dropped their equipment in the main room. It was indoor sleeping arrangements for them and a jail cell for the Lance Corporal. While his guards choose places to nap around the walls, Alerio spread out sailcloth and lay down.

Soon after, there was a commotion beyond the curtain.

"Where is Lance Corporal Sisera?" demanded a voice that was permanently horse and raspy from issuing loud field commands.

"He's in the supply room," the squad leader replied.

"If he's been injured, I'm going to draw my blade and put every one of you in the medical tent," Brictius threatened.

"We only marched him in and closed the curtain," the squad leader promised. "We were warned already by Centurion Carnifex. The Lance Corporal is not to be touched."

The curtain shot back and the Legion's First Sergeant stood in the door frame holding two lanterns.

"Lance Corporal Sisera. Let's you and I have a conversation," Brictius announced. He placed one lantern on the floor and he yanked the curtain closed.

Alerio rolled over, crossed his legs and leaned against the rough wall.

"I'm sorry about the lack of amenities, First Sergeant," he said indicating a place on the sails or a coil of hemp rope. "But there is a choice of seating. I'm afraid there is no repast. My mother would be embarrassed for me."

"Because you're under guard and heading for the punishment post in the morning?" Brictius asked.

"No, First Sergeant. Because she insisted every visitor to our Villa be served a meal and wine," Alerio explained. "It's common courtesy and tradition at the Sisera farm."

Brictius reached into a pack and pulled out a stack of oatcakes. He dropped them beside Alerio then he lifted out a wineskin. That joined the cakes on the sailcloth. The First Sergeant sat down with the meal and beverage between them.

"We must respect our mother's wishes," the Legion's Senior NCO said as he snapped off a small piece of oatcake and popped it in his mouth. Lifting the wineskin, he exclaimed. "To honoring the tradition of the Republic's mothers."

After he drank, he passed the wineskin to Alerio, who took a stream of a very fine vino.

"Do you do this with every Legionary destined for the punishment post?" inquired Alerio.

"Of course not. Most of them deserve the whipping and are right dēfutūta cūlī," admitted the First Sergeant. "You're a special case and I have an offer."

45

"An offer?" questioned Alerio. "Enough vino so I don't remember the lashes?"

"I want you to escape," replied the First Sergeant. "Leave Messina, leave the Legion and go home to your father's farm. No record will follow you. I'll see to that."

"But there's a squad in the other room and Legion troops between here and the harbor," Alerio reminded the First Sergeant. "And Qart Hadasht Navy ships on the Strait."

"You have two healthy Centuries from Claudius Detachment who will get you out of here and to the harbor," Brictius informed him. "As a matter of fact, I've had to stop them twice from busting in here and spiriting you away. Captain Frigian said he'd gladly row you up the coast of the Republic to a beach north of the Capital. Unless Captain Sisera, you want to join the Sons of Mars and command a ship of your own."

"How is Milon?" Alerio inquired.

"He has a nasty gash in his side. Tribune Eutropius doesn't have the guts to kill a man himself. I believe he just wanted the pleasure of inflicting pain and watching Frigian bleed. The Senior Tribune blusters and doles out punishment but he has political ambitions. And he couldn't chance the ramifications of butchering a Sons of Mars' Captain," Brictius offered. "Now, about your escape plan."

"I can't do any of those things, First Sergeant. First, it would put our Centuries in danger of decimation. I've sweated and bled with those Legionaries. I will not be responsible for every tenth man being put to death on my account," Alerio replied. "And I'm a Legionary, not a pirate. Besides, there's another reason I must take the punishment."

When the Lance Corporal didn't expand on the reason, the First Sergeant reached out and took the wineskin. After taking a drink, he handed back the vino.

"Care to explain?" inquired Brictius.

"General Caudex ordered the ten lashes as punishment, not for my actions but, for the sins of my patron," Alerio stated. "I've had a taste of the games powerful men play and it's bitter. Even so, the lashes are for Senator Spurius Maximus and as his protégé, I'm obligated to represent General Maximus with courage and honor."

"You will accept the wounds and pain to martyr yourself for a man who isn't here and probably will never know of your sacrifice?" insisted Brictius. "It makes no sense mixing Legion business with political revenge."

"Yet, we see it every day from the command staff and among some of the Centurions," replied Alerio. "I believe General Maximus will hear of the punishment and my reaction to it. In the future, I will show him the scars and collect my reward."

"If you intend to stand the punishment with a clear head and embrace the blessings of Algea," Brictius said. "I guess my offer of excellent, un-watered vino is wasted."

"I have no intention of having any more memory of the whip than is necessary," Alerio said as he lifted the wineskin. "Or of embracing the pain."

***

Alerio slept and, although the vino ran out before it could block the knowledge of what he faced in the morning, it did allow him to float on a haze of warmth with blurry thoughts. It did until he dreamed of battling giants with clawed hands. As the giants fought, he ran around their ankles dodging their stomping and shuffling feet. Occasionally, one would reach down and swipe at his miniature figure. After raking his back with sharp claws, the giant returned to exchanging flourishes with the other colossus. They fought and he raced around their trireme size feet with sweat stinging his eyes and blood oozing from painful wounds on his back. Then, one of the giant's toes nudged him in the side.

"Wake up, Lance Corporal," a voice ordered.

Peering up, Alerio saw Sanctus Carnifex standing over him. Rolling to his back, Alerio sat up and hugged his knees to his chest.

"Good morning, Centurion. Is it a good day to bleed for the Republic?" he asked.

"In the Legion, every day affords us a chance to mix blood with soil," Carnifex replied. "But the only good day is when it's the enemy's blood. Not a Legionary's."

"Has the sun risen?" inquired Alerio. "On my father's farm, I always enjoyed the sunrise. As you can assume, today I'm not so pleased with the idea."

"I've spent the night talking to your officers, NCOs and the Legionaries in Claudius Detachment. Both the healthy and the injured," the Legion's weapon instructor stated. "Your command staff is impressed with you but, any merda sucking mentula can cuddle up to his superiors. The true test of an NCO is the responses I received from the infantrymen."

Alerio chuckled and dropped his head.

"I can't imagine what they said about me," he ventured. "Between slaps with the blade, trips with my feet and hammering them with shields, it probably wasn't flattering."

"There were a few who volunteered to be the punishment Sergeant today. But the ones with minor injuries were more positive," Carnifex related. "However, it was the responses from the walking or severely wounded that told me the most about you."

"Is this part of the punishment?" inquired Alerio. "Because, if it is, I'd just as soon take the lashes, sir."

"Oh, you'll get the lashes, weapons instructor," Sanctus assured him. But the use of the title shocked Alerio. As the Legion's weapons instructor, Centurion Carnifex had the responsibility for certifying instructors in every Century to assure the Legionaries were proficient with their weapons and in maneuvering. To have the Centurion recognize Alerio as a weapons instructor showed a vote of confidence far beyond the young man's rank. "The wounded all had the same excuse for why they were injured. To a man, they explained that had they followed your instructions and training, they wouldn't have allowed the enemy to cut them. That, Lance Corporal Sisera, is the highest compliment a Legionary can offer his weapons instructor. Now, get up. You have an appointment with the punishment post."

***

In a Legion in the field, there were lots of activities. Such as collecting daily rations, cooking at the squad level, sentry duty, inspections, sacrifices to the Gods, both large and small, and there was training. Constant gladius, javelin, shield and bow work, until their arms and legs were exhausted. This put the Legionaries in sync with their squad mates and automatic in their response to an enemy. Then they ran, jumped and wrestled. There were activities aplenty in the field. The one thing missing was entertainment on a grand scale. And despite the thoughts of the command staff that someone sentenced to the punishment post provided motivation, in reality, it served to fill the entertainment gap.

On the days of a whipping, the punishment Sergeant was the ringmaster and center of attention. He strutted to the post, checked the bindings and proceeded to push Legionaries back to form a circle around the post. This was necessary as over a thousand Legionaries had crowded around to view the spectacle. Relieved of duty for the morning, they jostled for viewing spots and greeted friends from other units as they gulped down vino. Many had climbed on rooftops and walls while others stood on barrels or upended logs to see over the crowd. And, they placed bets.

How many lashes before the offender bled? Or passed out? Or cried out for his God or Goddess, or his mother were popular

49

wagers. And there was the one with the highest payout and longest odds. Would the Legionary die under the whip?

A row of Tesserarii had been arranged for the wagering. Who better to handle the coins than the Corporals who did the correspondence, kept logs, counted the Century's funeral funds and issued pay? Considering the age of the Legionary to be punished, the mother wage far exceeded any of the others. Although, the no cries for all ten lashes came in a close second. These placed mostly by the Sons of Mars who came for the sport of it and seemed to know something about the Legionary.

Oddly enough, the death bets began to pile up. At first, none of the Corporals paid much attention to the coins placed on the punished dying. But during a lull, one mentioned it.

"How old is the Legionary?" he inquired of the Tesserarius next to him.

"I don't know but I heard he's young. Why?" came the reply.

"Any illness or injuries?"

"He's fit as far as anybody knows."

"Then why all the coins placed on him dying?"

"Now that you mention it, I have three big stacks for the same wager," the Corporal noted. Then turning to the NCO on the other side, he asked. "Have you taken any death bets?"

The Tesserarius pointed to his camp table.

"Yes, and I don't understand it," the Corporal responded. "If he was old or sick, sure. But only ten lashes to a healthy man will put him in medical for a day. But kill him? No way."

Then a wave of newly arrived Legionaries lined up and the Corporals got busy.

***

Alerio and the escort squad left the house and marched up the street heading for the empty lot. Except the open area was no longer empty. Legionaries, Sons of Mars and residents crowded the lot and ringed the punishment pole.

"Big turnout for you, Lance Corporal," noted the squad leader.

"Glad I could be today's circus," commented Alerio.

Inside he trembled and his thoughts went to melancholy places. Maybe he should have escaped or run off and joined the Sons of Mars. At this instant, he visualized himself standing on the prow of a bireme with his oarsmen rowing towards a prize transport. But he was a Legionary and a protégé for one of the most powerful men in the Republic. He would accept his fate and abide the lashes like a man.

In the light of predawn, before shadows formed, the escort squad shoved into the crowd. Some people bristled and looked to see who dared push them from the rear. The sight of infantry shields, helmets and javelins dissuaded any argument and, the crowd parted.

The punishment Sergeant stood in the open with his implement of authority. The whip handle tapped against his leg, while his hand clutched a loop of braided leather. As he moved the handle, the loop of interwoven leather swung out and back showing the suppleness of the whip.

Behind the Sergeant, a thick pole jutted from a flat sandy circle. Another bet was how far beyond the sand would drops of blood fly. At the top of the pole, coils of rope covered a short length before the ends of the lines were allowed to dangle. Tied to the ends were leather cuffs with laces for a secure fit. As the crowd parted for the escort squad, some Legionaries stumbled into the cleared area. The punishment Sergeant stalked the perimeter shoving trespassers back into the crowd. Everyone jeered at the rough treatment but no one called out directly to the punishment Sergeant. Someday they might be sentenced to lashes and offending the man wielding the whip wasn't a good idea.

Once through the crowd, eight members of the escort squad dispersed around the cleared area. With Legionaries holding back the spectators, the Sergeant marched to the circle of sand and made a show of inspecting the pole, cuffs, and coils of rope. The final two members of the squad flanked Alerio. The three stood braced and waiting for an officer to arrive and read the charges.

Also waiting, but on a street to the rear of the crowd, was a Century, their Centurion and Corporal and, a medic. They had no interest in seeing their weapons instructor whipped. In fact, the eighty infantrymen ground their teeth, shuffled their feet and clinched their javelins until their fingers were white. None of them were happy about the punishment.

"He survived Syracusan phalanx attacks without a scratch. Works his cūlus off to train us," complained one of the infantrymen. "And now he has to take the whip. It's just not right."

"Stow it, Private," the Corporal ordered. "We went over this last night. When the tenth lash is delivered, we're going in and protect him while the medic does his work. It's the best we can do."

"It's merda, Tesserarius," another Legionary observed.

"I didn't say it wasn't," replied the Corporal.

***

A Centurion stepped into the cleared area and unrolled a short scroll.

"Legionaries. Attention to orders," he announced in a booming voice. "By command of General Appease Clodus Caudex, Caudex Legion, Senator, and citizens of the Republic, the following charges are levied, judged and directed against Lance Corporal Alerio Sisera, Southern Legion, Headquarters Planning and Strategies Section. The Lance Corporal has been charged with sleeping while on duty."

A grumbling went through the crowd of Legionaries. Sleeping on duty was an infraction usually settled by a Sergeant administering a few punches and extra duty.

"And being out of uniform at his post," the Centurion continued.

The Legionaries made no sound at that announcement. Most of them had mismatched armor and shields. Out of uniform had no meaning to them. Now, if the Lance Corporal had lost his gladius, they would understand the need for punishment.

"Desertion and avoidance of the enemy while his Century was engaged with the enemy," the line officer read.

A nasty growl arose from the attendees. Every man depended on his squad mates to cover his sides in a battle. If the Lance Corporal had ducked out of a fight, he deserved to be whipped. However, a few listened carefully and questioned the charges.

"If he was asleep at his post and out of uniform at his post, how could he have deserted his unit?" a few asked.

The questions raced around the crowd forcing the Centurion to hold up his hand for silence.

"And Lance Corporal Alerio Sisera willingly assaulted a staff officer."

The crowd roared, although, some of them with approval while others voiced disapproval. Nevertheless, the officer had finally called out a serious charge.

On the street behind the crowd, the Century from Claudius Detachment listened and judged the charges through their own experiences with Alerio.

"When's the funeral?" asked one of the infantrymen in Claudius Detachment.

"What are you saying?" demanded his Centurion.

"Sir, if our weapons officer assaulted a staff officer for real, there would be a sacrifice for the staff officer's passage to Hades and meat for the Legion," he explained. "Sisera doesn't know how to just assault. He kills, sir."

First Sergeant Brictius walked up just in time to hear the exchange. With a scowl, he warned the line officer against replying. The Centurion, unable to answer, stood and listened to the rest of the charges.

"Using the body of the staff officer, Legionary Sisera propelled the officer into a Lance Corporal dutifully charged with protecting the staff officer," the Centurion read.

The attendees didn't say anything, they simply broke out in laughter. What the Centurion read resembled a brawl in a pub rather than a breach of military discipline. Despite the sun almost topping the eastern heights, the line officer waited for the last chuckle to fade before continuing.

"By order of General Caudex, the accused Lance Corporal Alerio Sisera shall be tied to the pole and given ten lashes by the punishment Sergeant," the Centurion pronounced as he rolled up the scroll. "Punishment Sergeant, take charge of the Legionary. And do your duty."

"Yes, sir," the Sergeant replied. Then he marched up to Alerio, stopped and shoved his face into the weapons instructors face. "Are you going to give me any problems?"

"No, Sergeant," promised Alerio.

The two Legionaries on Alerio's sides were watching the Centurion and the crowd. They missed the stealth fist when the Sergeant landed an uppercut into Alerio's solar plexus. As the young Legionary bent forward, the Sergeant jumped back as if surprised. His response to the involuntary lunge was to pound Alerio in the jaw with the whip handle.

"There's always one," the punishment Sergeant stated. "Secure this man to the punishment pole. He is out of control."

Shocked by the violence from the docile prisoner, the Legionaries from the escort squad grabbed Alerio roughly by the wrists and dragged him to the pole.

"Make them tight," the punishment Sergeant ordered as the Legionaries laced up the cuffs. Then the NCO marched up and looped any slack in the lines around the pole.

Alerio hung with his arms above his head and his back stretched. He had no way to flex and bunch his muscles to absorb the lashes. Then a cold metallic object touched his neck before sliding down and a cool breeze let him know the tunic had been slit open.

The crowd grew silent preparing to shout out the number of lashes.

"The accused is bound to the punishment pole," the Sergeant announced to the Centurion. "With your permission, I will execute the order, sir?"

The Centurion glanced to the east to verify the location of the sun. Then with a blank face to hide his true feelings, he nodded and marched out of the clearing. He didn't stop until he was two blocks away. Only then did he allow his head to shake at the stupidity of the punishment.

"One!" screamed the crowd.

And the blood bets paid off. Even the distance long shot paid as splatters covered the sand to the edge of the circumference and a foot's length beyond. After the surprising early bleed, those with good locations inspected Lance Corporal Sisera's back from across the clearing. They expected a welt. Instead, the raw line resembled a knife cut on an overripe melon. A thin streak of red pulp stretched from under the Legionary's left shoulder blade to the top of his right hip. But he didn't call out or scream. The whip rose and cracked down.

"Two!" the crowd counted. This time with less enthusiasm.

A second gouged line ran from under the right shoulder blade to the top of the left hip. Again, the raw pulp of fat and tissue bled. And where the two lashes crossed, four corners of flesh lifted revealing the Legionary's back muscles.

Cries of alarm were shouted by the attendees and a couple of Legionaries ran into the clearing. The punishment Sergeant waited as the escort squad shoved them back.

***

The Century stood and they flinched with each count. They wanted to vent their frustration but the Centurion, Corporal, and First Sergeant Brictius walked the columns keeping them in line.

Then the sound of a horse in full gallop grew louder from behind them. The horse appeared beside the ranks and reared back as the rider savagely yanked the reins. He was dressed in dirty woolen clothing and even his hair was covered in mud. But his face glowed clean in the dirt wreath. It was the face of their Tribune and he shouted the order they wanted to hear.

"Second Century of Claudius Detachment," Gaius commanded when he recognized the Centurion. "Rally the punishment pole and secure the area. Centurion, go!"

"First squad and second, forward right. Third, fourth and fifth, forward left," shouted the line officer. "Sixth, seventh and eighth, draw. Forward right."

First Sergeant Brictius tucked in behind the First Squad as they plowed a path through the packed crowd. Bodies flew as the infantry shields hoisted people and launched them to the sides. The stomp reverberated off the street and Legionaries in attendance recognized the meaning. An armed unit was on the move. For their own safety, they scrambled to get out of First squad's way.

When they reached the clearing, First and Second squads began a tight circle to the right. Brictius sprinted directly to the punishment Sergeant who had his arm back for another strike. The First Sergeant hooked his arm through the Sergeant's and threw the man and his whip to the sand. Then Brictius glanced at the raw meat of Alerio's back. Without thinking, the First

Sergeant drew back his fist and punched the punishment Sergeant in the face.

Third, Fourth and Fifth squads came through the crowd and marched in a wider circle to the left. Following them, Sixth, Seventh and Eight squads, with naked gladii, circled right. Soon the punishment pole was surrounded by three ranks of circled Legionaries. The outer circle bristled with bare blades and javelin tips from the second rank.

The escort squad formed a line facing the Century. Before the Lance Corporal could issue an order, a voice called out.

"Hold where you are, squad leader," ordered Centurion Sanctus Carnifex. He marched by the squad and stopped in front of the neat circles of Legionaries.

"First Sergeant Brictius. I assume you have a good reason for this infringement on a lawful punishment," he called out.

"What do you call this, weapons instructor?" Brictius replied. Something long and thin sailed over the Centuries heads and landed at Carnifex's feet.

Reaching down, he picked up the whip and ran his fingers along the braids.

"Seashells woven into the leather braids," he offered. "It makes the whip a killing and maiming weapon."

"How bad is he?" a voice called from the open path. "Tell me, he is fit for duty."

"He needs a surgeon, Senior Tribune Claudius," the medic replied as Gaius stepped between the circled shields. "I can't do much more than keep pressure on the wound."

"Wound? You mean the welts?" questioned the Tribune.

"No, sir. Lance Corporal Sisera is flayed almost to his spine," the medic informed him.

"First squad, get me a shield," ordered the Corporal.

Two pairs of Legionaries placed javelins under a shield. Once Alerio was placed on the makeshift stretcher, the four men stood and marched for the opening in the crowd.

"First Sergeant Brictius. What do you need here?" Gaius asked.

"Leave me three squads, sir," he replied. "I'll report as soon as I know what happened."

"Centurion. Drop three squads and come with me," instructed Senior Tribune Claudius. Then to Brictius. "We'll be at the medical tent."

Chapter 7 – A Bribe and Murders

"That Century performed an unrehearsed rally around a flag," Carnifex observed as he and Brictius followed the three squads escorting the punishment Sergeant to where Alerio had spent the night. "It's usually a drill to impress the staff officers."

"Unrehearsed?" Brictius chuckled. "Every squad in Claudius Detachment can do it in their sleep."

"How? Why?" questioned the weapons instructor.

"The first time Lance Corporal Sisera taught it, the troops circled in the wrong direction, tripped, and bumped into the other squads," Brictius explained. "I told him maniple troops didn't require fancy drills. But the Syracusan cavalry watching laughed at us. Suddenly, the squads were begging Alerio for instructions. What he did was tie javelin tips to the right and left sides of everyone's helmets. After a few stitches, they learned to circle and form circular ranks. The Syracusans stopped laughing."

"What do you make of this situation?" asked Carnifex holding out the coiled whip.

"The Sergeant doesn't know Alerio. Someone had to put him up to the murder," suggested the First Sergeant.

They were a block from the punishment pole when a Tesserarius jogged up.

"Centurion. First Sergeant. I heard what happened," he said. "You should know, we took a lot of bets on the death of the Legionary."

"Didn't you think that was unusual?" questioned Carnifex.

"For a while but then we got busy. They spread out their bets between all of our stations," the Corporal recounted. "We discussed it later and realized all the bets were placed by only four Legionaries."

"Do we know their names?" inquired Brictius.

"No, First Sergeant," the NCO admitted. "But we know what unit they're from."

"If you don't know their names, how can you know their unit?" questioned Carnifex.

"Because, no other outfit smells as distinct as mule drivers," the Corporal responded. "And they have calluses between their fingers on both hands. An infantryman only has them on the right hand."

"Centurion Carnifex. Would you round up the drivers for questioning?" asked the First Sergeant.

"Give me two squads," Carnifex responded as he handed the whip to the First Sergeant. "We'll search all of them for betting slips."

"And I'll start questioning the punishment Sergeant."

***

Once in the house and away from prying eyes, the First Sergeant sent the squad to stand guard outside. His instructions. Let no one in and keep the presence of the Sergeant a secret.

"We'd be happier taking him to the harbor and pushing him off the dock, for what he did to Lance Corporal Sisera," the squad leader suggested as he herded his Legionaries out of the house. "But first we'd tie him to a very large stone."

"A vivid description. Are you an educated man? Did you study theater in the Capital, by chance?" Brictius inquired. "Or maybe elocution and the mysteries in Athens?"

"No, First Sergeant, I didn't," the squad leader responded.

"Then leave the matter to me and Centurion Carnifex," urged the First Sergeant. "Go see to your squad and mind the orders."

"Yes, First Sergeant," the Lance Corporal said as he walked out of the house.

When the door closed, the punishment Sergeant exhaled loudly.

"Thanks for getting me out of there, Brictius," the Sergeant said. "When that Century circled, I feared for my life. And imagine that squad leader mouthing off about an Optio like that. If I had him on my post, he'd learn to keep a civil tongue in his mouth. How long do you think I'll be here before it's safe to go back to my transportation Century?"

"Why do you suppose the infantrymen came in and surrounded the punishment post?" Brictius asked.

"Some confusion between the command staff, I imagine," the Sergeant replied.

"Yes, it must have been," Brictius agreed holding out the whip. "While we're waiting for Centurion Carnifex, explain this."

"It's what the messenger wanted," the punishment Sergeant informed him. "Make Sisera bleed for what he did to Tribune Eutropius. And if the Lance Corporal dies, no one will care. Legionaries sometimes die on the punishment post."

In his career with the Legion, First Sergeant Brictius had killed barbarians, pirates, thieves and even another Legionary in a knife fight. But the idea that a punishment Sergeant would willfully murder a Legionary went against his sense of honor.

"This messenger, did he come from Tribune Eutropius?" Brictius inquired.

"I don't know," admitted the punishment Sergeant. "One of my Privates was contacted and given the message."

"Then how did you know it came from the command staff?"

"The sack of coins," the NCO boasted. "A big sack of coins doesn't accompany a message unless it's a serious matter and from a wealthy noble. Now Brictius, I've answered your questions. When can I get out of here?"

"It's First Sergeant Brictius and you aren't going anywhere," the Senior NCO explained. "And I suggest you sit down before I knock you down."

"I don't understand," the punishment Sergeant begged.

"No, you don't," replied Brictius.

***

A Legionary walking guard at the back of the Citadel turned a corner and began to pass the staff officers area.

"Private Hippolytus. Come into my office," Maris Eutropius called from his desk.

The Private stopped and looked around. His Lance Corporal from the Tribune's protection squad would be angry if he left his post. But the staff officer had ordered it. Deciding Eutropius had the authority and seeing as no one was watching, the guard marched into the room. Standing stiffly in the center of the Tribune's office, the Legionary didn't make eye contact with the aloof staff officer.

"Sir. What do you need?" the Private asked.

"Come closer to my desk," urged Maris with a wave and a smile.

Hippolytus marched to the desk and bent forward.

"Sir, if it's about the message," he whispered. "It was delivered as well as the coins."

"To a friend of yours?" Maris inquired.

"No sir. Just like you instructed, I found one of the punishment Sergeant's Century and passed the message and coins to him," Private Hippolytus reported. "I caught him alone and no one saw us."

"Excellent work, Private," Maris gushed.

"There is one thing," admitted the Legionary. "The man asked why. I couldn't think so I told him it was payback for Sisera attacking you."

Maris Eutropius' jaw clenched down and his hands closed into fists. Once the anger passed, he reached out and picked up a mug of wine.

"Of course, you can't think," Eutropius delivered the backhanded compliment with a wink. Then Maris offered a mug to Hippolytus. "Have a drink with me to celebrate the successful completion of our mission."

The confused Private took the mug and held it at waist height. In the weeks his squad had guarded the Tribune, the staff officer hadn't spoken to any of the Privates. Until the mission. And then only to him. Now, the Tribune wanted to drink a toast.

"Come on Private. Drink up," urged the Senior Tribune. "I've never seen a real Legionary pass up a drink of fine vino."

"If you say so, sir," Hippolytus responded while lifting the mug to his mouth. He gulped it down thinking it was a far better vintage then he was accustomed to drinking. "It's excellent sir."

"Yes, it is," Maris stated as he watched the Private drain the mug. As he placed the empty vessel on the desk, the Senior Tribune noted the missing ear on the Private's left side. Briefly, Maris wondered about the wound, before commanding. "Now, get back to your duties. And remember, say nothing about the mission."

"Upon my life," promised Private Hippolytus. "You have my word, sir."

"I'm sure I do," Tribune Maris Eutropius replied.

***

While First Sergeant Brictius hid his feelings as he questioned the punishment Sergeant, Centurion Sanctus Carnifex didn't.

"What is the Sweet Butcher doing here?" asked a wagon driver as Carnifex marched into the transportation area with a squad of infantrymen.

"I don't know. But whenever the weapons instructor shows up, it's never good," another driver replied.

The Centurion stopped in the center of the yard. Soft, churned-up dirt where wagons and mules crossed, sank under his boots. After signaling the squad to spread out around the area, he put his hands on his hips and glared around.

"Transportation Century, form up, on me" he bellowed.

A Centurion and Corporal came rushing from a building.

"Now see here, Sanctus," the officer began.

But the Legion's weapons instructor grabbed him by the shoulders, pulled him close and put his lips beside the transportation officer's ear.

"This is trouble that might go up to the General's staff," whispered Carnifex. "I suggest, you go back to your office and make busy with your scrolls."

Visibly shaken, either from the rough physical contact or the idea of dealing with staff issues, the Centurion turned to go.

"Corporal. Come with me," he ordered.

"No. Your Tesserarius stays here," Carnifex informed the Centurion.

The transportation officer was an old campaigner nearing mandatory retirement age. If he lost his position in Caudex Legion, he probably wouldn't find another Legion to recruit him. In his younger days, he might have disputed the challenge to his leadership. But, Sanctus Carnifex understood personal combat and knew death intimately. Whatever the trouble, he'd let the weapons instructor sort it out. For now, he'd seek the sanctuary of his office.

"Corporal. I'm looking for four of your men," Sanctus stated as the mule drivers and transportation personnel shuffled into the yard. "Let me know if any of your troops are missing."

"Yes, sir," the NCO replied. Then he ordered. "Transportation Century, form up on me."

More men came from stables, tents, and warehouses commandeered by the Legion. When the flow of men stopped, the Tesserarius began looking over the assembly.

"There are eleven missing," he announced. "Two are at medical. And five are on assignment delivering supplies to the defensive lines. I don't know about the other four."

From between the tents, two men appeared. An infantryman nudged a mule driver with the tip of his gladius. The mule driver looked as if he'd rather be anywhere else except marching towards the weapons instructor and the Corporal.

"This one tried to sneak out the back of a tent," the infantryman exclaimed. "The Lance Corporal found a betting slip on him."

As they approached the center of the yard, Sanctus reached out and took the mule driver by the throat and drew his dagger.

"Can you handle a mule team with one eye?" he inquired.

"Yes, Centurion," the man replied.

"Good. Because I wouldn't want to short the Legion a man while we're in contact with the enemy," Carnifex explained. "I'm going to ask you a question, then I'm going to carve out your eyeball."

"Wait, weapons instructor," the man begged. "Don't you mean, if I don't answer, you'll take my eye?"

"No. If I have to work to get information about the mistreatment of Lance Corporal Alerio Sisera, I'm taking an eye as payment for my labor," Carnifex stated.

"It was Caratcus' idea to place the death bets," the wagon driver blurted out. "He claimed he had a message and coin for the punishment Sergeant to hurt Sisera, bad. Knowing our

64

Sergeant, we figured the odds of the Legionary dying were worth the coins ventured."

"And where is Caratcus?" demanded the Corporal.

"I don't know, Tesserarius," the driver replied. "After the infantry surrounded the Sergeant at the punishment post, we ran back here."

From a warehouse, two infantrymen dragged a driver out of a building and across the yard.

"We found him hiding under the grain," one of the Legionaries said. Then he slapped the driver across the top of his head. "Nasty piece of merda, putting your dirty cūlus in our grain."

"That's Caratcus, sir," the Corporal said identifying the wagon driver.

"Take him to the First Sergeant," Carnifex ordered the two Legionaries holding the driver. Then he yelled. "Squad leaders, form up on the road and report to your Century."

From the tents, buildings, and warehouses, the other squad assigned to Centurion Carnifex emerged. They fell into columns next to the squad in the transportation yard. Together they marched away with the Legion's weapons instructor marching behind them.

***

"Sergeant. Is this the Private who brought you the message and the sack of coins?" demanded Carnifex as he shoved Caratcus into the house.

"Yes, Centurion," he replied.

First Sergeant Brictius pulled out his gladius and held the weapon at his side. It hung motionless but the punishment Sergeant and the wagon driver both cringed at the unspoken threat of the naked blade.

Turning to the Private, Carnifex inquired, "Who brought you the message?"

"I don't know his name, sir," pleaded the Private. "But I recognized him. He's on the squad protecting Tribune Eutropius."

"Now look here, sir," the Sergeant blustered. "Enough of this game. Your questions are dangerously close to accusing a Senior Staff Officer of committing a violation. But we all know you'll do nothing, except get all of us a session on the punishment post. Maybe not you, Centurion, but First Sergeant Brictius, Private Caratcus and me. We're the ones who will be up on charges."

"You aren't wrong, Sergeant," replied Carnifex. "That's why this is a secret inquiry. Private Caratcus. Describe the Legionary who brought you the message."

"He is average height, stands with his back real straight and he didn't look me in the eyes," Caratcus related. "Plus, he's not very smart. When I asked why the orders to hurt the Lance Corporal, he got confused before telling me. Oh, and he's missing an ear on the left side."

"That's Private Hippolytus," announced Carnifex. "Sergeant. Take your man back to the transportation Century. I don't want to hear any gossip about the message or what we discussed in this room. And if you ever get another bribe to hurt a Legionary, I want to hear about it."

The Sergeant nodded his understanding, put a hand on Caratcus's back and shoved the Private out of the door. Before leaving, he locked eyes with First Sergeant Brictius.

"Don't get over your station, First Sergeant," he warned before following Caratcus out of the house.

Brictius sheathed his gladius and cocked his head in a questioning manner.

"What now, Centurion?" he inquired.

"You go tell Tribune Claudius what we discovered," directed Carnifex. "I'm going to speak with Private Hippolytus."

Chapter 8 – Bees' Wax

The infantry tents were neatly arranged in Legion squares. In the center of the camp, the line officer's large tent anchored the Century's area. While the First Century, Headquarters guarded the General and access to the Citadel, patrolling the structure, fell to infantry squads of rotating Centuries. The duty would end when the Legion went into combat.

Legionaries sat in front of tents repairing or cleaning their equipment. Sanctus Carnifex located the tent he wanted and marched to it.

"Centurion Carnifex. What can I do for you, sir?" the Lance Corporal asked as he looked up from where he was sharpening his gladius.

"I need to speak with Private Hippolytus," Sanctus stated.

"Sir. I'm aware of Hippolytus' actions," the squad leader admitted. "I'm waiting for my Centurion and Sergeant to get back from inspecting the northern defensives. I'm sure they'll administer the appropriate punishment."

"And you had nothing to do with it?" inquired Carnifex.

"No, sir. I'm studying my numbers and letters," replied the Lance Corporal. "Someday, I'd like to be a Tesserarius. Permitting my men to get blind drunk while on duty would hurt my chances of being selected."

"Drunk on duty?" asked a confused Carnifex.

"I promise you, sir. I inspected the guards before they were posted," reported the squad leader. "Hippolytus was sober. I didn't even smell vino on his breath. You can imagine my surprise when I was informed one of my Legionaries was passed out behind the Citadel. That's why you wanted to speak with him. Isn't it, sir?"

"Where's Hippolytus now?" demanded the Centurion.

"In the tent sleeping it off," the Lance Corporal said pointing behind him at the squad's tent.

Sanctus rushed to the tent, tossed back the flap and stepped into the muted interior. One bedroll was occupied. The Centurion knelt down and felt Hippolytus' forehead. It was wet and cold. After placing a hand on the Private's neck and finding a weak pulse, he shouted.

"Get this man to medical," Carnifex ordered.

***

"And we know a Private Hippolytus from Tribune Eutropius' protection detail delivered the coins and the message," related First Sergeant Brictius. As he talked, Senior Tribune Claudius paced outside the surgery tent forcing Brictius to turn his head back and forth as he reported. "And that's as far as I dare take the investigation, sir."

"I want to speak with Private Hippolytus, later," Gaius Claudius informed the First Sergeant. "For now, I need Lance Corporal Sisera."

They both looked up the street to see Centurion Carnifex and four Legionaries carrying a man on a shield.

"Medic!" one of the porters called. A tent flap opened and the men and the stretcher vanished through the opening. Moments later, the Centurion emerged and marched to Gaius Claudius.

"Who was that, Centurion?" Gaius inquired.

"Private Hippolytus, sir. I've seen food poisoning from spoiled grain and meat and illness from bad water and vino," Carnifex offered. "But I've never seen any of those put a man down as hard as whatever the Private drank."

"You think he was intentionally poisoned?" asked the Senior Tribune.

"I wouldn't know about poisons, sir," Carnifex replied. "That's a weapon only wealthy people can afford to wield."

Gaius Claudius' forehead creased and his lips pressed together hard. Before he could say what was on his mind, a doctor, wiping his bloody hands with a rag came from the surgery tent.

"Your Legionary is stitched up and bound," the doctor announced. "He'll need a few days of rest. The lashes didn't rip the muscles, just scratched them. But his flesh was jagged and I had to stretch it to sew the stitches."

"I need him on his feet," demanded the Gaius.

"If he moves around too much, he'll break the linen stitches," advised the doctor. "And if the wound isn't flushed with vinegar twice a day, it'll get the rot. He could die."

"If he isn't on his feet, we may all die," Gaius informed the Doctor. "What can you do to get him back on duty?"

"I could apply a compress of honey and olive oil and seal it with bees' wax," replied the Doctor. "That should keep the flesh around the stitches supple. And a tight binding will hold it together. But, he wouldn't be able to hold a shield or swing a gladius."

"I'm not putting him in a shield wall," explained the Senior Tribune. "I just need his eyes and his voice."

"Let me prepare the balm and dressing," the Doctor informed Gaius. "But this goes against my recommendations."

"Noted. Now get Lance Corporal Sisera patched up," ordered the Senior Tribune. Then to the First Sergeant. "I'm going to clean up and get on my armor. As soon as Sisera is released, bring him to Citadel Hill."

"Yes, sir," replied Brictius. "How should we transport him?"

"As fast and as comfortably as possible, First Sergeant," Gaius suggested as he swung onto the horse's back. "Try not to open the wound. It wouldn't do him or us any good if he bleeds out before finishing the mission."

The Senior Tribune trotted west through the city and Centurion Carnifex glanced at the First Sergeant.

"Any ideas?" he asked.

"Maybe, but I need a messenger," Brictius said. Glancing around he saw a young man squatting beside the medical tent. "Legionary. Come here."

"Yes, First Sergeant. What can I do for you?" asked the medic in training.

"I need you to find Captain Frigian from the Sons of Mars," Brictius instructed as he pulled coins from a pouch. "Gives these to him and ask him…"

***

Senior Tribune Gaius Claudius, General Caudex, and Senior Tribune Maris Eutropius stood on the crest of Citadel Hill gazing to the south. Only Gaius was actually watching anything. To the General and Eutropius, the Syracusan troops appeared as discoloration on the grass in the distance.

"King Hiero is running commanders through his tent as if they were a festival parade," described Claudius. "It must be in preparation for an attack."

Messengers and Junior Tribunes sprinted from the Citadel building and raced down the hill. The messengers continued to run and the young Tribunes leaped on horses and galloped away. After the surge of pounding legs and cranking elbows, Palaemon Nicephrus and Pericles Requiem calmly strolled from the Citadel building.

As the Colonels drew closer, General Caudex turned from the vista and focused on his Division commanders.

"Can we hold Messina?" he asked.

"Against the Syracusan troops, yes," Nicephrus replied.

"Against the Qart Hadasht mercenaries, positively," Requiem added.

"What about their combined forces?" questioned Caudex.

"It'll be an epic battle," Nicephrus commented.

"One for the annals of the Republic," Requiem assured the General.

"Colonels. Those are not answers," Caudex observed.

"Because, General, there are no answers," explained Nicephrus.

"We need additional Legionaries in the south to handle the phalanxes and cavalry to counter the Syracusan horsemen," Requiem said analyzing the requirements. "In the north, we'll need additional ranks to fight through the pinch point between the marsh and the Strait."

"Neither campaign is insurmountable," Nicephrus exclaimed. "It's just we don't have the Centuries to do both at the same time."

"Senior Tribune Claudius. Besides your voyeur preoccupation with King Hiero," inquired the General. "Do you have anything to add?"

"My plan is to prevent them from coordinating their attacks," Gaius stated.

"I don't see any movement on that front," commented Maris Eutropius.

Gaius snapped his head around and glared at the other Senior Tribune. General Caudex caught the tension between the two and pointed a finger in their direction.

"Gentlemen, we have troubles enough," scolded the General. "Maris, do you have any ideas you would like to share?"

"We send advanced units to the north to keep the Qart Hadasht occupied," Maris Eutropius proclaimed. "Then we march on the Syracusans. Drive them across the river and return to finish the mercenaries."

"A bold plan. Colonels, your thoughts on Senior Tribune Eutropius' battle strategy?" Caudex asked.

"Six thousand Qart Hadasht troops and a narrow strip of land," Requiem pondered. "The Spartans did it at Thermopylae.

Would you like to lead the three hundred at Messina, Tribune Eutropius?"

"Before you answer, remember the Spartans died," Nicephrus reminded the Senior Tribune. "And the width is a lot wider than a seaside mountain pass."

"I like the plan where we don't fight on two fronts," suggested Colonel Requiem.

"Is that an option?" Caudex inquired.

Then, Colonel Nicephrus pointed to a street beyond the toe of Citadel Hill.

"What is that?" he asked.

"When I was a young man, I traveled to Egypt on family business," General Caudex explained. "What you see approaching is a Lectica. Although most are public transportation and, except for nobility, don't have extra porters, an elaborately carved car, and gaudy cloth. This one seems to have silk or fine Egyptian linen curtains."

Multilayers of cloth blew around a box of dark wood. Four large men, two in front and two behind carried the box on poles. Marching beside the litter, First Sergeant Brictius gave a cross chest salute to the command staff on the hill. Only Tribune Gaius Claudius returned the salute and he did so with a smile.

"I believe, Lance Corporal Sisera has arrived," exclaimed Gaius.

"Where?" asked Eutropius. When Gaius pointed to the royal box, Eutropius demanded. "Have the Lance Corporal climb out of his royal Lectica, come up here and present himself properly."

Tribune Claudius snapped his fingers and a messenger came running up with a pouch. Gaius reached in and pulled out a coiled length of leather. Then he let it unspool to the ground before he flicked his wrist. The whip snapped a few hands width in front of Maris' face. Yelling in shock and surprise, the Senior Tribune jumped back.

72

"Notice the seashells woven into the leather weaves," explained Gaius as he snapped the whip again. "Lance Corporal Sisera took lashes from this whip this morning. The surgeon, who sewed him up, said he's lucky to be alive. I disagreed with the doctor. It is us, the Legions, who are lucky he's alive."

"That's the man who can identify the royal messenger?" questioned General Caudex. "And how do you propose a man wounded by such a whip can get around and find the messenger."

"Because General, we will bring the messenger to the Lance Corporal," announced Tribune Claudius. "Now if you'll excuse me, I need to have a conversation with my emissary catcher."

***

Senior Tribune Claudius approached the litter which the porters had rested on the ground.

"What have you got?" Gaius asked as he stopped in front of the First Sergeant.

"Lance Corporal Sisera as fast, portable and comfortable as we can make him," announced Brictius.

Gaius leaned over and parted the billowing curtains. He stared at Alerio's back for a moment before realizing the Lance Corporal was sitting backward in the chair. Moving around to the rear, he again parted the curtains.

"Senior Tribune Claudius. My apologiges for not greeting you properly," Alerio said. He sat with the chair back under his arms to support his upper body. "I don't seem to be at my best, sir."

"Can you recognize Macario Hicetus from in there?" inquired Gaius.

"Yes sir, as long as I'm facing in the right direction," Alerio assured the Tribune. "What's the plan, sir?"

"Still working on it. Stand by," Gaius said as he dropped the curtains.

From inside the litter, he heard, "Standing by, Tribune."

"We plan to use tax collection and census as a ploy to search for the messenger, sir," Brictius announced. "I'm sending two Centuries to the western foothills. They'll herd anyone passing through to a survey point. Lance Corporal Sisera will be off to the side in his chariot watching as the Tesserarius collect a fee and take names."

"Which Centuries?" asked Gaius.

"One from second maniple and one from Claudius Detachment to watch Alerio's back," replied the First Sergeant. "And I placed four archery squads on the arm at Messina harbor. In case they try rowing the messenger by us."

"Be sure the Centurions know to treat the civilians with respect," warned Gaius. "If we start being heavy-handed, the messenger might wait for nightfall to attempt crossing our lines. I want him to feel safe when he lies about his name."

"Gentle it is, sir," Brictius assured him.

Chapter 9 – Hunting Stand

Fourth Century, Second Maniple, marched through the western gate. While they rapidly marched up the first of the nodes creating the foothills, the litter transporting Lance Corporal Sisera moved more slowly. Although the powerful Sons of Mars oarsmen could easily handle the weight, the Medic warned against jarring the wounded Legionary. They held to a restricted gait. Third Century, Claudius Detachment, sauntered along behind, enjoying the easy pace.

Three ridges from the wall of Messina, a farmer and herder trail provided a flat ribbon wandering along the ravine. The Fourth crossed the rough road and began dropping squads out of their columns. Where the foothills ended and a mountain cliff prevented further travel, they dropped the last squad. With a picket line established, their Centurion and Tesserarius doubled back to the road.

While the Fourth of the Third established the high positions, the Third of Claudius dropped squads on the lower foothills and sent half-squad patrols to the north and south. The Centurions and Tesserarii from both Centuries set up tents and desks on either side of the path. In front of one tent, the litter was placed facing northward.

"How are you feeling, Sisera?" asked the medic assigned to the mission.

He leaned against the Lectica and spoke through the curtains.

"I've been better and more comfortable," Alerio replied. "But I have a good view of the southern trail."

"Let me know if you feel dizzy or need to nap," the Medic requested. "I'll have the Corporals delay passing people through until you are rested."

Alerio shifted and sharp pains rippled from the center of his back up to his shoulder blades and down to his hips.

"Unless I pass out, I don't think sleep is in my future," Alerio replied as he shifted trying to ease the tightness in his back.

***

Shortly after the checkpoint was established, a cart approached from the south.

"Name and cargo?" asked the Corporal. "We're taking a census and collecting a travel tax."

"I'm a simple farmer with five little ones and a wife to feed," complained the man as he dragged an old mule to a stop. "Taxes. For what?"

"What are you hauling?" asked the Corporal as he walked to the rickety cart.

The Tesserarius glanced at the litter. After the medic spoke into the curtains, he shook his head indicating the farmer wasn't the royal messenger.

"I'm hauling melons to market. What's this robbery going to cost me?" inquired the farmer.

"Two melons tax," the NCO said picking out two midsized melons. "Move along."

"Two melons you take? Do you know the sweat I spend cultivating the land before planting?" the farmer stated as he nudged the mule into motion. "Days of my labor went into growing those. Here I am on the way to Synes and you pluck two of my melons out of my load. And just like that, I'm two melons short. If…"

The Legionaries could hear the farmer grousing even when the cart was almost at the bend in the road.

"This is going to be a long and boring assignment," the Tesserarius exclaimed as he handed the melons to his Centurion.

"Find us some more melons and it'll at least be a tasty duty," the Centurion commented.

The bleating of goats reached them before the herder and his flock came from the north. Turning, the officer and NCO watched the other Tesserarius.

"There's a tax to pass," the Corporal said as he walked between goats to reach the minder.

"I've only thirty heads," pointed out the herder. "Would you take a full goat when I'm just trying to reach new pastures?"

"Your tax is two containers of goat's milk," the Corporal said.

He combined the contents of four clay water pots. After pausing long enough to milk two nannies, the herd moved on.

"I'll trade you one milk for your two melons," one Centurion offered the other.

"One for one," countered the line officer.

"Done." And they made the trade.

As they put their taxes in separate tents, a wagon came from the north.

Two men walked beside a mule team pulling a covered wagon. One wore a green cloak, the other a blue garment and a third man, strolling behind the wagon, had on a brown travel coat. Under the hood, he coughed and sneezed. All three had the hoods of their travel cloaks up to keep the rising sun off their heads.

"Names, and there is a tax," the Tesserarius stated to them. "What's in the wagon."

"Linen, silk and thread," the man in the green cloak replied as he tugged the mule team to a stop. "How many coins will this cost us?"

As the Corporal walked around the wagon lifting the cover and peering into the bed, the mules shuffled sideways and the man in the blue cloak placed a hand on the side of a mule's head and shoved the stubborn beast hard. The mule stepped back in line and the team steadied.

"Two copper coins," the Legion NCO said as he arrived back beside the animals.

"We're just meeting our partners to turn over the cloth," stated the man. "If you charge us two now, will we have to pay when we come back?"

"No, I'll let you through," the Corporal informed him. He remembered the instructions to make civilian passage as easy as possible. "But let's see your faces so I know when you come back."

The three men tossed back their hoods. Two were clear-eyed but the third had a runny nose and wet red-rimmed eyes.

"Move along," ordered the Corporal as he clutched the two coins in his hand.

The wagon rolled away and the Corporal strolled to his officer.

"Two coins, Centurion."

"At this rate, we'll be able to feed and pay the Legion from the taxes," teased the officer.

The sun passed overhead and traffic slowed.

"Here Lance Corporal Sisera," the Medic offered as he handed a bowl of Legion stew to Alerio.

"I'd rather face a phalanx than sit here being useless," complained Alerio as he took the bowl.

"You have a mission," the Medic reminded him. "How are you feeling?"

"I felt a little wetness back there," Alerio informed the Medic.

"Let me check your bandages," he said as he stepped between the curtains. "Ah, Hades, you're bleeding. I wish I could do a full dressing."

Without the supplies of a medical unit, the Medic settled for a field alternative.

"This is going to hurt," he warned.

"Can't be worse than," began Alerio before he inquired. "What's going to hurt?"

Suddenly, his back was drenched and he smelled vinegar. The stinging and burning, almost as bad as when he was whipped, caused him to convulse. Shaking and moaning, he dropped the half-eaten bowl of stew and squeezed the back of the litter chair. Finally, the pain settled into a throbbing along the x-mark and he relaxed his grip.

"You could have told me," suggested Alerio.

"I did. Let me get you another bowl."

"Don't bother. My stomach can't handle food right now," explained Alerio. "Maybe some water?"

The afternoon saw farmers, tradesman, travelers and herders filtered to the Legion checkpoint. In all of those heading northward, Alerio checked and discounted them. None were Macario Hicetus or even men of military age.

Then, a caravan of farmers came from the south. Five carts pulled by men or old mules. Each cart needed to be checked and all of the people spoken to by a Corporal. The returning cloth merchants joined the end of the line. Feeling sorry for them, the Corporal waved them around the line of carts being inspected.

"Thank you for remembering us," the man in the green robe said. "We're trying to get home tonight and not spend another night under the stars."

"Just let me check your load," the Corporal assured the man as he walked to the wagon.

"My brother is resting in the back," the tradesman informed the NCO. "I fear this trip has drained all his strength."

Alerio looked at the men through a haze of pain and exhaustion. Vaguely, he remembered them from what felt like a lifetime ago. His throat was dry and he wanted a drink of water. But, he feared taking his weary eyes off the tradesmen.

The Tesserarius poked something in the wagon before the man in the brown cloak sat up. After looking closely at the man's face, the Lance Corporal discounted the brown cloak. Then, he shifted his attention towards the front of the wagon to check on the man in the blue cloak.

Far back in the procession of carts waiting to be inspected, an old farmer began screaming and beating his mule. If there was one thing beyond their shields, javelins, and gladii understood by Legionaries, it was mules. Each squad had one and, to a man, they were glad for the pack animal's capacity. If not for the mule, the tent, squad cooking supplies, and other gear would have to be carried by the Legionaries.

With the enthusiasm of the old farmer, the Corporal feared his Legionaries would soon have to drag a mule carcass off the path. In a rush, he raised an arm to wave the cloth merchant onward. But one of the mules on the wagon team stepped sideways in the direction of the blue cloak.

Alerio chuckled as he recalled the exact action from the morning. The motion caused his back to spasm and he lost focus for a heartbeat. Recovering enough to see a blurry image, the Lance Corporal waited for the head shove.

Standing quietly at the side of the mule, the merchant in the blue cloak reached out and caressed the animal's neck. Not a gesture used to correct a stubborn pack animal. It was the reaction of a cavalryman.

"Medic. The man in the blue robe," croaked out Alerio. With his throat partially closed, his voice didn't carry far. In frustration, the Legionary took hold of the light frame supporting the curtains and he snapped the posts. The effort racked his back with pain while the curtains collapsed burying him in Egyptian linen.

"Sisera! Are you in pain?" cried the Medic as he grabbed hands full of fabric and pulled them off his patient.

"Blue cloak. Blue cloak," Alerio whispered. "Don't worry about me. Blue cloak, get him."

The two Centurions noticed the destruction of the upper carriage of the litter. Mesmerized by the quaking fabric and the final toppling of the frame, they laughed when the Medic began frantically ripping away the linen. Then, the Medic spun and pointed a finger at the cloth merchant's wagon.

"The man in the blue cloak," the Medic yelled. "He's the messenger."

The shout also reached the man in blue and he raced away from the mule team. One of the Centurions put two fingers between his lips and emitted three shrill whistles.

Legionaries were trained to respond to commands from their squad leader, NCOs and their officer. From over the crest of the hills bordering the rough road, two half-squads leaped the ridges and sprinted to the road. They converged on the blue

80

cloak. When he attempted to force his way between two shields, he was slammed to the ground.

A pair of Legionaries grabbed his arms and they dragged him back towards the checkpoint. To the horror of the waiting farmers, every Legionary had lowered his javelin. All the civilians stood with an iron tip at their chests.

"Get me out of this," wheezed Alerio.

The four oarsmen, who had been lounging in the shade of a tent, strolled to the litter.

"Captain Sisera. You've ruined Captain Creon's favorite chair," one of them remarked.

"He's not going to be happy about that," another of the big men said as he reached in and yanked Alerio out of the wreckage.

Lance Corporal Sisera, heavy infantryman, weapons instructor, Legion Raider, certified combat rower, and veteran swordsman cried. Tears ran down his face as he crumpled to the ground. Withering in the dirt, he tried to reach his back to clutch at the pain and find a less agonizing position.

"What have you done?" screamed the Medic as he knelt beside his patient.

Seeing the blood soaking through Sisera's bandages and tunic, the oarsman jumped back.

"I didn't know," he pleaded. "I thought the Captain was hiding like in a hunting stand."

"It seems, he needed the litter," another oarsman commented. "I wondered why it stunk of vinegar."

"Help me get him up," and the Medic paused. Where could he put the wounded Legionary?

The oarsman who had jerked Alerio out of the litter went to the vehicle and wrenched the chair from the lower frame.

Setting it down by the Medic, he suggested, "Put the Captain back in the chair."

The Medic and an oarsman picked the moaning Legionary off the ground. They placed his legs on either side of the seat and leaned his chest against the chair back. Alerio's head hung and he fought to get control of the pain.

"Is this the messenger?" a voice asked.

Blinking his eyes to clear them, Alerio raised his head and stared into the face of Macario Hicetus.

"Lieutenant Hicetus. Good to see you again," Alerio said softly.

"You! The spy," spit the Syracusan noble. "I should have killed you when I had the chance."

"And I should have left you for the street gang," Alerio replied weakly. "But that's history and the fates have brought us together briefly."

"Briefly?" Hicetus asked.

"Yes. Senior Tribune Gaius Claudius wants to have a conversation with you," advised Alerio. "And you should know, the Tribune is tired. He was out last night killing Qart Hadasht troops with his bare hands. If you want to keep your body parts, you'll answer his questions, quickly."

The Centurion assigned three squads as escorts.

"Double time back to Citadel Hill," he ordered. "If the prisoners can't keep up. Kill the other two and carry the messenger. Go."

When the squads, Macario Hicetus and the brown and green cloaks vanished over the crest of the first hill, the Centurion turned to Alerio.

"The Tribune was only observing the Qart Hadasht troops last night," the officer stated. "I don't think he participated in any combat."

"No, sir. But the Syracusan messenger doesn't know that," replied Alerio. Then he groaned and went limp over the back of the chair.

Chapter 10 – Missives and Responses

"The day after tomorrow when the sun is overhead," Tribune Gaius Claudius stated as he unrolled a scroll and placed it on the table. "There are no other couriers. When threats didn't reveal other messengers, I resorted to something Lance Corporal Sisera said to get to the truth."

"And what was that?" asked General Caudex.

"I handed Macario Hicetus a wineskin and waited," Claudius informed the Legions' command staff. "When he was dancing with Bacchus, Lieutenant Hicetus admitted that he was the only royal messenger."

Colonel Requiem reached out, snatched up the scroll and read the document. When he finished, he offered it to Colonel Nicephrus.

"I don't read Greek," Nicephrus admitted as he waved off the scroll. "Four Gallic languages because I need to know my enemies. Until now, they hadn't been Hellenes."

"What's your opinion of the message, Pericles?" General Caudex questioned.

"Just what the Tribune reported," Requiem explained as he scanned the message. "The day after tomorrow both King Hiero's forces and the Qart Hadasht mercenaries will...Let me see. Become the swords of Nemesis and punish the arrogance of the Republic. With the Goddess' blessing, the streets of Messina will run red with the blood of our mutual foe."

"That's plain enough," Nicephrus observed. "It's a battle on two fronts."

"Not yet, Colonel," Caudex suggested. "I'm going to send missives and emissaries. We will seek peace and a resolution."

"When General? Before they attack and kill us all," accused Maris Eutropius. "We have one option, withdraw from Messina. Row back to the Republic and forget this ill-advised adventure."

Colonel Nicephrus and Colonel Requiem stared open-mouthed at the Senior Tribune. Then they glanced at each other before looking across the table at General Caudex.

"It's a good thing Senior Tribune Eutropius is on the General's staff," Nicephrus stated. Then he looked over his shoulder at the junior Tribunes, Legionary runners, and servants standing against the walls.

"Why is that, Colonel?" inquired General Caudex.

"Our Centuries fight aggressively based on the assumption that we will be victorious," Requiem exclaimed. "Starting our plan of battle with a retreat will demoralize the Legionaries. Now that Tribune Eutropius has voiced a defeatist attitude and predicted our demise, we have to repair the internal damage."

"What has that got to do with whose staff he serves on?" asked the General.

"If he suggested a retreat before a battle near a Centurion, the line officer would stab him in the gut to silence him. And to show that Senior Tribune Eutropius was, literally, full of merda," Colonel Nicephrus informed the General. "As it is sir, you'll need to give a rousing speech to the Legions to reassure the men of our victory."

"I'll make the speech after I craft the missives and dispatch the representatives," promised General Caudex. He looked around at the onlookers. "Once we get the replies, we will formulate a plan that does not include another night crossing of the Messina Strait."

***

Two emissaries with Legion cavalry escorts galloped from Messina. One went to the Syracuse King in the south and another to the Qart Hadasht General in the north. After they rode out, Legionaries began crowding the streets of Messina. Colonels Nicephrus and Requiem had sent orders to their Divisions. It was compulsory for every Legionary, not required to man the defensive positions, to come and stand at the foot of

Citadel Hill. There, they would bask in the words of their General and hear the truth about their situation.

General Caudex marched from the Citadel with the Colonels flanking him five steps back. At the crest of the hill, he paced as if inspecting the units. After long moments, he raised his arms to silence the men.

"Legionaries! Citizens and defenders of the Republic, I am General Appease Clodus Caudex. There are rumors running like city rats through our Centuries. I am here to smash the rats and clear the ranks of these ugly untruths. Be of good cheer and not downcast. For we have the enemies of our Republic where we want them."

A murmur of confusion ran through the crowd of Legionaries at the comment. They were trapped with warships preventing resupplies on the Strait and armies to their south and north. Yet the General assured them it was a positive condition.

"I see you lack the vision to see the true nature of our situation. Allow me to rip away the fog before your eyes and show you reality. Victories do not fall to the better-equipped or the undisciplined masses. Victory, my Legionaries, is earned by men of valor. Legionaries who display better skills than those of their opponents. You've run until your feet are calloused. You've swung your gladii until your muscles are hard. And you've marched until the men at your sides resemble Phobos and Deimos to the enemy."

Comparing the Legion ranks to the God of Fear and his twin brother, the God of Terror, brought cheers from the Legionaries. The exuberance at the compliment by their General flowed from those in front to those standing far back on side streets. As his words were repeated, more cheers erupted. Gazing at his Legionaries, Caudex stood absorbing their adoration.

"You see the Strait and the seas as deep woods and the Qart Hadasht warships as unstoppable wolves. But I tell you, the Republic will soon acquire the science of seafaring. Sea warfare skills can be obtained by men who give their minds to it and mastered by practice. Bravery, on the other hand, when not in a man's nature cannot be acquired. Bravery comes from the heart, not from numbers, positions, instructions, or the giving of coins. Let them row around for now. Soon, they will feel and fear the sea might of the Republic."

More cheers erupted and the General paused until they subsided.

"I trust my life and the health of the Republic to the bravery of my Legions. To your hearts and the strength of your shield and gladius arms. To your Squads, your Centuries and the unbeatable ranks of our maniples. From the power of my veterans in the first maniple to the steady skills of the second. And even to the untested Legionaries of the third maniple. The enemy's numbers tremble in the face of my Legionaries. Their leaders should fall to their knees and beg for our mercy. They do not have your heart! They do not have your courage!"

And the Legionaries shouted back, "Ita Vero! Ita Vero! Ita Vero!"

"Legionaries of Caudex Legions, standby," ordered the General.

Seven thousand hobnailed boots stomped the streets of Messina and the Legions replied.

"General. Caudex Legions, standing by," they roared.

Appease Clodus Caudex slammed his hand into his chest. After the salute, the General spun on his heels and marched away. Down Citadel Hill, Legionaries strutted back to their units, their chests bursting with confidence.

"Nice speech," commented Palaemon Nicephrus. "Bucked up the men."

"And made them unafraid of the armies flanking us," replied Pericles Requiem. "I wish I had the same confidence."

"Why Colonel, did you not hear the words of our General?" inquired Nicephrus. "Are you not inspired?"

"I'll let you know Colonel when the emissaries return with the replies," Requiem offered. "Until then, I'll hold my enthusiasm in check."

They turned and followed the General into the Citadel.

***

As the sun touched the western mountaintop and shadows grew long, a rider reined in at the foot of the hill. He slung a leg over the horse's neck, jumped to the ground and ran up the slope. At the top, he sprinted for the Citadel.

"Sir. A message from the Qart Hadasht General," the Tribune announced as he handed Caudex a folded and sealed piece of parchment.

"What did he have to say?" inquired the General as he took the reply.

"He said nothing, sir," responded the messenger. "He took your missive into his tent and returned directly with that piece of parchment."

General Caudex pulled his dagger, slit the seal and unfolded the message.

"We have our answer from the Qart Hadasht forces," he exclaimed while handing the paper to Colonel Requiem.

Requiem glanced at the short message and passed it to Nicephrus. He read it and handed the parchment to Senior Tribune Claudius.

"The General is a man of few words but elegant in his brevity," Gaius stated as he slid the message to the other Senior Tribune.

"*Verminum Curre,*" Maris Eutropius mouthed the two words on the reply. "Run vermin."

"We have one answer to my olive branch. Let's see if the other is dashed to the dirt as well," stated Caudex. "I believe it's time to assemble a war council. Colonels, call in your

87

experienced Centurions, your cavalry officers, and our First Sergeants."

"Yes General," Nicephrus and Requiem said at the same time.

They turned and waved runners to their sides. After issuing orders, the messengers ran for the door to collect the other leaders of Caudex Legions.

As darkness fell, Senior Centurion Valerian, First Sergeant Brictius and, Southern Legion's First Sergeant Gerontius marched into a full meeting room. They had just cleared the doorway when the second emissary appeared.

"General. King Hiero sends his regards," the messenger announced as he handed a scroll to Caudex.

"That's a promising start," suggested the General as he unrolled the scroll. Then his face fell. He finished reading it and slammed the scroll onto the tabletop. "This is unacceptable."

Colonel Palaemon Nicephrus spun the document around and began reading.

Consul Appease Clodus Caudex of the Republic,

It lightens my heart to read you are weary of playing General. Not every man is destined to be a victorious war leader, such as myself. I understand the difficulty of your situation, although as a strategist, I've never felt the embarrassment of your hopelessness.

In response to your plea for help, I grant you and your army of farmers, safe passage away from Messina. Once you have laid down your weapons and retreated from the city, I will march in and, after crucifying the Sons of Mars, proclaim the city as part of Syracuse. But you will not be forgotten.

Bulls will be sacrificed in your honor and I will declare a yearly festival honoring you as a benefactor of Syracuse. Even as you have no choice, I await your humble reply.

King Hiero the Second, Supreme Ruler of Syracuse, General of the People's Army and Protector of Sicilia.

"General. Do you have a reply?" questioned Colonel Pericles Requiem

"Put the map on the table," ordered the General. Once the thin leather was unrolled, displaying Messina and the surrounding countryside, Appease Caudex made a fist and hammered a location south of the city. "We attack here, first. Give me a plan for victory."

Chapter 11 – Horse, Infantry & Irregulars

In the center of Messina, Colonel Pericles Requiem patted his horse's neck. Behind him, runners stood waiting and his contingent of Tribunes sat beside him on their mounts. Two hundred and forty Legion cavalrymen trotted up from the lower reaches of the city and turned left. Once they reached the southern wall, the units split with half going left and the other half reining right.

Then, twenty-one Centuries of heavy infantry marched from the upper areas, turned right and marched through the south gates. Following behind, seven Centuries of skirmishers made the turn and marched through the gates. Off to the side of the marching and cantering, Requiem and his staff watched without expression. Only when Colonel Palaemon Nicephrus and his staff appeared, did Requiem react. He waved and gave a nod to his fellow Legion battle commander.

When General Caudex passed with Senior Tribunes Maris Eutropius and the rest of his staff, the Colonel saluted. Headquarters First Century jogged around the General as if the unit was already in contact with an enemy. Javelins leveled, the Centurion, Optio, and Tesserarius directed the unit to keep the General's path clear and to make their Legionaries aware of perceived threats.

"Watch those Qart Hadasht mercenaries," shouted the General as he turned right and rode for the gates.

"Absolutely, General," Requiem called to Caudex's back. He looked across the road at a Senior Centurion. "Bring up your reserves."

"Yes, sir," the line officer replied.

Soon, the streets on either side of the gates hid the remaining fifteen Centuries from Nicephrus' Legion plus fifteen additional Centuries of heavy infantrymen from Requiem's.

"I want a continuous line of Tribunes and runners from here to our northern defenses," Pericles Requiem instructed. "If the Qart Hadasht troops move, I want to know immediately."

"Yes Colonel," his staff replied. They moved off and began taking up stations a block apart stretching from their commander, across Messina, to the northern wall.

Colonel Requiem sat calmly on his horse dividing his attention between the open gates to the south and the line of his staff stretching out towards the north.

"Do you think Hiero will come out and fight?" asked Senior Tribune Gaius Claudius.

"Gaius, he better," commented the Colonel. "If he waits for tomorrow, we'll be ground meat for Legion stew. As it is, how can he refuse the sacrifice of twenty-two hundred Legionaries to his six thousand soldiers."

***

The twenty-one Centuries marched through the defensive positions, over the footfall trenches and out into no man's land. At directions from their Centurions, the units to the rear changed their lines of march to diagonal paths. As they moved further from their defenses, a formation appeared - seven Centuries to the front spaced widely apart with the others stacked behind them.

"Legion, halt in ten!" ordered Colonel Palaemon Nicephrus.

The signalmen began waving flags while others shouted the command. Soon, every Centurion, Sergeant, and Corporal was repeating, "Legion halt in ten, nine, eight, seven, six, five, four, three, two and halt."

As if a hand had descended to still each Legionary, the Centuries suddenly stopped. They stood motionless in the mid-morning sun.

"Palaemon. It seems as if your maneuver has gotten the Syracusan's attention," remarked General Caudex. In the Syracusan camp, men scurried around pulling on armor and strapping on weapons.

"It has, General. Let's show them how few we are and see if they'll take the challenge," Colonel Nicephrus suggested. "Legion, form maniples in ten."

The orders were flagged to the end Centuries while it was passed verbally from the center of the Legion. Again, the air rang with officers, Sergeants and Corporals counting down. At ten-and-form-maniples, the first column in each Century marched forward. The lead man turned ninety degrees and soon the column was a single file. In quick order, the blocks of Centuries were dissolved and replaced by three rows of five hundred and sixty Legionaries.

When the maniples were formed, the cavalry trotted forward to flank and protect the infantrymen at each end.

"Send out the Velites to keep their cavalry off our infantry," instructed Nicephrus. "Execute!"

Flags waved and the passing of his orders rolled over the three ranks. From behind the infantrymen, five hundred sixty skirmishers, their officers, and NCOs stepped through gaps in the first maniple, crossed the narrow space and marched through the second maniple. On the other side of the third maniple, the Velites spread out in squads. Behind them, the holes in the rows closed as fast as they had formed.

The relatively short lines of Legionaries weren't impressive or intimidating. Syracusan cavalry raced forward but changed direction when a hail of javelins from the skirmishers rained down on them. The mounted soldiers settled for racing up and down the Legion lines. But they stopped short of engaging the Velites or the Legion cavalrymen.

"They seem to be giving our horsemen some respect," commented General Caudex.

"No, sir. I've seen the tactic used by the Gaels up north," explained Nicephrus. "They hope to lure some of our horsemen out of formation. Once in the open, the enemy will turn and cut them down. My Centurions know to keep their men in ranks."

All the while, the skirmishers rotated their squads to face the enemy horsemen keeping them away from the relaxed infantrymen. The maniples would have work enough when the heavy infantry of the Hoplites arrived.

***

King Hiero's irregular soldiers came online and shuffled forward to face the maniples. Grass torn and uprooted by the cavalry, allowed the soldiers' sandals to scrape dirt and raise dust. Haze blocked the view of what was amassed behind them.

Suddenly, seven wide gaps appeared in the soldier's ranks and, from the dust cloud, groups of iron tips appeared. Supporting the tips were long spears who's ends vanished into a wall of shields. More long spears jutted from the sides and the shield covered formations moved relentlessly forward. King Hiero II had accepted the challenge and committed his phalanxes.

"Centurions make the call," ordered Colonel Nicephrus.

Flags waved, voices shouted and the line officers glanced from side to side. Those with Legionaries in the paths of the phalanxes raised their hands.

"So that's a phalanx," observed General Caudex as the tightly locked shields approached the third maniple. "Frightening display of power. How do you get past their shields and crack the egg?"

"You don't crack a phalanx, General," responded Colonel Nicephrus.

"You just gave authority to your line officers," Caudex stated. "I assumed they would attack the Greek formations."

"A phalanx is like a carriage without horses rolling down a hill," described Nicephrus. "Stand in front and it'll run you over."

"Then what can we do against them?" inquired a panicked Caudex.

"Watch, sir. This was Colonel Requiem's tactic," explained Nicephrus. Then to the Senior Centurion. "Valerian. Call them out."

"Yes, sir," the Senior Centurion replied as he kneed his horse towards the gates.

After jumping over the defensive line, his horse burst through the gates and he reined it in a tight circle.

"Centurions. Seven phalanxes," he shouted to one side then repeated the announcement to the other. "Four Centuries on each. The last two, go to the ends for containment. Forward!"

From the left side of the gate, fifteen Centuries jogged into view. On the right side, another fifteen appeared. The Centurions of the first four Centuries through the gates shouted and their formations headed towards the Centurions holding up their arms. The same orders were given on the right.

"I thought you were hiding the reserves to entice Hiero to go to battle against a weaker force," offered General Caudex. "But you seem to have them ready to take on the unstoppable. How will they do what you said was impossible?"

"I apologize for the incomplete analogy, sir," expressed Nicephrus. "A wagon careening down a hill has one weakness. It can't change course without turning over. When it turns over, the wagon breaks up. And so, the phalanxes will break formation when they turn."

"You'll have three hundred twenty Legionaries for the Hoplites in each of their formations," ventured the General. "And you've managed to slip your reserves on the battlefield in the process."

"We have sir. Now let's offer a prayer to Tyche that our good fortune holds," the Colonel suggested. "Because we still have to trim the barbs from the eggs."

***

Private Eolus of the Seventh Squad, Sixth Century, third maniple couldn't see clearly. It might have been the sweat dripping into his eyes, or the helmet that kept shifting as he shuddered or maybe, it was the blinding fear that caused both of the above. In any case, his vision blurred as a line of Syracusan soldiers closed with his position. Sure, his squad mates stood to either side and, the more experienced second maniple stood behind him, but to the young Private, all the soldiers in front seemed to be coming directly towards him. Then the soldiers parted and a horror from his childhood came through the dust.

A giant centipede with barbed legs squirming and reaching out for him approached. In his dreams as a child, he ran from the beast. Before he could bolt, a fist slammed into his shoulder.

"Just like we practiced, correct, Private Eolus," a voice from behind growled in his ear.

"Yes, Optio," he stammered in reply to his Sergeant's statement.

"Good. You are our Pivot man," the Sergeant informed him.

The Optio's muscular and hairy arm pressed on his shoulder armor and the NCO's forearm and fist appeared in front of the Private's face. Uncurling his fingers, the Sergeant pointed at the centipede.

"Those cowardly Hoplites have made a grave mistake," the Sergeant said with his fingers pointing at the approaching phalanx.

"Mistake, Optio?" inquired Eolus.

"Absolutely. They picked the position of my most ferocious Legionaries," the Sergeant replied. "Poor Hoplites, they are perfututum now."

"I don't understand Sergeant, what mistake?"

"They choose to enter the gates of Hades, courtesy of Seventh Squad, Sixty Century, third maniple," the Optio declared. "And their true error was picking your position. When they get to the underworld, they'll be asking who was the gatekeeper? Was it the God of War himself? No, Pluto will reply as he sorts them. The butcher on the Legion line was Private Eolus!"

The Sergeant felt the tightening of the Private's muscles and the straightening of his back as confidence flooded the inexperienced Legionary.

"When I give the word, guide your section back. And Private Eolus," the Optio directed. "Keep their shields tight and in line."

From the fear that racked the young Legionary, a new sense of confidence and duty took over. He was acting Pivot and as the barbed ends of the centipede closed, he worried more about his squad's performance than the iron tips.

Behind him, Sixth Century, third maniple's Centurion shifted his attention between the reserve Centuries running towards him and the phalanx approaching his line. When both were close, he dropped his arms.

"Open the gate!" the Centurion ordered.

"Eolus. Pivot," commanded the Sergeant.

"Pivoting. Step back," Eolus ordered as he paced off the line. Glancing to his right, he corrected the half squad moving with him. "Keep it tight. Straighten those shields. Step back. Step back."

As if a set of doors were opened inward, the Legion lines parted leaving a hole for the phalanx. Except the hole led to a corridor of Legionaries. While the three maniples parted, a section of first maniple rushed forward bowing out the Legion line and filling in the gap. They would hold the line against the Syracusan soldiers until the phalanx passed completely through.

"Draw," ordered the Sergeant and, Eolus and his squad pulled their gladii.

As the shields of the phalanx passed by and the spears jabbed out and pulled back, the Legionaries forming the corridor parried the iron tips with their shields and hacked at the shafts with their blades.

Eolus slammed a spear tip to the side while he hacked at another. Then a third iron tip traveled forward. With his shield out of place and his gladius off to the side, the spear was traveling straight for the young Legionary's face. Eolus didn't think about ducking or dodging. Instead, he shifted his shield to protect the Legionary beside him from another Hoplite spear. Figuring it was his duty and his fate, he waited for death.

A big arm bumped his head and a gladius whirled with terrifying speed across his vision. The spear shaft was hacked almost in half. The shaft angled downward and the tip dug into the dirt.

"What's your name?" demanded a voice he didn't recognize.

"Eolus," he answered as he fended off another spear and hacked at the shaft.

Then the area in front of him cleared and he could see a line of bloody Legionaries standing on the other side of the corridor. Like him, they were breathing hard, bent over trying to catch their breath. Glancing at each side, he expected to see his squad mates. But something was wrong, he didn't recognize any of the Legionaries from the third maniple.

"Eolus? Which one of you is Eolus?" demanded a huge Sergeant.

"Here, Optio," he responded raising his gladius.

"Is that the man?" the NCO inquired of two Legionaries flanking him.

"That's him," one assured the Sergeant.

"What's your unit, Private Eolus?" the Optio asked.

Before Eolus could respond, his Sergeant marched up.

"He is Seventh Squad, Sixth Century, third maniple," Eolus's NCO answered. "Why? Is something wrong?"

"Optio. Two more engagements and I'm voting him into second maniple," the Sergeant announced. "And if he stays true, I'll draft him into my Century. The man is a warrior."

"I agree, Eolus is my gatekeeper to Hades," responded his Sergeant.

When the Legionaries went to rejoin their unit, Private Eolus gazed at his Sergeant in confusion.

"What happened?" he inquired.

"Most of third maniple was overwhelmed with the task of attacking the sides of the phalanx. Not really their fault being inexperienced. It was an ugly job," related the Sergeant. "As they fell back, the second and first stepped up to fight the spears. Except for one Legionary. He stayed on his line and fought until the monster passed. During the fight, you saved two Legionaries from first maniple. Imagine the embarrassment of two veterans owing their lives to a third maniple Legionary."

"I did that?" questioned Eolus. He didn't remember anything except the never-ending thrusts of spears. "Who was the Sergeant?"

"Third Century, first maniple's Optio," replied his Sergeant. "Seems you have a patron. Now, hero, let's get back in this fight."

Twelve paces away, soldiers and Legionaries clashed shield to shield. Bloody javelins and gladii created sparks as they raked against swords and spears. Above the din of battle, wounded and dying men cried out. Their pleas just slightly softer than the war cries of their brothers at arms. Private Eolus sheathed his gladius, snatched up a javelin and ran to the battle line. There, he shoved his way into the rank of third maniple and retook his place between his squad mates.

***

The Centurion of Headquarters Century was screaming in anger and rage.

"Fold your line back," he ordered for the third time. His Sergeant and Corporal ran around the collapsing circle moving Legionaries to critical areas.

Two phalanxes had broken formations and made a run for the Legion's command staff. Two groups of one hundred twenty-eight Hoplites surged towards the General coming at his guards from two sides. The move by the Hoplites took them by surprise. Only the First HQ Century stood between their commander and Hiero's Greeks. It was an attempt to cut the head off the Legion. As the reserve Centuries were still sprinting to cover the distance and had yet to form squad ranks, the First Centurion made a decision.

"Optio. Pull four squads off the perimeter," he ordered. "Turtle the General."

General Caudex sat pivoting his head. All around him, Legionaries and Hoplites hacked and chopped at each other. Further away, segments of the battle line appeared through the dust. Men pushed and hacked, and javelins and spear tips came over their shoulders stabbing down into both ranks. Then the dust rose again to veil the battle.

"General. My apologies," his First Optio said. Then the veteran NCO reached up and yanked Caudex from the horse's back.

From a height where he could scan the battlefield, the General's view was reduced to hobnailed boots, legs, and the bottoms of armor skirts. Their shields clamped together and as if in a tent, the light became muted. Sitting in the dirt, General Caudex shook his head trying to make sense of the sudden change.

Colonel Nicephrus had ridden to the far right to get an idea of the fighting in that sector. When he looked back at the center, he saw the General's horse standing riderless. Then, he noted Tribune Eutropius pounding on a mound of shields. Finally, he took in the Hoplites pushing into the First Century's protective circle.

"Centurion. Give me half of your cavalry," he shouted to a mounted officer.

While the infantry line was locked in a deadly dance, on the ends, the mounted Legionaries fended off Syracusan cavalrymen and skirmishers. Without waiting for reinforcements, Nicephrus kicked his horse into motion. His Tribunes, caught by surprise, followed a moment later.

The Colonel reined his horse to the side and pulled back. As the horse reared up, Nicephrus swung his gladius at the edge of the massed Hoplites. A spear grazed his thigh but he remained mounted, fighting from horseback. The Tribunes came in and attempted to defend their Colonel. Seeing a new threat and the gold on Nicephrus' breastplate, the Greeks sent men to kill the Legion battle commander. The shift took a little pressure off the embattled First Century.

Then, eight squads of heavy infantry marched into one side of the Greeks and that side went from attacking the General's formation to fighting for their lives. And still, Nicephrus leaned in and chopped ignoring the blood running down his leg.

Seventy mounted men riding in a single file could be compared to a saw blade. Each rider, acting as a sharp tooth, rode by the Hoplites. By the time the Legion cavalrymen wheeled for a second pass, fifty Hoplites laid on the ground dead or wounded. The Greeks realized their numbers were diminishing and their officers shouted for a retreat.

The seventy Hoplites, still mobile, ran for the end of the Legion line. Colonel Palaemon Nicephrus sat straight, raised his blade and pointed it at the running Greeks.

"Cut their threads and send them to Hades," he ordered the cavalrymen. *"Non capimus!"*

The Colonel nudged his horse around wounded Legionaries to reach the mound of shields.

"Uncover," he ordered and, as the shields unlocked, a sputtering Appease Caudex rose up and looked around as if in a daze.

"Mount your horse, sir," directed Nicephrus.

"Palaemon. Someone dragged me off my horse," shouted the General. "I want him found and whipped."

"Maybe later, sir. Right now, I need you on your horse," Nicephrus insisted. Then to a Legionary, he directed. "Select a Greek sword. No, not that one. Dig the one out of the body. Yes, that one. Give it to the General."

Without looking, Caudex took the sword then almost dropped it when he noticed it was coated in wet blood.

"Nicephrus. This is filthy," scolded the General.

"Raise it above your head, sir," ordered the Colonel. "Tribunes to me."

General Caudex sat on his horse with blood flowing down the sword and onto his hand and arm.

"Really, Nicephrus. It's disgusting and about to ruin my tunic," Caudex warned.

Ignoring the plight of the General, Nicephrus motioned the Tribunes in close.

"I want this repeated to every Centurion personally. Word-for-word," he directed. "King Hiero sent assassins to kill our wounded. General Caudex seeing the vile act, rallied a small force and led them against the assassins to protect the injured Legionaries. With great personal risk, General Caudex fought off King Hiero's killers until reinforcements arrived. The General single-handedly slew ten Greeks today. He wants to know how many Syracusans have you have killed today?"

After having the Tribunes repeat the story, he sent them to tell the line officers. There was little doubt the tale would spread rapidly throughout the Legion.

"General. You are holding that sword as a display of your power," Nicephrus explained. "Our men saw you off your horse. Fear is a strong force and if the Legionaries thought their General was dead, they would lose heart."

"But someone pulled me off my horse," complained Caudex. "I want that man punished. Who dared?"

Maris Eutropius, who had unsteadily climbed onto his horse's back, lifted an arm and pointed at the Headquarters' Sergeant.

"He pulled the General off his horse," accused the Senior Tribune with a sneer in his voice.

"First Optio. Did you see the General off his horse?" Nicephrus demanded.

"Yes, sir. I saw the General off his mount," replied the First Sergeant of Headquarters Century.

"And what was the General doing off his horse?" he inquired.

"Sir, the General was leading us to intercept Syracusan assassins," the Sergeant stated loudly. "It was an unselfish act of bravery. And, I might add Colonel, I am proud to serve under a man with that quality."

"General. With your permission, I would like to send a letter to the Capital boasting of your heroism," ventured Nicephrus.

"Well Colonel, if you insist," Caudex replied.

"But Appease, that Legionary...," stated Eutropius but the General cut him off.

"Of course, you may add your name to the letter, Senior Tribune," Caudex explained. Then, he noticed the bleeding leg. "Medic. The Colonel requires a Medic."

Two Medics and a Doctor jumped at the announcement. As the Colonel's leg was bandaged, there was a roar from the infantry line. Looking around, the commanders watched as the first maniple shoved the second aside and jerked the third off the battle line.

"What just happened, Colonel?" asked Caudex.

"Our veterans have accepted your challenge to kill at least ten Syracusans," Nicephrus exclaimed. "Seems they want to win the admiration of a General who protects wounded Legionaries."

***

The Syracusan infantry gave ground to the first maniple but, a line only five hundred and sixty shields wide was no match for six thousand soldiers. The mass alone of the Syracuse army soon overcame the savagery and, the Legion stalled.

"Signalman, flag the reserve cavalrymen," ordered Nicephrus as he rode to the left of the battle line. "Let's show King Hiero our numbers."

The Legionary, running beside the Colonel, jerked his flags in a preset series and a signalman at the center repeated the sequence. When the signal was seen from the gates of Messina, it brought relief to one man.

Senior Centurion Valerian mumbled, "It's about time."

Anger and frustration at helplessly watching the Hoplites attack his General almost caused him to ride back to the battlefield. But, duty and years of military experience held him at his post. When he saw the flags, he stretched his arms out to his sides and pointed at the Legionaries staged on either side of the gates.

"Mount up," he shouted. His arms extended, pointing to the left and right. As the two hundred and forty Legion cavalrymen jumped on their horses, he added. "Victory goes to the brave. Standby."

"Standing by, First Centurion," the horsemen replied.

Slapping his hands together in front of his chest, he indicated the gates and bellowed, "Forward!"

**

The thirty Centurions from the reserve Centuries supervised the clean-up of the Hoplites. Unfortunately, the attack on their General changed the original plan. Instead of taking prisoners, who could be sold as slaves, the Legionaries took revenge on the wounded Greeks. While they watched the gladii stab and their Legionaries wander around in groups, the line officers also kept eyes on the gates. When the cavalry galloped through, they began organizing their infantrymen.

Fortunately, the dust and haphazard distribution of the reserve Centuries prevented the Syracusans from getting an accurate count of the Legionaries in the back. They might recognize that a large number of Legionaries were milling around behind the fighting but none of King Hiero's commanders knew or understood.

"Rotate the first off the line," Nicephrus instructed his signalman as he returned to the center near General Caudex. "Forward the second maniple."

Flags waved and shouts were passed through the Legion. On the shield wall, the Syracusan soldiers at the front got a face full of Legion shields followed by a pause in hostilities. Then, the veterans stepped back and were replaced by the unbloodied second maniple. With fresh Legionaries coming on the battle line, the fighting intensified.

Strengthened by the extra mounted units, the Legion cavalry pushed forward. With shouts of glory, the Syracusan horsemen rushed to engage them. They clashed three horse lengths in front of the battle line. Thinking to use the cavalry fray to get around the ends of the Legion, King Hiero's commanders sent their skirmishers and free units into the dusty gap between the horses and the ends of the Legion line.

Bellowing their war cries, the Syracusan soldiers charged through the haze. Expecting to end around the Legion, the lead elements were in full stride. Their charge faltered when they splattered against Legion shields and had their guts split open by gladii. The line of Legionaries had expanded by four hundred shields. Then the now thirteen hundred and sixty men of the third maniple stepped behind the second and added their javelins to the fighting.

Senior Centurion Valerian galloped towards the battle, reining in only a spear's throw from the fighting. Sitting his horse and looking along the Legion lines, he resembled Aenaeus, one of the judges of Hades. In fact, the Senior Centurion was sterner than the trio of judges from the underworld. Runners and signalmen fell in around him.

"Tell that Centurion if he can't keep his shields straight, I will come down there and run a javelin up his cūlus to demonstrate straight," he ordered a runner. To another, he instructed. "Tell that Centurion if he wants to be a bowman, join an archery unit. I do not want bowed lines in my infantry."

Weak points, sagging or arching sections in the Legion line soon disappeared and the Legionaries fought as if they were guided by a *Groma* surveying instrument. It wasn't. The alignment came from the sharp eyes of the Senior Centurion. Once happy with his Legionaries, Valerian twisted around and saluted his Colonel.

"Ten advances," ordered Colonel Nicephrus after receiving the sign that the Legion was ordered and ready. "Let's see what the Syracusans are made of."

Flags and shouts, messages sent and received, and along the line Centurions, Sergeants and Corporal counted down. By the count of four, every Legionary was either saying the numbers or, in the case of the second maniple, they thought the numbers saving their breath as they blocked and stabbed.

"Three, two and Advance, advance, advance...!"

The second maniple's thirteen hundred plus shields powered forward, slamming into the soldiers. Then the shields drew back and the blades of thirteen hundred gladii struck like snakes. The line stepped forward into the gap created by the dead or wounded Syracusan soldiers. They repeated the synchronized assault and stepped forward again. The third maniple kept pace while stabbing with their javelins and stomping on soldiers, living or dead, who littered the ground.

***

The Syracusan soldiers, stacked sixth from the front of the fighting, waited for their opportunity. Pressure from the back and from the front trapped them, preventing forward or rear movement. With nothing to do, they spoke with their rank mates, stopping occasionally to shout encouragement before returning to the conversation. Some of them talked with bravado and others whispered their fears. Most couldn't see the Legion shields. On the fifth Advance, the rank in front was thrown back or vanished below the big red shields. Then, the Syracusan sixth rank was hammered and stabbed to the ground before hobnailed boots stomped them into the dirt.

The Legion systematically eliminated seven ranks of soldiers. But, the addition of disciplined Syracusan troops to the fight and the Legionaries uneven footing on a carpet of dead caused the Legion's advance to falter.

"It's going to be bulls locked in a mating dance," announced Nicephrus seeing the line stop. "I'm betting on mine. Send the first maniple forward."

Flags and orders passed on his command and the Legion's veterans shoved between the third maniple and replaced the

Second. And soon, the Colonel's prediction came true. The best of the Legion clashed with Hiero's professional soldiers.

Grunting, heaving, and slashing, the line moved but the toll on both sides had the stretcher-bearers and Medics racing to the line and dragging back wounded or dead.

Colonel Nicephrus trotted his horse back and forth watching the state of the enemy troops. When he felt he had a feel for them, he pointed at the signalman.

"Send up the third maniple," he directed. "It's time they earned their coin. And earned their place in the Legion."

Flags and shouted orders carried his message, and the inexperienced maniple tossed down their javelins, drew their gladii and shoved between the first maniple, shouldering the veterans back and out of the way. Behind them, the second hustled up and began stabbing over their shoulders.

"Three advances," ordered Nicephrus as General Caudex rode up beside him.

The Tribunes around the commanders were confused. The first maniple could only manage a few steps forward against King Hiero's best soldiers. Now their Colonel wanted three steps from his least experienced line. But no one questions a battle commander and, the orders were flagged and passed.

"Advance, Advance, Advance," the Centurions, Sergeants, and Corporals shouted.

To everyone's amazement, the Legion moved forward. Following the violent thrust of their shields and the follow-up stabs with their blades, the puppies of the third maniple advanced. The motions were repeated and the third maniple stepped forward again. After the third advance, the line halted and set their shields as they hacked and stabbed at the soldiers.

"How did you know?" inquired Caudex.

"They committed their best all along the line," the Colonel explained. "They only had one rank and no second rank to relieve them. Our veterans wore them down and our pups had the advantage of facing exhausted troops. They've been properly bloodied. Send up the second maniple."

For the rest of the day, the Legion advanced one step at a time. On the flanks, the horsemen came at each other in waves but their injured or killed was far less than the shield wall fighting of the heavy infantry.

"They're pulling back," observed General Caudex. "Are you going to chase them down?"

"No, sir. We hurt them enough. They'll think twice about coming against us again," replied Colonel Nicephrus. "Now it's up to Colonel Requiem."

"Aren't you afraid the Syracusans will attack when the Qart Hadasht attack?" offered Caudex.

"I am General. But if we pursue King Hiero, it'll be a fight late into the night," explained the Colonel. "We'll end up camped too far from the city to respond. Besides, the Legionaries have to repair their equipment and rest. Tomorrow, when the sun is high, they'll face the Empire."

Chapter 12 – In a Day of Illusions

Colonel Palaemon Nicephrus limped into the medical tent. A doctor, seeing the blood soaking through the bandage on the battle commander, ran up.

"Colonel. We'll clear an area and get you treated," the Doctor exclaimed.

Nicephrus glanced around at the Legionaries waiting for medical attention ranging from amputations to minor stitches.

"I'll wait until you finish treating the more seriously injured of my men," the Colonel announced as he hobbled to a stool at the back of the tent. He sat stiffly, folded his arms across his chest, dropped his chin and began snoring.

The Doctor stared at the Colonel for a moment before stepping over to the patient laying on his surgery table. He shoved the man's intestines back into his stomach and sewed the sword wound closed. Shaking his head at the futility of bothering to close up the dying man, he pointed to a pair of Medics who lifted the Legionary off the gore-soaked table.

"Water," demanded the Doctor and another Medic tossed the contents of a bucket and washed the blood and tissue off the tabletop. "Bring me the next patient."

Two blood splattered veterans pushed through the flap and marched into the tent. Their leather and metal armor creaking and their gladius sheaths snapping against their armored skirts.

"Medic. We're looking for a wounded infantryman," one called out loudly.

"Take your pick, we have plenty," a Medic walking across the tent replied. He pointed around the tent. "Take two if you want."

"Don't smart mouth me," warned one of the infantrymen. "You might end up keeping your teeth in a bag and sucking your mush through a hole in your throat."

The other veteran smiled but rested a hand on the hilt of his gladius. He seemed prepared to carry out his companion's threat.

From the side of the tent, a clerk at a table called to the men, "What's the name and unit of your friend?"

"Not a friend. Don't know more than he was third maniple," one stated as he strutted to the table. "His name's Eolus."

"I have a Private Eolus from Seventh Squad, Sixth Century, third maniple," the clerk reported as he read from a long scroll. "He came in at midday."

"Where is he?" demanded the veteran.

Colonel Nicephrus woke to the sounds of the rough voices and followed the infantrymen with his eyes. From their exchanges with the passing Medic and the clerk, they needed their leashes jerked for their boorish manners.

"Follow those two Medics," the clerk instructed.

The Medics, carrying the Legionary with the fatal stomach wound, were going through a slit in the tent. As the infantrymen stomped after them, Nicephrus struggled to his feet and limped across the tent towards the slit.

An awning attached to the Medical tent covered an isolated area. Laying on blankets around the area were butchered Legionaries. Their arms too weak to raise, their bodies displaying holes and slashes from swords and spears, contrasted with their clean faces. The reason for the freshly washed faces was obvious. A young man in a dirty tunic kneeled in the dirt beside an injured Legionary washing his face. He chanted in a grating voice.

Nenia Dea
You hover just out of sight
But death is called
To claim his life
With gentle hands so light
Take him with care
As is a worthy man's right
Goddess of Death, Nenia Dea
Hear our plight
As you hover just out of sight

"You there, Priest, Medic? Where is Private Eolus," shouted one of the infantrymen.

The man continued chanting as if the veteran hadn't called out.

Allow him to pass bravely
His comrades call his elegy
We sing Memento Mori
For this man's end

remembering we will all die
Release this Legionary
This son of man
This best of friend
Grant him an end
Goddess of Death
Allow him to pass bravely

The man wiping the Legionary's face glanced up as he chanted. Then he looked down and went back to removing the blood and dirt from the deathly pale skin.

Nenia Dea
You hover just out of sight
But death is called
To claim his life
With gentle hands so light
Take him with care
As is a worthy man's right
Goddess of Death, Nenia Dea
Hear our plight
As you hover just out of sight

"I'm talking to you," one of the infantrymen cautioned as he stormed down an aisle between the wounded. "Ignore me at your own peril, Priest or Medic, whatever you are. I asked you a question."

Nicephrus arrived at the slit in the tent as the infantryman lifted a foot preparing to kick a kneeling man. A bucket of water sat next to the young man and a sopping wet rag was clutched in his hand.

Before the battle commander could call out, the man in the dirt tossed the wet cloth in the infantryman's face. Snatching up a rustic cane made from a tree root, the kneeling man used it to swipe the blinded infantryman's leg out from under him. One

110

end of the cane had a large knot and, as the veteran fell and fought to get the cloth off his face, the knot hammered him in the head. Then, the man in the dirt used the cane to get unsteadily to his feet.

"If you pull that gladius," warned the man with the cane in a low voice. "You'll be back in the Medical tent and on the Doctor's table. Your call. What will it be?"

While the veteran near the slit pondered the possibility of being hurt by an obviously injured man with a tree root, his companion on the ground stirred. The young man poked him with the blunt end of the cane. "Stay down and you'll walk out of here. Move and I'll be washing your face and chanting to the Death Goddess for you."

Nicephrus was tempted to let the drama play out, but his thigh hurt and, he could feel blood running down his leg.

"What in Hades' name is going on here?" he demanded as he stepped through the slit.

The man with the cane and the upright infantryman snapped to attention at the sight of the silver breastplate with the gold inlay.

"Colonel. We were looking for Private Eolus," the infantryman explained.

"Did you and him locate the Private?" questioned the Colonel while pointing at the embarrassed infantryman laying in the dirt.

"No, sir. We, ah, seem to be having an issue," the veteran stammered.

"And what are you doing?" the battle commander inquired of the man with the cane.

"Teaching a lesson, sir," the young man replied. Then glancing down at the infantryman. "You began your kick too close. It left you open for a preemptive strike. Next time, get a handle on your temper and kick out from a distance. Now get off the dirt in the presence of the commander."

111

All three stared at the cane in the man's hand and at his feet. Although standing stiffly, his feet were spaced for balance and the cane held as if was a gladius.

"Explain the rag and bucket of water," requested the Colonel. "And your soiled tunic."

"Sir, this is the staging area for those waiting for the touch of Morta," he informed Nicephrus. "The Medics, as you saw, are busy. I was unable to fight today so I decided to comfort the dying. They fought and lay waiting for their threads to be cut. They will not pass alone or with dirt and blood on their faces."

After watching the infantryman scramble off the ground and stand at attention, the Colonel asked, "Who are you, that you care for my critically wounded in their last moments? And put one of my veterans in the dirt from your knees?"

"Sir. Lance Corporal Alerio Sisera, Southern Legion and weapons instructor," he answered softly. "I apologize for the melee. But, this duty weighs heavily on the heart."

"I would imagine. Do you know the whereabouts of this Private Eolus?" Nicephrus inquired.

"Yes, sir. He's at the edge of the overhang," Alerio said pointing at a covered body. "He went hard. To the last, he fought to stand up and return to his squad and the battle."

"There's your answer," Nicephrus said to the infantrymen. "What now?"

"Nothing, sir," one replied as they dragged coins from pouches.

They walked to Private Eolus' corpse, pulled back the blanket and placed coins on his eyes. With coins placed so Eolus could pay Charon, the ferryman, and secure passage to Hades, they marched off, one of them limping from a sore ankle.

"Lance Corporal Sisera. You were the one who apprehended the Syracusan messenger," ventured Nicephrus.

"Just the eyes for the Century who caught him, Colonel," Alerio replied. He sagged and his knees almost buckled. "Sorry, sir."

"I heard about the punishment post fiasco. One more thing before I leave you to your chanting," questioned the Colonel. "What would you suggest we do with Macario Hicetus? Put him on the wood or stone him?"

"Neither, sir. Send him back to King Hiero and let him explain that the Qart Hadasht army won't be coming to support him," suggested Alerio. Indicating the dying Legionaries around the isolated area, he added. "Without their aid, he might have second thoughts about creating Legion corpses."

"Carry on Lance Corporal Sisera," Nicephrus ordered before turning towards the slit in the medical tent. "Doctor, I'm cutting into the line."

"Yes, sir. Come in and hop on my surgery table," the Doctor replied from inside the tent. "Water!"

***

The sun was low when Colonel Nicephrus nudged his horse up the steep hill. After handing the mount off to a servant, he limped into the Citadel.

General Caudex, Senior Tribune Eutropius, Colonel Requiem and Senior Tribune Claudius, along with a handful of Tribunes, sat around a table.

"Palaemon, come. Have a celebratory drink with us," called out the General. "I was just explaining how our strategy of deception would make the God Dolos blush. Where have you been?"

"Getting fifteen stitches and visiting our wounded," replied the Colonel as he crossed the room. He took a chair offered by one of his Tribunes. "And getting sage advice from a Lance Corporal."

"What advice could a junior NCO offer you?" inquired Colonel Requiem. "Today you seemed to have a genius for all

113

the right moves. Except for when you failed to dodge the Hoplites' spear."

"That was unavoidable," Nicephrus defended his wound as he picked up a mug. After a sip of wine, he looked General Caudex in the eyes. "General, we need to release Lieutenant Macario Hicetus."

Tribune Eutropius slammed a hand on the table.

"No. The Syracusan is to be crucified tomorrow," Maris slurred. "The Legionaries will enjoy the sight of him up on the wood."

"Or is it you looking forward to the man's pain?" questioned Senior Tribune Claudius.

"Tribunes, the Colonel was about to explain his idea," Caudex said hushing the staff officers. "Please continue Colonel. By the by, who was this Lance Corporal?"

"Lance Corporal Sisera and he..."

Another rap, this one harder than the first, came from Maris' hand on the tabletop.

"I will not suffer the name of that disrespectful...," but he never finished.

Colonel Nicephrus stood quickly, grimaced from the pain in his thigh, and leaned on the table.

"You interrupt me again Tribune and I will send you to the Medical tent for stitches of your own," threatened Nicephrus as he lifted a hand and rested it on the pommel of his gladius. "I will not be shouted at by you. This is a battle council, not an orgy with your sycophants sucking at your family's nipples. Sit quietly while men of reason discuss important issues."

Nicephrus sat but his eyes remained locked on Maris Eutropius. Despite the warning, the Senior Tribune opened his mouth to reply when an open hand slapped the back of his head. His head rocked forward before he jerked around to see who dared strike him.

"Go ahead, challenge me," offered Colonel Pericles Requiem. "Colonel Nicephrus is exhausted and injured. I am neither. Should we draw blades?"

"Colonel Nicephrus is correct. This is a battle council," declared General Caudex verbally stepping in between the two men. "Let's get back to the matter of King Hiero on one side of us and Qart Hadasht forces on the other. Please, Colonel, inform us of Lance Corporal Sisera's contribution."

Maris Eutropius slouched in his chair and pouted. But his eyes burned and he shifted them between the Colonels. His evil eye went unnoticed by the General and his battlefield commanders, but not by Senior Tribune Gaius Claudius.

"We release Macario Hicetus and allow him to see a parade of fresh, unsoiled Legionaries," explained Nicephrus. "Then we put him on a horse and let him report to his King. What else can he say except that he saw fresh Centuries."

"The King will overestimate our strength," declared General Caudex. "It might be enough to make him pause when we go against the Qart Hadasht army."

"You are correct, as always, General," Colonel Requiem exclaimed. "With your permission, I'll send Senior Tribune Claudius to roust the cleanest Legionaries and have them marching around when he escorts the Syracusan through Messina."

"Order it, Colonel," instructed Caudex as he lifted his mug. "In a day of illusions, let us hope for the success of one more. I propose we drink to the Goddess Tyche. To her continued blessings and good fortune."

Everyone at the table raised their mug high overhead and whispered their own prayer.

***

Lieutenant Macario Hicetus expected to be blinded by the sun when Tribune Claudius guided him from the dark room.

Instead, the light of early evening allowed him to open his eyes fully. And what he saw surprised him.

"Be careful," urged Gaius Claudius as a Century of Legionaries stomped by. "Our heavy infantry is disappointed in missing out on today's skirmish. They're looking for a fight and a Syracusan cavalry officer is tempting."

"What skirmish?" asked Hicetus.

"Some of our Legionaries formed a battle line and your troops came out to play," Claudius said nonchalantly. "When King Hiero called them back, the Legionaries let them go before the rest of our lads had an opportunity to join the fun."

They strolled up the main boulevard and as they walked, Century after Century marched by in both directions. By the time they turned at the road leading to the gates, Macario Hicetus had lost count of the units. The parade didn't end when they approached a cavalry unit milling about besides the gates. Even then, Centuries came from side streets crossing the road and vanishing behind buildings as if Messina was bursting at the seams with Legionaries.

"Of course, discipline is always an issue when you pack so many Centuries into a small place," offered Claudius. "At least when some are out fighting Syracusans and others leave to fight the Qart Hadasht army, I'll have a chance to organize my Centuries around the walls and set up proper defensives."

"How many troops do you have in Messina?" Macario Hicetus inquired as they reached the Legion cavalry unit.

"Lieutenant. I'm not going to tell you that," laughed Claudius. "You'd just tell your King and he would send to Syracuse for more men. Get on the horse and leave."

"Thank you, Senior Tribune," Hicetus said as he mounted the horse. Once on the animal's back, he looked around at the huge number of Legionaries marching up and down and across the streets. Then he jerked the horse around and trotted through the gates with the escort.

116

A big shape separated from the shadows and marched towards Gaius.

"How did we look, Tribune Claudius?" inquired Senior Centurion Valerian.

"As if we have five Legions quartered in the city," replied Gaius. "You can stand them down now. Lieutenant Hicetus and the escort are well beyond the defensive line."

"Very good, sir," Valerian stated before facing up the street, cupping his hands around his mouth, and calling out. "First Sergeant Brictius. Stand the Centuries down."

From far away, Brictius shouted back, "Senior Centurion, standing them down."

"Out of curiosity Senior Centurion, how many Centuries did you have on the streets?" asked Claudius. "It looked like thousands."

"We started with twenty but they kept running into each other two blocks away," Valerian explained. "After eliminations, we settled for using ten. You should have seen them running to make the next cross street for another march by."

"You did all of this with only eight hundred and thirty Legionaries," Tribune Claudius observed. "I'm impressed."

"No offense Senior Tribune, but it's not you who needed to be impressed," Senior Centurion Valerian suggested as he pointed through the gates at the fading shapes of the riders. "It's Lieutenant Hicetus who had to be impressed."

Act 3

Chapter 13 – A Hero is Anointed

At Legion posts around Messina and along the southern and northern defenses, Legionaries relieved those on guard duty. All the posts reported no contact during the late evening changing-of-the-guard.

Soon after the positions settled down for the long night, a guard on an eastern position detected movement in the dark.

"Trouble," whispered the sentry. "Squad, up and armed. Runner to the Corporal."

Around him, eight of his squad mates leaped to their feet and snatched up javelins and shields. The ninth man ran off in search of their Corporal. By the time the runner reached the duty NCO, the outlines of two men emerged from the darkness and stopped at the foot of the mound. Following the alerted squad's example, the adjacent positions woke and formed ranks. A stillness fell over the shields lining the mounds and the infantrymen waited.

Following the runner, the Century's Tesserarius sprinted to the mound with another squad and three runners. If it was an attack, two runners would wake the rest of the defenses while the third went to warn their Centurion.

"You, in the dark, identify yourself," called out the Corporal.

"Velites, Second Century. Sergeant Griffinus," the man replied. "I need to speak to your Centurion, right away."

"Give me a covered light," ordered the Corporal. "Come forward so I can get a look at you."

In a sheltered hollow behind the mound, a Legionary struck flint and ignited a fish oil lamp. The skirmisher Sergeant and his man came through the·defenses and huddled with the Corporal. Moments later, the three of them sprinted for the Centurion's campsite further behind the defensive line.

***

Maris Eutropius rolled out of his rack with a smile on his face and joy in his heart. After pulling on a tunic with the Tribune insignia, buckling up his gladius belt and strapping on sandals, he quietly climbed down the ladder.

"All is quiet, Senior Tribune," reported the Centurion at the duty desk.

"Fine, fine," Maris Eutropius replied as he searched the chest beside the duty officer. He located the whip with the interwoven seashells and lifted it out. "I'm going to review the guard positions."

"Yes, sir," the infantry officer acknowledged. Inside, he shuddered and thought about sending a runner to warn someone that the sadistic Tribune was on the prowl. But, he didn't know Eutropius' route and, short of an all-out alert, he was helpless.

Maris strutted through the doorway of the Citadel and searched the moonlit night. Two men with cloth masks covering their faces left the deep shadows and approached.

"Good evening, Senior Tribune Eutropius," one greeted him.

"Did you locate his quarter's, Private?" inquired Maris.

"Yes, sir. We spread some coins around and a couple of street urchins identified them," the Legionary reported. "He's spending a lot of his time there. His roommates are out most nights at a pub called the Pirate's Pride."

"Good. Take me to the rooming house," Maris commanded.

The sentries watched as two of the Headquarters Century Legionaries and the Tribune marched down the hill and vanished into Messina. None of them wore their armor and, as usual, the Privates had their faces covered. No one wanted to be identified later by the squadmates of those summarily disciplined by the Senior Tribune.

Maris Eutropius inhaled deeply and his stomach quivered in anticipation. If he couldn't have the delight of watching the Syracusan, Macario Hicetus, on the cross, he'd have the pleasure of delivering justice too long delayed.

They trekked through the city until one of his bodyguards held up a hand.

"Wait here, sir," the Legionary said. Then, he slipped into a dark alleyway. Moments later, he came back. "The urchin said he is inside alone. The rest are out at the pub."

"Excellent. You two wait here," instructed Eutropius as he let the whip uncoil. "He's owed eight more lashes to satisfy the General's sentence. I will deliver the punishment and return."

"Yes sir," the two bodyguards replied.

Maris approached the door and, as he reached for the latch, he noted his hand trembling in anticipation. His one regret was not bringing a wineskin of good vino. It would be nice to quench his thirst between delivering the lashes. With that sad thought in mind, he shoved opened the door and stepped into the dark interior.

The door closed on its own, a hand clamped over his mouth and powerful men on each side grabbed his arms and lifted him off the floorboards.

"Senior Tribune Eutropius. So nice of you to join us this evening," a voice spoke cordially as if greeting a guest. "Tie him and take the staff officer to the basement."

Maris' hands were bound and a piece of cotton cloth thrust between his lips. Then, he was lifted and dropped. He fell expecting to hit the floor. But the drop lasted until he passed the boards and crashed into the hard dirt far below. Other hands lifted him off the basement floor. A light flared to life and Maris saw the bottom of a trap door above his head close.

120

"I don't suppose you remember me, Senior Tribune," a man standing out of the light ventured. "Let's get reacquainted. I'm Captain Milon Frigian."

"You're the pirate from the harbor barricade," replied Maris as Milon stepped into the light. "Now you've committed a capital offense. I'll see you and your scum crucified by tomorrow afternoon."

"You might want to rethink your position before you go insulting my fine crew," warned Milon. "Get the Tribune dressed and subdue his bodyguards."

In the alleyway, the street lad received a signal. He crept to the end of the alley and hissed for the Legionary's attention.

"What?" asked one of the bodyguards as he crossed the street and stepped into the dark.

A club came from overhead and the Legionary crumbled to the ground. Across the street, the other bodyguard watched as his companion fell. Before he could pull his gladius or call out, another club drove him to his knees. A second swing laid him out. Both men were dragged into the alleyway.

***

A cavalry unit galloped from the southern gates, leaped the trench and raced towards the Syracusan lines

"If your claim is verified, Griffinus, tomorrow is going to be an easy day," the Centurion stated.

"I thought the only easy day in the heavy infantry was yesterday?" questioned the Velites' Sergeant.

"Some are easier than others," the line officer suggested.

They sat, leaned against the wall and waited. The moon moved against the sky and the Legionaries shifted uncomfortably and shivered in the cool night air. None of them were able to sleep.

They leaped to their feet when the sounds of hooves, dangerously pounding the ground in the dark, reached them. Fast moving horses burst through the gates and pulled up.

121

"It's confirmed," the cavalry Centurion said breathing hard from the ride. "Clear a mount for the Sergeant."

One of the Legion horsemen jumped to the ground and handed the reigns to Sergeant Griffinus. Once the skirmisher NCO was seated, the cavalry officer put heels to his horse and led the unit towards the Citadel.

The duty Centurion heard the horses as they galloped up Citadel Hill. A moment later, they snorted and stomped the ground outside the door. Before he could go and investigate, a cavalry Centurion and a Sergeant raced through the doorway.

"Wake the duty Colonel," ordered the Centurion.

"Why?" requested the duty officer.

"It's an important field report and I would rather not repeat it and waste time," the cavalry officer replied.

The Centurion ran into a side office. He and Colonel Requiem emerged almost immediately.

"Report!" ordered Requiem as he buckled on his gladius.

"The Syracusans have withdrawn, sir," the cavalry officer announced. "Sergeant Griffinus was making a night reconnaissance and crept closer when he heard noises. He assumed they were preparing to attack our lines. But, when he got close, he saw wagons being loaded. I took a detachment and rode to check. And, Colonel Requiem, their camp is empty. All I could find was a long line of wagon lights stretching across the River Longanus heading towards the mountains."

"Take four Centuries of cavalry and check every approach to confirm they haven't left forces behind," instructed the Colonel. "Good work both of you."

As the cavalry officer and the Velites' Sergeant marched out, the Colonel turned to the duty Centurion.

"Wake Senior Tribunes Claudius and Eutropius. And fetch Senior Centurion Valerian," ordered Requiem. "Have servants bring food to the conference room."

"What about the General, sir?" inquired the Centurion. "Should I wake him?"

"Not yet. I want to see if we have an opportunity here first," Requiem replied as he walked towards the large room. "And get me a Centurion of the signal corps and runners. Lots of runners."

"Yes, sir," the Centurion assured him. After the Colonel was out of sight, he pointed to one of his runners. "Go into Messina, find Senior Tribune Eutropius, and inform him he is needed at the Citadel."

"Where in the city, sir?" asked the Legionary.

"Start at the punishment post," suggested the officer remembering the Tribune had taken the whip. "If he's not there, just keep searching."

After the one runner was gone, the duty officer began issuing orders to the other runners. Once they were off, he marched towards the ladder leading to the second floor and Senior Tribune Claudius' quarters.

***

Centurion Faustinus of the Headquarters Century and his Optio came into the room and stood off to the side. Gaius Claudius and Pericles Requiem were leaning over the map pointing out features north of Messina. As they talked, the battle commander made notes based on the Tribune's recent visit to the Qart Hadasht lines. They didn't notice Senior Centurion Valerian and Centurion Sanctus Carnifex march in and take seats. Also unacknowledged were pairs of junior Tribunes wandering in and taking seats.

"Where is Senior Tribune Eutropius?" Requiem inquired looking up from the map.

"He went into town," Claudius informed him. "The duty officer sent a runner to find him."

"This is only a 'what if' meeting," declared the Colonel. "If the Syracusans have left the field, I want ideas from everyone.

Tribune Eutropius' absence isn't critical but it is annoying. Someone, instruct the duty Centurion to send out more runners. Now let's talk about the situation."

Colonel Eutropius rested his hands on the tabletop and glanced at the junior Tribunes.

"Someone, give me a thought," he requested. "Don't get fancy, that's my job."

"Attack at dawn, sir," mumbled a young nobleman. "We can flood the battlefield with all of our Centuries and crush the Qart Hadasht forces before they know what hit them."

"That's an interesting idea, Tribune Castor Ireneus," commented Requiem before he looked across the table at Valerian. "Senior Centurion, how many fresh Centuries do we have?"

"Twenty-one Centuries of heavy infantry, Colonel. They were on the defenses or in Messina and didn't participate," Valerian reported. "Unfortunately, all of our cavalry and our Velites were bloodied."

"Alright Tribune Ireneus. You have sixteen hundred eighty fresh infantrymen without the support of Legion horses or skirmishers," Requiem explained to the junior Tribune. "They are going to surprise six thousand entrenched mercenaries. What tactic do you employ?"

"Ah, Colonel, I'm not sure," young Castor stammered.

"Well, Senior Tribune Claudius has firsthand knowledge of the enemy positions," instructed Requiem. "And Senior Centurion Valerian and Centurion Carnifex have spent the evening evaluating the rest of our infantry. What do you do?"

"Ask them questions," Castor replied looking from the Senior Centurion to the Senior Tribune.

"And that's the lesson for you staff officers," explained Colonel Requiem. "Gather intelligence about your enemy and his position before fixating on a plan of attack. Know your resources and the state of your men. Tired men die and lose ground. Fresh Legionaries kill and take ground. You started this, ask questions."

Young Castor Ireneus swallowed and focused on Gaius.

"Tribune Claudius. What defenses will we face?" he asked.

"They have a reinforced farm wall across their front," related Gaius. "It cuts across a narrow finger of land between the Messina Strait and marshland. It's a gooseneck that will force a collapse of our attack line."

"Prospect of using cavalry?" inquired Requiem.

"Flanking can be handled with several Velites' Centuries next to the swamp," Claudius suggested. "There is no open ground for our Legion cavalry or for their horsemen."

"Valerian. This is going to be an infantry confrontation," ventured Requiem. "What is the state of our Legionaries?"

"The third maniple as you can guess was hurt badly," stated the Senior Centurion. "The second and first fared better. Overall, we can field fifty-one Centuries. But, we'll need to rotate them more than is customary."

"I agree. Four thousand eighty Legionaries against six thousand mercenaries it is," exclaimed the Colonel. "I'd prefer a few days rest and an open battlefield. But, in light of King Hiero's actions, we need to take advantage of the situation."

A commotion in the outer room drew everyone's attention to the doorway. Four cavalry officers marched into the conference. All four were smiling.

"Colonel. We've searched all the approaches and likely staging areas," one reported. "It is the considered opinion of your mounted Centuries that the Syracusans have withdrawn. The southern defensive line is unopposed."

"Gentlemen, now we plan for war," announced Colonel Requiem. "First Centurion Faustinus. Wake the General and request his presence here. Then, take two squads, locate Senior Tribune Eutropius and bring him back here."

"Yes, sir," the officer replied.

125

As he marched out of the room, Colonel Requiem gave a bring-it-on hand sign to the table. First Centurion Faustinus left the room as voices requested more information from Tribune Claudius and Senior Centurion Valerian.

***

First Centurion Faustinus did as the Colonel suggested to the young Tribunes. He gathered information before setting off to find the Senior Tribune. Based on a conversation with his Tesserarius, he discovered that Tribune Eutropius had tasked two of his Privates with locating the quarters of Lance Corporal Sisera. Then from the duty Centurion, he learned Maris Eutropius had taken the lethal whip. Putting those facts together, along with his knowledge of the Senior Tribune's propensity for inflicting pain on others, gave him a starting point.

His two squads marched to the rooming house and he sent two half squads to search the surrounding streets. He and two Legionaries went directly to the front door and opened it. The main room was dark and empty. After a search of the rooms, Faustinus realized the entire house was deserted. With no other leads, except for something concerning the Lance Corporal, he marched his squads to the area where the detached Southern Legion Centuries were camped.

The twenty squad tents, neatly spaced, occupied sections around two large command tents. Each tent had an on-duty guard with two additional men walking around the command tents. Legionaries, not away on Legion sentry duty, were sleeping.

"Lance Corporal Sisera. Front and center," Faustinus bellowed as his squads approached the sleeping encampment.

"Something the Southern Legion can do for you, Centurion?" the guard at the closest squad tent inquired.

"Get Lance Corporal Sisera out here, now," the First Centurion ordered.

126

Turning to face the camp, the sentry shouted, "Get Lance Corporal Sisera over here."

"Can't do that," a guard on the other side of Southern Legion's area called back.

The guard turned to face the First Centurion, raised his arms as he shrugged and announced, "Can't do that, sir."

"Was I not clear?" Faustinus blustered. "Get Sisera over here now."

A youthful Centurion and an older Sergeant pushed aside a flap on one of the command tents. They marched to where the First Centurion stood in front of his squads.

"What can Southern Legion do for you?" asked the line officer with a yawn.

'What kind of an outfit are you running here, Centurion?" demanded Faustinus.

"One that was on the shield wall all day," responded the Southern Legion Centurion. "My Legionaries have earned a night's rest. If you had any manners, you would have asked for me before disturbing my people. Now, I asked you again. What can the Southern Legion do for you?"

"Senior Tribune Eutropius is missing and I've been tasked with locating him," replied the First Centurion.

"Optio. Have you seen the Tribune?" the officer asked his Sergeant.

"No, sir," the NCO replied.

"Sorry, Faustinus. We haven't seen him," the Centurion reported. "And so, it's not my problem. But you rousing my Legionaries is a problem. So good night."

"I demand to speak with Lance Corporal Sisera," Faustinus threatened. "Which squad is he in? I'll have my men drag him out of the tent."

The rattle of armor and the snap of javelins settling in on top of shields came from deep in the camp. Then, two squads in battle formation marched from between the tents.

"What's this? Are you looking for a fight?" asked the First Centurion.

"Stand down," the line officer instructed the two Southern Legion squads. "First Centurion. Lance Corporal Sisera is not here. If you had asked me to start with, I would have told you he is at the Medical tent."

"Malingering, no doubt," offered Faustinus. "I witnessed his assault on the staff officer. Out of uniform and hiding from his duty, he was probably drunk as well."

"Be careful of your words, First Centurion," cautioned the young Centurion.

"My words?" stammered Faustinus. "I'll say what I want when I want, and there's nothing you can do to stop me."

"It's not me, First Centurion," replied the Southern Legion line officer. "Just a word of advice. Don't threaten Death Caller."

"Who?" questioned Faustinus but he didn't wait for an answer. "Squads left face forward."

As the Headquarters squads marched away, the Sergeant glanced at his Centurion.

"Why didn't you tell him, sir?" asked the NCO.

"He wouldn't have listened," the line officer replied. "Let's check our sentries and try to get some sleep."

"Yes, sir," the Optio said agreeing with his Centurion.

***

Even in the middle of the night, the Medical tent bristled with activity. Legionaries moaned or cried out from pain and Medics gave sips of water, bathed feverish foreheads, or poured vinegar on wounds to prevent the rot as they changed bandages.

The worst aftermath of a shield to shield fight lay in three ward tents. All the surgery was done for the day. Now it was up to the individual Legionary to heal or die. The surgeons had turned in for the night because tomorrow there would be amputations for the men who contracted gangrene. As all of the

Medics were Privates or Lance Corporals, none were prepared to face an impatient First Centurion.

The goat leather flap popped against the tent's side as Faustinus strutted into the ward.

"Where is Lance Corporal Sisera?" he demanded.

Medics and injured Legionaries, those cognizant enough to care, peered at the First Centurion. But, no one replied.

"I asked a question and I will have an answer," announced Faustinus. "If you are hiding him, I'll have you on the punishment post for insubordination."

"First Centurion. Go through surgery and out the slit in the back," instructed a Medic holding up a blood-soaked bandage. "But keep your voice down."

"Do not tell me to keep my voice down," Faustinus thundered. "I'll speak anyway I choose."

As he marched out of the ward and into the quiet of the surgery area, he fumed at the night. Trying to find a lost Senior Tribune was bad enough. But having a junior officer and a Medic tell him to be cautious and to keep his voice down tried his patience. He was a veteran and the officer in charge of keeping General Caudex safe. To be hushed as if he was a school lad, was an insult to his position.

The noise of the ward faded and, in the silence of the surgery area, he heard words mumbled. As he rounded a butcher's block, as most Legionaries thought of the surgery work surface, words became distinguishable.

See the man is broken
For him, others have spoken
Although not a proper temple
Yet a hero lays
In a modest Legion chapel
Recognize this man
Dying wasn't his plan
His face is clean

You can see
Gaze peacefully
Goddess of Death
See the man is broken

First Centurion Faustinus stepped halfway through the slit and stopped. An awning blocked the moonlight, and he waited for his eyes to adjust to the unusual darkness. While he listened to the sound of trickling water dripping into a bucket, a ragged voice chanted.

Nenia Dea
You hover just out of sight
But death is called
To claim his life
With gentle hands so light
Take him with care
As is a worthy man's right
Goddess of Death, Nenia Dea
Hear our plight
As you hover just out of sight

The Centurion's eyes finally adjusted to the dark and he saw men sleeping in rows. One figure knelt beside another, running a wet rag over the sleeping man's face.

"Lance Corporal Sisera. Wake up, I will have words with you," Faustinus boomed.

He glanced around expecting Legionaries to stir from their sleep at the order. When none moved, he stepped fully through the slit and the odor reached his nostrils. The aroma of fresh corpses caught him by surprise and he involuntarily stepped back.

As the First Centurion recovered his balance, the kneeling man dipped the rag in a bucket and turned to wash another face.

Reach out for my brother
His light fades as do others
Ease his struggle to survive
As his strength wanes
Pacing steadily to his demise
Grip his hand in yours
Take him from this plain
Free his soul
Cease his pain
Goddess of Death
Reach out for my brother

First Centurion Faustinus shook off the surprise assault on his senses and he opened his mouth to demand that Lance Corporal Sisera identify himself. Before he could utter the words, an old, yet robust, Centurion appeared at the edge of the awning. He held a lantern over his head. In the light, Faustinus could make out scars on big arms that identified the Centurion as a veteran.

"First Centurion, do not disturb Death Caller," growled the grizzled line officer. "If you want conversation, join us. If not, go the Hades away, quietly."

"I am…" then the First Centurion stopped his sentence as the large Centurion's gladius leaped from its sheath and appeared in the man's big fist.

"I asked you nicely," advised the old Centurion. "Say another word and Lance Corporal Alerio will be washing your face and calling Nenia for you."

Nenia Dea
You hover just out of sight
But death is called
To claim his life
With gentle hands so light
Take him with care

131

As is a worthy man's right
Goddess of Death, Nenia Dea
Hear our plight
As you hover just out of sight

First Centurion of Headquarters Century Faustinus had never backed away from a fight in his life. But here, in the murky darkness as if in the shadows of the Death Goddess herself, a chill ran down his spine. He glanced at the Lance Corporal for a moment and when he looked up the old Centurion had sheathed his gladius. As he followed the ancient campaigner, he heard the kneeling man's gravel voice chant.

Sense beyond the shell
Yes, he has been through hell
Feel beneath his genocide
As the spirit thrives
Trapped in the ruined outside
Embrace his essence
In your arms, we ask
Release him
From this task
Goddess of Death
Sense beyond the shell

They walked around a wagon to a campfire. Another line officer sat and stared into the flickering flames. Strangely, the chanting faded as they approached the fire.

"My apologies, First Centurion," the large man explained. His voice coming from deep in his chest in a low baritone. "That's my Optio being washed by Death Caller. He is a fierce and competitive man and a terror in the battle line. A Syracusan spear through his chest and out his back fell him near the end of the fighting. The surgeon showed me the bones coming through the hole and explained he couldn't live much longer. But he is a fierce and competitive man. As if waiting for all the Legionaries to go first, my Sergeant lingers. I couldn't have Death Caller disturbed until the last hero of the battle passes."

"And so, you sit late into the night waiting for your Optio to leave," ventured Faustinus. As he sat and warmed his hands by the fire, he questioned the other line officer. "And you Centurion?"

"The Lance Corporal of my First Squad took a sword slash to his shoulder," he answered. "As he drew back, a spear reached under his shield and ran the iron head through his gut. He is a stallion of a lad. First to help and first to volunteer to fight. Unfortunately, the spirit that drives him, won't let go of his body. When I came to check on him, the Medics had already placed him under the awning. That's the second time I witnessed Death Caller work."

"You mean Lance Corporal Sisera," corrected Faustinus.

"Yes. He's been here, washing faces and chanting since the first fatal casualty was placed under the awning," explained the younger Centurion. "There are two holding onto life and Lance Corporal Sisera has vowed to stay until Nenia Dea comes for the last one."

"We were fifteen around the campfire at sundown," offered the large Centurion. "Now we are two as there are two dying and waiting for the Goddess to release them."

"You said this was the second time you've watched Lance Corporal Sisera work," inquired Faustinus of the younger Centurion. "Do you mean him chanting to the Gods?"

"No, not chanting. I've seen Death Caller fight and send scores of Syracusans to the dirt to wait for the Death Goddess. At least some of them, the others he killed without waiting for the Goddess' permission," described the Centurion. "I believe Lance Corporal Sisera has a special relationship with Nenia."

"As do I," added the old Centurion. "No one that young should have the scars of a veteran and be alive. He is truly blessed by death herself."

"What scars?" inquired Faustinus. He'd only seen the Lance Corporal in a tunic and by lamplight. "Do you mean the punishment welts?"

"No. During the day and earlier, Medics came to change Sisera's bandages and clean the wounds from the whip," the old Centurion informed him. "He has knife, sword, gladius and arrow wounds on his body. During the time he was treated, he didn't whimper, but continued to chant."

"If he's been here all day and evening, I don't need to interrupt him," declared Faustinus. He stood and, as he rounded the wagon heading for the front of the medical tent, he heard the strained voice still chanting.

Allow him to pass bravely
His comrades call his elegy
We sing Memento Mori
For this man's end
remembering we will all die
Release this Legionary
This son of man
This best of friend
Grant him an end
Goddess of Death
Allow him to pass bravely

***

The First Centurion marched into the Citadel, passed through the great room and entered the conference room.

"General. Senior Tribune Eutropius has vanished," he reported.

"Do you mean you can't find Tribune Eutropius?" asked General Caudex.

"We've searched and sent runners to all of our positions," explained Faustinus. "He didn't report to any of them. Also missing are two of my Privates who accompanied him, sir."

Caudex's face paled and he clenched his fists. The General really didn't care what happened to Maris Eutropius but he couldn't let the feeling be known. Maris' father was a big supporter of Senator Caudex and losing the man's support would cost him politically.

"Colonel. As soon as the assault on the Qart Hadasht army is over, I want every pirate from the Sons of Mars lined up," instructed the General. "And every tenth man killed until one of them confesses. If none do, we'll start at the head of the line and start over again."

"Yes, sir. The decimation of the Sons of Mars," Requiem assured him. "Now, General. As I was saying, we'll attack at dawn. Maybe catch the Qart Hadasht mercenaries asleep before they realize we've climbed over their wall."

"I thought the men were exhausted? When I suggested this earlier, you had a pouch full of reasons against it," complained the General.

"Sir, that was before King Hiero pulled back," the Colonel informed him. "We had to withhold assault Legionaries to guard our southern defensives. In light of the new information, cavalry and skirmishers are adequate to the task."

"Show me how this is going to work," demanded Caudex.

Colonel Requiem handed his stick to junior Tribune Castor Ireneus. It was an honor for the young nobleman who had suggested the dawn attack.

"Explain our strategies to the General," instructed Requiem. "This was your idea."

General Caudex sat up and smiled at the very young Castor Ireneus. The Colonel had just handed the briefing off to the son of the powerful Ireneus family. Maybe he wouldn't miss Maris after all. But, he would still punish the Sons of Mars.

Chapter 14 – Assault at the Wall

The chill of predawn and the exhaustion from yesterday's fight weren't the things bothering the Legionaries. It was the low visibility in the darkness making the silhouette of their squad mate indistinguishable from other squads causing the frustration. Stumbling around in the dark was the opposite of their usually precise maneuvering. Helping, although not fast or efficient in the dark, were the Centurions, Sergeants, and Corporals shoving, grabbing and questioning Legionaries to locate and position their men.

"Squad leaders, Pivots, say your unit's number," urged Centurion Sanctus Carnifex in a hushed tone. "Line them up in columns of twos."

All he could see were javelins jutting into the night sky held by a shifting mass of shadowy clumps. When the mass congealed and the javelins became wavy lines, he called out.

"Requiem Division, First Century, First Squad, on me," he directed. Two shapes of lines of Legionaries stepped in front of him and he began walking down the corridor checking to be sure all the squad members were present and in the correct unit. "First Squad? First Squad? Good. Second Squad? Second Squad, good."

The Centurion located the start and ends of the First, Second and Third Centuries. They would make up his first maniple. Then, he called for the Eleventh Century and walked the line through them and the Twelfth and Thirteenth, his second maniple. As expected, when he called for the Twenty-fifth Century, they were having difficulty sorting themselves out.

"Requiem Division, Twenty-Fifth Century, First Squad, on me," he directed. And slowly, his least experienced Centuries began to form columns. "First Squad? Good. Second Squad, good."

At the tail end of the Twenty-Seventh Century, Centurion Carnifex marched to a man sitting on a horse.

"Senior Centurion Valerian. Your maniples of three Centuries each are formed and ready to march," Carnifex reported.

Valerian turned and addressed the mounted shape behind him, "Colonel. The assault force is standing by awaiting your orders."

"It is ordered, take them out," Requiem instructed.

"Yes, sir," Valerian responded. Turning back to the front he said. "Centurion Carnifex forward your maniples."

"Yes, First Centurion," Sanctus Carnifex acknowledge. He turned and marched back through the seven hundred and twenty heavy infantrymen of his assault force. Along the path as he marched between the squads and the Centuries, he repeated. "Stand by. Stand by."

At the head of the First Squad, First Century, he located a man standing off to the side.

"Senior Tribune Claudius. We are ordered forward," Carnifex reported.

"Lead them out, Centurion," directed the staff officer. "And good luck to you."

***

Centurion Sanctus Carnifex walked the boards placed over the trench and down the steep hill. At the bottom, he strolled through the dale and climbed the shorter hill before descending to the narrow plain. As quietly as men try, armor, shields, and sheaths rapped and squeaked and hobnailed boots kicked rocks and scraped the ground. The Centurion heard the sounds and cringed, knowing eventually the Qart Hadasht sentries would also hear the racket.

Far across the open ground, a shape materialized from the dark and fell in beside him.

"I've stationed my Velites at the marsh and at positions across our line," the skirmisher Centurion reported. "Your Legionaries are loud."

"They're supposed to be loud. They're heavy infantry," Carnifex explained as he continued to walk through the tall grass. "It scares the enemy."

"Not good form for clandestine maneuvers," observed the officer.

"It doesn't matter," replied Carnifex. "Do you really think we'll make it over the wall before six thousand mercenaries wake up?"

"Not a chance Sanctus," agreed the Velites' officer.

They walked onward, the night raced towards dawn and the nine Centuries stumbled through the dark as they followed.

***

A new shape appeared in the dark and the Velites' Centurion reached out and stopped Carnifex.

"My line is twenty-four paces from here," he advised.

"Centurion of the First and Second Centuries stand here and put the first maniple online," ordered Carnifex. "Pass the rest through."

He stood and waited until the Eighth Squad of the Third Century was guided off to the side. When the Centurion of the Eleventh Century reached the gap, he fell in and marched the line officer six paces before stopping.

"Stand here and direct the second maniple to their line," he instructed. "Pass the rest through."

Again, he stood and waited. When the Eight of the Thirteenth turned to get online, Carnifex took the arm of the Twenty-Fifth's Centurion and walked him six more paces.

"Third maniple line forms here," he directed.

The Velites' officer moved away and vanished into the night.

Although Centurion Sanctus Carnifex couldn't see, he visualized three ranks of Legionaries. Each rank had two hundred forty shields stretching from the marshland across the grassy plain to the shore of the Messina Strait. In front of his formation, eighty skirmishers kneeled in the grass. All were waiting for the sky to lighten. So far, there had been no sign the Qart Hadasht sentries were alerted to the presence of the Legionaries. That would change when his assault force attacked the wall.

"Sanctus. We have a mystery," the Velites' officer whispered as he reappeared. "My line near the shore found three dead men."

Six lightly armored Legionaries following him came out of the night. Each pair carried a body balanced on their javelins.

"Who are they?" Carnifex asked.

"We don't know. They're wearing rough woolen clothing," he replied. "But all three are armed with Legion gladii. It's too dark to make out their features."

"Mercenaries with captured weapons?" ventured Carnifex.

"All have short haircuts and two are wearing hobnailed boots," the skirmisher officer replied. "One has on quality sandals."

"Have the bodies taken back to Messina," instructed Carnifex. "Maybe someone there can identify them."

The Velites were given instructions and they vanished in the dark.

"You've got a crack," the line officer informed Carnifex.

Glancing at the eastern sky, the Centurion saw a light haze identifying the top of the mountains. Although still dark, Carnifex decided to commence the assault.

"Have your skirmishers remove the guards," Carnifex ordered. "We're moving forward."

Senior Centurion Valerian stood in torchlight at the northern defenses. When he noticed the skirmishers carrying bodies up the hill, he panicked. If the assault force was already engaged, they had been discovered early and the result would be disastrous.

"Casualties?" he called to the bearers. "How many?"

"Just three bodies we found in the field, Senior Centurion," the lead skirmisher replied.

"Bring them over here," Valerian instructed while pulling a torch from the ground. Leaning over, he waved the light in front of the three faces. Then the Senior Centurion instructed. "Take them to headquarters and show them to the First Centurion."

The General had moved his staff to the center of Messina and Faustinus wasn't happy. It was one thing to protect the General on a battlefield where he could see the enemy. Or during trips from the Citadel in daylight. But in the center of a city at night, with different Legionaries arriving and leaving because of the planned attack, his Century was almost overwhelmed with checking each man. While his Century guarded the approaches, the Centurion, Optio, and Tesserarius remained close to General Caudex.

"First Centurion. You are needed at the north road," the squad leader of his Third Squad informed him.

"Isn't it something you can handle Lance Corporal, or another NCO?" asked Faustinus not wanting to let the General out of his sight.

"No, sir. We've located Senior Tribune Eutropius and our men," the Legionary replied.

Faustinus hurried out of the command tent, crossed the open area and stopped where the street and boulevard intersected. After peering at the pale faces of the deceased, the

First Centurion pointed at two of his Legionaries and the command tent.

"Carry Senior Tribune Eutropius to the General," he ordered. "Give me four to take our men to the Medical tent. We'll collect them for burial later."

First Centurion Faustinus held the tent flap and allowed the Legionaries to enter.

"What's this First Centurion," asked Caudex.

"We've located Tribune Eutropius, General," he replied. "He was found by the Velites as they got into position for the assault."

Appease Caudex walked around the map table and approached the body.

"Why is the Senior Tribune dressed in workmen's attire," he inquired. Then looking down at the body asked. "Maris. What were you doing near the Qart Hadasht lines'?"

"Sir, we don't know why he is dressed like that," Faustinus admitted. "Could he have been trying to emulate Senior Tribune Claudius' night reconnaissance?"

General Caudex jerked upright and rested a hand on his chin. After a moment of contemplation, he smiled.

"Maris died on a secret mission. That makes Maris Eutropius a hero of the Republic," announced the General. "I'll see to the commendation and be sure his father is recognized in the Senate."

In his private thoughts, Appease Caudex rejoiced. Without the return of his son's body or a satisfactory story, the Senator could lose the father's support. However, by singing the son's praises, he'd keep the elder Eutropius' support by anointing the son a hero.

"With your permission, General, we'll take him to the Medical tent," suggested Faustinus.

"Yes. And be sure they pack him in salt for the journey back to the Capital," instructed Caudex. Then quickly changing topics, he inquired. "What news of the assault?"

"It's still dark outside, General," Faustinus said as he indicated for the Legionaries to lift the Tribune's body and leave the command tent. Just before he ducked out of the tent, the First Centurion added. "I'm sure you'll carry the day, sir."

"I do believe the Qart Hadasht General will have something to say on the matter," Caudex replied to the closing flaps.

Chapter 15 – Dawn and Death

Legionaries train consistently. They run, jump, drill for immediate responses to commands and vault trenches, mounds, tree trunks, and any other obstacle they might encounter during a battle. The third maniple vaulted the chest-high stone wall and their shields slammed into the unprepared Qart Hadasht guard force. Driving them back, the Legionaries killed and stomped as they annihilated the stunned mercenary units. But all surprise attacks lose the element when the enemy realizes the situation and turns their spears towards the fight.

Five Legionaries were down. Seven more of the two hundred and forty men, who began the assault, staggered back to the stone wall with debilitating injuries. Pacing behind the shields of the third maniple and the thrusting javelins, the Centuries' Sergeants, Corporals, and Centurions shouted to their squads.

"Enthusiasm kills. Lethargy gets you dead," the Sergeant of the Twenty-fifth Century screamed to be heard over the heavy breathing, grunting, and rattling of javelin tips on enemy shields. "Close the gaps."

His words were repeated on the line by the squad leaders and the Left and Right Pivot men. Although they seemed to add to the racket and chaos, the words reached and comforted all the members of his three squads. His words, even in the midst of a blade to blade fight to the death, let the Legionaries know their command was intact. With enemy warriors a blade's length away and their vision restricted by their helmets and infantry shields, the Optio's voice and forwarded words assured the infantrymen that their line was unbroken.

On the other end of the Twenty-fifth, the three squads under the Corporal also repeated his words of encouragement and orders to keep their shields tight. While the NCOs controlled three squads each, in the center, their Centurion directed only two squads. Between his words, the line officer glanced back regularly to watch the assault commander.

Centurion Sanctus Carnifex stood on the stone wall holding an infantry shield he'd taken from a wounded Legionary. High above the fray with legs spread wide, shield swinging to deflect spears and arrows, the Legion's weapons instructor peered around calmly as if this was a training session. His confidence transferred to the line officers whose inflections reached their NCOs and by their tone spread to the eight squads of each Century. But inside, Carnifex's mind raced as he weighed his thinning line against the mass of Qart Hadasht soldiers staging behind the engaged mercenaries. Before the wave of professional fighters could form and sweep away the third maniple, the assault commander twisted around and held up two fingers. Then he held up one finger and pointed at the backside of the stone wall.

"Third maniple. Throw, push, push, draw," Carnifex bellowed while drawing his own gladius.

Until this point, the personal duels along the Legion line had been unconnected stabs with javelins and individual blocks with Legion shields.

"Throw. Push. Push. Draw," the line officers shouted and the orders were repeated by the NCOs.

As quick as three hand claps, the orders echoed along the line. Suddenly, over two hundred and twenty-five javelins arched from the Legion side. As they impacted with the rear ranks of Qart Hadasht mercenaries, the ones to the front of their formation got smacked by a coordinated surge of Legion infantry shields.

The change from individual fighting to a unified thrust shocked the mercenaries. Then a second push drove them back half a step. But they recovered quickly as the rank behind held them up against the power of the moving shields.

"Advance. Advance. Five steps back," Carnifex commanded while mimicking a thrust with his shield and a stab with his gladius.

Again, his orders filtered rapidly to the Legionaries. This time, when the shields shot forward and withdrew, gladius blades stabbed into the Qart Hadasht's front rank. But this time, the second rank couldn't hold them up as the mercenaries in the front rank fell from stab wounds. Those on the ground ate hobnailed boot leather as the Legion line stepped into the empty space. Shields powered forward and back, followed by a glint of over two hundred and twenty-five blades thrusting out and pulling back. Then the locked shields of the Legion stepped back from the devastated second rank of mercenaries. An area opened as the Legionaries hurriedly put five paces between the combatants.

Seeing the mercenaries hesitate from the shock of the advances, Centurion Carnifex ordered, "Back six paces and brace."

The third maniple back stepped raggedly and their officers and NCOs screamed at them to straighten their line and lock their shields. By the fourth step, the line solidified into a rail straight entity. On the sixth step, the line stopped and the Legionaries bent their forward legs and flexed their shield arms.

As with all withdrawals during contact, the issue concerned backing away and giving the enemy room to gain speed as they rushed forward. The Qart Hadasht mercenaries took the advantage and sprinted at the Legion line hoping to bust through and break up the formation.

"Brace," Carnifex ordered again as a reminder. He could see the battle was wearing on his less experienced troops. With fatigue, their thrusts weren't as crisp and their line fell apart until ordered to straighten it. Looking out beyond the mercenaries, he could see units of Qart Hadasht soldiers forming up and marching towards the fight. "Brace. Impact. Advance. Advance."

The bravest and fastest mercenaries launched themselves. They hoped to bust through the shields and allow their comrades to flow through and attack the Republic line from the rear.

"Brace," echoed through the line as the bodies of the flying mercenaries smashed into the shields. But, Legionaries trained for this. Those hitting the shields high were flipped to the rear and the shields dropped back into place. Behind the line, Sergeants, Corporals, and Centurions rushed over as the tumbling enemy fighters crashed to the ground. One pass hammered their heads to keep them down. Then, the line officers and NCOs backtracked stabbing throats.

The low flying mercenaries hit and bounced off the shields. Some of them fell to the ground while other staggered back in a daze. As their comrades attempted to avoid trampling their own men, the enemy's charge faltered.

"Advance. Advance," ordered the Centuries' commanders after the impact. And the solid wall of shields hammered forward and gladii snaked out leaving dead and wounded mercenaries. Hobnailed boots stomped, the shields shot into faces and gladius blades found flesh and then the Legion line locked in place.

"Back six and brace," called out Centurion Sanctus Carnifex.

The line moved unevenly with gaps between shields as they stepped back. Some of the gaps were from inexperience while others were from missing Legionaries. It was time to disengage the third maniple.

Carnifex twisted around, flashed two fingers, then one finger, indicated throw, and raised his gladius over his head. When the third maniple reached six steps back and braced, the assault commander waved his blade in the air to be sure the Centurions and NCOs saw it.

"Third maniple. Stand by," and Carnifex's words penetrated the hard breathing and foggy minds of the exhausted Legionaries. "Drop!"

As if the two hundred and fifteen surviving infantrymen, NCOs and officers of the third had their legs cut out from under them, they crumbled to the ground. Shocked at the actions of their enemy, the mercenaries stood looking at the still bodies, shields and bloodied blades. Then, assault commander Sanctus Carnifex dropped his arm.

From behind the stone wall, second and first maniples stood up, drew back their arms and threw javelins. Two hundred and forty javelins arched into the sky and mercenaries ducked and cringed as the shafts glided over and fell towards the Qart Hadasht ranks. Before the rain of iron tips touched a single mercenary, another two hundred and forty javelins skimmed over third maniple. There was no time for cringing or ducking as the almost flat trajectory of the shafts took the javelins from the hands of second maniple immediately to the bellies, arms, legs, and faces of the Qart Hadasht troops.

"Third maniple, fall back," ordered Carnifex before he jumped from the stone wall, sailed over the maniples and landed lightly on the grass. Spinning around, he watched as Centurions, Sergeants, and Corporals stood on the stone wall.

For the line officers and NCOs, this was the most dangerous part of a retreat while in contact. But, it was necessary. Delaying their withdrawal showed the infantrymen their leaders had courage and, they cared about every Legionary making it off the line. Once the last Centurions leaped from the stone wall, Carnifex instructed. "First and second maniples, step back twenty paces."

***

As if the skirmish at dawn had never taken place, silence descended on the narrow slip of land. The mercenaries had not crossed over. In fact, they pulled back from the stone wall. Centurion Sanctus Carnifex prowled behind the maniples keeping an eye on the stone wall as he talked with the Centurions.

"It was a good workout for the third," he stated. "If they keep progressing, I can send the rest of you back to Messina."

"And have your mentula dragging in the dirt when Qart Hadasht regulars jump that wall," warned a line officer from the first maniple.

"Suppose they just go back and have breakfast?" inquired an officer from the second.

"Then you'll be taking your lads over there and kicking over their cooking pots and spilling their camp stew," Carnifex offered. "But I don't think that will be necessary."

Everyone turned as a mounted man in gold armor rode up and gazed over the wall and across the field.

"I believe he has on more gold plating then General Caudex," observed one of the Centurions.

"I didn't think that was possible," another shot back. "Even the staff officers are pretty."

Reining up beside the gold armored man, a gaggle of riders in fancy armor crowded around. While their General sat his horse stately, they pointed and gabbed excitedly to each other.

147

"Like they've never seen a Legionary before," another Centurion commented.

"All they have to do is come over that wall and we can introduce them to a few," suggested a Centurion loudly. "It'll be fun meeting new people and exploring new cultures. Right, infantry?"

Laughter came from the center of the maniples and mumbling passed the line officer's words to all the Legionaries.

"Centurion. Are you suggesting they might have ill feeling towards us?" asked another Centurion loudly. His voice carried to the center squads and word of mouth assured the line officer's question traveled through both sides of the maniples. After a moment, he added. "We are but few and they are so many."

"I'll put my heavy infantry against any in the world," boasted Centurion Carnifex. "Besides, we have a secret weapon. Our third maniple is available."

The men in the second chuckled and laughter rippled through the first maniple. Just the thought that the pups would have to save the veterans was beyond comprehension. But Carnifex wasn't referring to the third's prowess in battle.

Two men with bags hanging from their shoulders marched from the direction of Messina and joined the third maniple. Stretcher-bearers carried stretchers to each area as the Medics treated wounded Legionaries. What the Qart Hadasht General and his staff missed were the piles of javelins dumped out of the stretchers and into the tall grass before the wounded were loaded.

"Centurions. Get them off their rumps and in line," Carnifex shouted to the officers of the Third. "We are on display and I demand a good show."

"Yes, sir," one of them replied as he began ordering his men up.

Soon the Third stood behind their shields. Hidden by the shields, men squatting down distributed the javelins evenly across the field.

***

For the most part, the Qart Hadasht General wasn't concerned with less than seven hundred of the Republic's troops. His army numbered in the thousands and he was content to post a couple of companies to prevent a reoccurrence of the morning's raid.

"General. Why would they send so few to attack you?" questioned the diplomat. "Could it be their main force is occupied on the south side of Messina. Possibly fighting King Hiero's forces?"

"And if they are?" inquired the General.

"Then it is as if an Impala held up a pride of lions," suggested the diplomat. "We laugh at their pitiful force because it is no threat. However, while we wait, the Syracusans may take Messina and claim it as part of their Kingdom."

"Just the other day," pondered the Qart Hadasht General. "Weren't you suggesting we wait to attack?"

"Then, I was proposing we wait for word from King Hiero," offered the diplomat. "This seems to be a delaying tactic on the part of the Republic. And, a broken alliance by the King."

"What do you think I should do?" inquired the General.

One of his Captains nudged his horse between the diplomat and the General.

"Sir. We crush this insult and take Messina for the Empire," the young field commander stated as he shook his fist in the direction of the Legion lines. "My men are embarrassed. We request, no General, we demand the satisfaction of butchering those wild beasts who attack in the night."

***

"I wasn't sure the General wanted any part of us," commented a Centurion as the group of Legion officers watched the General and the man in the fancy robe talk.

"I don't think he did until tall, dark and angry inserted himself in the negotiations," another added. "He seems to be my kind of man."

"I didn't know you had a kind of man," teased another Centurion.

"What I meant was, someone who isn't afraid of a fight," the line officer said in defense of his statement.

The hot-headed Captain wheeled his horse and shortly after leaving the General's side, trumpets blared.

"Are we ready for this?" shouted Sanctus Carnifex.

A roar went up from the Legionaries and the conference of line officers ended as each Centurion marched back to his Century.

***

It started when six ranks of heavy infantry appeared at the wall. Easily fourteen hundred men strong, they looked imposing with their midsized shields, tall helmets, shiny breastplates, and spears.

Assault commander Carnifex observed the Qart Hadasht infantry scrambling over the stone wall. While he watched, the line officers watched him.

"Let's make them mad. And bloody them up a little," Carnifex announced as the fourth rank climbed over the stone wall. "First maniple. One javelin. Throw."

The first was his experienced veterans and in three heartbeats, two hundred and forty javelins arched over the twenty paces. It was a long throw for the heavy weapons so only the first and second ranks of the Qart Hadasht soldiers caught the iron tips, leaving the rear, unorganized ranks ignorant of the danger. But the attack got the attention of their Lieutenants.

Suddenly, the Qart Hadasht infantry organized into thirty-five units of seven columns and they marched towards the Legionnaires. The movement showed them well trained and probably superb at field maneuvering. Except the field was narrow and only one hundred forty shields wide. All of their knowledge and experience couldn't overcome the geographical restrictions of the battlefield. They stacked up with no way to spread out and circle around the smaller force of Legionaries.

Assault commander Carnifex watched them bunch up creating a thick target.

"First and second maniples. One javelin. Throw," ordered Carnifex and the air filled with shafts. Being closer, the soldiers deeper in the ranks of tall helmets fell. "First maniple. Back five steps."

As his veterans backed up, Carnifex called for another flight of javelins from the second. This time, they only targeted the front rank of the Qart Hadasht infantry. But the second maniple had used their last javelin, as had the first maniple. This fact didn't escape the Lieutenants or the Qart Hadasht Captain.

Orders in a language most Legionaries didn't recognize resulted in actions they understood. The first two ranks of Qart Hadasht infantry lowered their spears.

"Second maniple, fall back to the third," Carnifex shouted. Now, with the second backing up to join with the third, his veterans stood alone waiting for the Empire's soldiers. "First maniple. Draw."

***

Centurion Carnifex waved his arm and forty Velites sprinted from the swamp. Their legs and light armor caked with splatters of mud, the skirmishers resembled clay brick makers instead of light infantrymen. Without being told, they fell in behind the third maniple reaching the line just as the second arrived.

"Take the spears," bellowed Carnifex as the Empire's heavy infantry marched towards the Republic's heavy infantry. His orders filtered quickly through the first maniple.

The Qart Hadasht Empire dominated the known world through its sea power. Land warfare to them meant forming a large army of mercenaries and crushing any city-state or tribe resisting the edicts of the Empire. For this, they depended on their spearmen to intimidate and eliminate the offending party or preferably bring them begging to the bargaining table. Long, thin shafts with sleek iron tips made the weapons light and deadly to unarmored foes. Or so numerous, armored troops were overcome by the sheer number of Empire soldiers. Unlike the heavy tipped Legion javelins, the spears weren't meant for throwing.

"Take the spears," was on the lips of the first maniple and their officers and NCOs when the spear tips reached out for the Legionaries. Rather than wait until the shields touched and the spear tips stabbed into armor or flesh, gladii swept up and chopped into the shafts. Not all of the shafts broke. But enough cracked that the first rank of Empire soldiers stepped back to rearm and the second rank rotated forward.

"Step. Advance. Advance," ordered Carnifex.

The veteran Legionaries stepped in, disrupting the rotation. Their shields shoved forward and they stabbed with their blades. Soldiers fell and were stomped as the shields shot out again.

"First maniple. Fall back. Fall back," Carnifex commanded.

While the Empire officers attempted to organize their third rank, the Legionaries, still holding their shield wall, backed away and kept backing until they filtered through the third maniple.

"I'd say they are good and mad, Sweet Butcher," commented the Centurion from the Second Century using the weapons instructor's nickname. He and Sanctus Carnifex walked back through the lines of Legionaries.

"Not mad enough," replied Carnifex. "I can see the end of their unit and daylight to the stone wall. Let's see if we can get them to commit another company or two. Javelins!"

From the deep grass, the seven hundred and thirty-five Legionaries scooped up javelins and held them at shoulder height.

"Stand by to throw one," he commanded. "Throw!"

The Empire company had taken casualties from javelins and gladii. Their Captain jumped around yelling at his Lieutenants. His anger caused by his company's inability to inflict more injuries on the Legion's infantry. During his tirade, the sky filled as if a flock of birds was flying overhead. But the black dots were heavy iron tips with shafts that arched over and fell among his troops. Not all the javelins killed. Some were deflected by shields, others missed completely but, a lot of them found flesh and maimed soldiers.

Of the fourteen hundred and forty who came over the stone wall, five hundred and ten soldiers of the Qart Hadasht Empire were dead or wounded. Only fifteen Legionaries had been seriously injured.

"That almost evens us up," remarked a Centurion.

"That's what I was thinking," replied Carnifex. "Third and second maniples. At a jog, forward."

With their Centurions and NCOs shouting to keep the line straight and shields tight, the maniples raced across the open ground. There was no need for any orders from assault commander Carnifex. As he ran, keeping pace with his lines, he scanned the Lieutenants and their Captain. As he hoped, the Qart Hadasht commanders hadn't expected an offensive move and were out of place to warn those further back in their columns.

At the initial surge, the big Legion shields deflected spear tips and drove the first two ranks of soldiers back. Gladius blades hacked and hobnailed boots stomped as the Legionaries fought their way into the soldier's formation. But the aggressive tactic took a toll.

"Disengage. Fall back," Carnifex ordered when eighteen of the third maniple toppled back from spear thrusts. "Second, give the third cover."

Dragging the eighteen injured, the third ran for the first's line while the second maniple back stepped, keeping their shields towards the soldiers. As the Legionaries pulled back, Qart Hadasht trumpets sounded from behind the stone wall.

"I believe they have called for reinforcements," suggested the Centurion from the Thirteenth Century. "I noticed you've saved the Second. Is there a reason?"

"Yes. And the reason is coming over the stone wall," Carnifex answered. "Not to worry, you'll earn your rations today."

A seemingly never-ending wave of Empire soldiers were jumping the stone barrier.

"Second maniple, you have the rear guard," Carnifex shouted as he reached the Legion line. "First back them up. Third maniple and Velites disengage."

The second maniple, shields still locked, stepped back while watching the gathering of Empire companies. Close behind them, the first also backed up while the third and the Skirmishers picked up the wounded and jogged towards Messina.

The assault detachment had completed their mission of rousing the Qart Hadasht army and bringing them out from behind the stone wall. All they had to do now was survive the retreat.

Chapter 16 – Sweet Butcher

Centurion Sanctus Carnifex glanced back to see the injured, the inexperienced Legionaries, and the light infantry disappear in the distance. Swiveling his head around, he surveyed the narrow spit of land in front of his retreating formation. Starting at twenty paces in front of the second maniple, Qart Hadasht soldiers and mercenaries filled the landscape to the stone wall with more coming over.

Twice several ranks of Empire heavy infantry had charged forward. Twice, the second maniple had left ranks of dead and dying soldiers in their wake. Unfortunately, several of Carnifex's Legionaries also died with them.

'This can't go on,' the assault leader thought as he motioned a Centurion from either side to come to him. Carnifex looked to his right rear. Tall grass on mostly flat land ran to the waters of the Messina Strait. Not directly, there was a drop about the height of a man to the deep water. He'd need to station several men there in case the Empire sent swimmers to attack from the rear. Then he noted a pair of trees in the distance. Their branches offered some protection from arrows and would give his Legionaries a focal point for their defensive formation. "I'm going to order the first to flake off the line in squads. I want them heading towards Messina until the last squad is off. Then, they head for those trees and set up a defensive half circle. On my command, the second maniple is to turn around and run after them."

"That will put our backs to the Strait," offered one of the line officers.

"At least we can wash off afterward," added the other. "Better than sucking mud from the marshland."

"Inform the command line," instructed Carnifex. "I don't want to order it until we are ready."

The Centurions strolled behind the maniples stopping to casually chat with every Corporal, line officer, and Sergeant.

When they reached the ends of the lines and started back, Centurion Carnifex glanced right and left and, pointed at his officers and NCOs. Forming fists with his hands, Carnifex extended his thumbs and jerked his hands over his shoulders.

"Execute!" he shouted. After issuing the command, the assault commander stood calmly and relaxed. The Empire officers were watching him trying to get a hint of his intentions.

Along the Legion line, nothing happened at first. Then as if a strip of bark was peeled off a tree trunk, the last Legionary in the first maniple turned around and marched off the line. Then the adjacent man about faced and fell in beside him. By the time fifteen Legionaries formed lines moving away from the front, the Qart Hadasht commanders took notice. But the second maniple's solid line of shields remained in place. The Goddess Tyche blessed the Legion detachment and the Empire didn't attack.

The staggered squads of the first maniple drew parallel with the pair of trees and their Centurions shouted, "Break."

Until that moment, the Qart Hadasht commanders assumed the Republic forces were falling back towards Messina. It was the direction they wanted to go in and they were satisfied with quick attacks while following. When the Legion squads turned and ran towards the trees, they realized their mistake. Fighting a retreating line maintained their forward movement. If the Legionaries formed a defensive position, the army of the Empire would have to stop. They couldn't leave an active enemy force at their rear. Besides, this Republic unit had embarrassed them and must be crushed.

"Second maniple, turnabout and run!" cried out Centurion Sanctus Carnifex.

Along with the other training, Legionaries sprinted. It provided conditioning and was required for quick maneuvering tactics. With a twenty-pace head start, the right wing of the maniple easily outran the charge by the Qart Hadasht infantry.

But, the far reaches of the left wing had to cross the field at an angle and sprint twice the distance.

"First maniple, Javelins," ordered Carnifex as he ran towards the trees. He slid to a stop in front of the shields and allowed Legionaries to run by. Ignoring the Empire soldiers bearing down on him, the Centurion focused on those converging with his men racing across the field.

Two squads were caught. Shoved sideways, they stopped running and defended themselves. Although they moved as they fought, Empire soldiers began to flow around them.

"Punch them a hole. Throw," commanded Carnifex.

Two hundred javelins tore into the tightly packed soldiers standing between the trapped Legionaries and the defensive circle. For a moment, a path cleared and half the Legionaries scrambled over the impaled bodies on the ground. A clamshell opened in the defensive line and slammed shut once the ten men entered the half circle. The other ten Legionaries disappeared beneath jabbing spears and hacking swords. Sanctus Carnifex shook his head at the loss and walked between the shields.

"Your defensive circle is too big," he called out. "Pull every third man back and close up."

The first maniple complied, shifted and locked shields just as the Qart Hadasht infantry smashed into them. Shields clashed, javelins and spears dueled at shoulder height, and men crowded together in a crush of bodies attempting to murder the man across from them.

***

In the chaos of a shield wall, things stood out. A man ignoring cuts while splashing drops of blood around as he continued to stab at his foe. When Sanctus Carnifex observed those, he'd rotate the injured Legionary back for treatment. Or, three or more adjacent Legionaries falling into a rhythm and carving up the soldiers across from them. Those he simply watched in appreciation of their teamwork. Small instances of heroism, sacrifice, and selfishness were the little things unseen by most of the combatants.

Then, there were the big events that could momentarily halt a fight.

***

A Legionary's body fell inside the defensive circle and his split shield was tossed back landing on his lifeless form. Centurion Carnifex noticed the cleaved shield from across the defensive formation. When another body and another split shield joined the first, the assault commander rushed to that section of the arc.

Towering above his fellow Empire soldiers, a giant of a man swung a two-handed sword with one arm. A piece of Legion shield flipped into the air as the huge warrior drew back his great sword for another strike.

"Shields forward, defensive posture," Sanctus shouted as he snatched up an abandoned shield and fitted it to his arm.

This time the massive sword smacked against and rattled the faces of overlapping Legion shields. It created little damage but while the Legionaries were defending, they couldn't stab or slash. In the absence of offense, Empire soldiers crowded forward.

"Rotating up," growled the weapons instructor as he drew his gladius. "Protect my flanks."

Carnifex shouldered aside two Legionaries and joined the defensive line. In front of him stood a massive warrior. Seeing the Legionary with the bright comb on his helmet, the soldier raised his sword and smiled.

The idea of killing an officer, any officer, pleased the giant. Now he had one from the Republic in arms reach and he wanted a one strike kill. He was already counting the bounty as the sword chopped downward.

Sanctus Carnifex bent his knees to allow the bottom of his shield to rest on the ground. Anchoring his body with his shield arm, he braced and raised his gladius horizontally. As the long blade descended, Carnifex powered out of the squat just as the blades clashed. The giant's sword slid along the Centurion's gladius and was guided off to the side. Momentum carried the redirected blade around and it chopped into the Empire soldier fighting beside the giant. As the soldier and his split shield flew back into his own company, the fighting in that sector stopped. A personal duel between champions constituted an event.

The warrior, pulled to the side by the weight of his great sword, received a hasty slash along his ribcage. But, he was powerful and managed to bring his shield around before Carnifex was able to line up for a stab. The two-handed blade arched up and across, forcing Carnifex to lean back. A deep furrow on the face of the Legion shield marked the passage of the blade's tip. Rising to shoulder level, the long blade hung for a moment as the giant tightened his muscles preparing for a targeted downward slash.

Carnifex spun in a circle. Using the edge of the Legion shield, he bumped the giant's shield, briefly, off center. Thrusting into the closing gap, the gladius sliced the massive warrior's other ribcage to the bone. Reacting to the pain, the Empire warrior jerked the two-handed blade downward in an uncontrolled hack.

The Centurion relaxed his left arm. Instead of being thrown to the side by the heavy blade, the power of the giant, and the weight of the Legion shield, Carnifex allowed the arm to float in the direction of the force. Although his arm overextended, he remained balanced. The only real damages: a corner of the Centurion's shield was sheared off and he was exposed.

The massive warrior seethed with anger. His strikes had done no damage to the broad-shouldered Legion officer. Now, he had his enemy open with the big shield out of position. But, his sword was outside that shield. He needed to draw it back in order to deliver a killing strike. To give him time to withdraw the long blade, he slammed the Centurion in the chest with the Empire shield.

Legionaries trained with their shields. Besides their gladii and javelins, shields were their most effective weapons. The natural inclination when receiving a face full of wood and leather was to back away. But that would throw a Legionary off his attack line, leaving a breach and his squad mates unprotected. Training included attacking with a shield and defending against attacks by a shield. Legion instructors delivered a lot of smashes with shields during drills to teach the proper techniques. Conversely, weapons instructors ate a lot of oiled hardwood from irate Legionaries returning the favor.

Weapons instructor Carnifex dug in his left foot to anchor his place and bent his left knee to brace against the Empire shield. As he set one side of his body, he rotated his right leg back, pivoted his upper body and bent away from the full force of the blow. The warrior's shield connected with the left side of his chest and shoulder. While he absorbed the impact, Carnifex swung his right arm down and twirled the gladius in his fingers. From forward facing, the weapon flipped, putting the blade to the rear. Then, he raised his arm and stepped forward with the right leg.

The giant had his sword arm back, bringing the long blade up in an arc. In a heartbeat, it would swing over his shoulder and chop the Legion officer killing him instantly. Then, a hand, holding a gladius, appeared above the Empire shield. Before the massive warrior's sword rose further, the gladius stabbed down into the Empire soldier. The short blade entered his lower throat and shattered the top of his sternum before piercing the giant's heart.

As the huge soldier dropped to his knees, Sanctus Carnifex pulled his gladius free and stepped back.

"Close the gap," he ordered while shaking off the Legion shield. It tumbled onto the other broken shields. The Centurion sheathed his gladius and clasped his hand over his elbow.

"Trouble, Sweet Butcher?" inquired a line officer.

"He hits like a mule," replied Carnifex.

"Not anymore," the Centurion stated. He pointed towards a group of Empire soldiers carrying the giant on their shoulders away from the fighting. "Thanks for that. He was about to carve a hole in my lines."

"I thought he was going to carve a hole in me," Carnifex responded while indicating the three broken shields. "Or, begin to remove body parts. Where are we in this ugly fight?"

***

The wounded lay between the trees being tended to by the less seriously injured. Around the defensive line, they were down to two ranks. Soon, the injured, those able to hold a javelin or handle a gladius and shield, would be required to man the lines again. Before it came down to the last man defense, Qart Hadasht trumpets sounded and the attacking soldiers pulled back.

In the distance, assault commander Carnifex saw Senior Tribune Claudius and Senior Centurion Valerian ride into view. As they drew closer, ranks of Legionaries, grouped around unit flags, trotted ahead of the staff officer and Centurion.

The army of the Empire retreated trying to get their companies back over the stone wall. But there were too many mercenaries and soldiers in the narrow field. With no room to maneuver or time to flee, they set lines preparing to fight.

"Centurion Carnifex. Are we going to get into that?" a blood-splattered Private inquired.

"No. We've completed the mission," Sanctus replied. "And, we've had enough fun for one day. Let's enjoy the show."

Centuries spread out forming the front attack ranks. Behind them, Legionaries stacked up twenty ranks deep waiting for their chance to fight. Like a saw blade through dry wood, the Legion began chewing up the army of the Empire. Once they had advanced beyond the trees on the banks of the Strait, the Senior Tribune and his runners rode to the battered assault detachment.

"Senior Tribune Claudius. Good morning, sir," Carnifex said while delivering a cross chest salute. "We are glad to see you."

Looking around at the wounded, Gaius Claudius ordered a runner to fetch a medical team before he replied.

"I thought you'd bring a few of their units over the wall," Claudius explained. "But it seems you've drawn half their forces."

"We couldn't help it, sir," Carnifex reported indicating the exhausted and wounded Legionaries around him. "Every time they attacked, we beat them. They kept sending more and more units over the stone wall after us. And we kept beating them."

"Colonel Requiem will be along shortly with General Caudex. Give them your report," instructed Claudius. "Then get your detachment back to Messina. From the looks of it, you all need to report to the Medical tent."

Tribune Gaius Claudius reined his horse around and galloped off with his runners.

"Colonel Requiem is trusting the Legion to the Senior Tribune," remarked one of the Centurions.

"I guess he wants to make a battle commander out of him," Carnifex replied. "Let's get this detachment cleaned up and ready for the General. Legionaries, on your feet."

Act 4

Chapter 17 – Canes Venandi

Gaius Claudius trotted from the assault detachment to the center of the field. Legionaries behind him waited in ranks. To his front, two rows of Legionnaires battled with the army of the Empire. A third rank passed forward new javelins when one broke.

"I don't think the stone wall will be a problem," Gaius announced as he rode up beside the Senior Centurion.

"No, sir. They have so many scrambling over it, we'll simply tag along," responded the senior line officer. Then he called a Centurion to the rear of the attack line. "You are lagging behind. We need to hit that wall as one. Make it one!"

The line officer and his NCOs shouted to their Century and the slightly concave shape in their section straightened.

"Third maniple to the front," Valerian ordered. Holding up two fingers, he turned his head and instructed. "Bring up two."

On the attack line, the commanders passed on the order and the fighting Legionaries at the front angled their shields to create uniformed gaps. The third rank shuffled through the second maniple, who were thrusting javelins at the enemy, and surged a full step into the enemy line. There, they took over the hard work of shield to shield fighting.

What had been the front rank, stepped back. Gasping to catch their breath and shaking out tight muscles or applying pressure to cuts, they walked towards the rear of the Legion formation. As they ambled back, two fresh lines jogged forward to the assault line. For a brief moment, the rotation left only two maniples at the front.

"Second maniple, fall back," Valerian ordered as the two fresh lines filtered into place.

It only took a few heartbeats and the Legion personnel on the attack line completely changed. Fresh Legionaries maintained the intensity and forward momentum. On the other side of the fighting, the Qart Hadasht Captains and Lieutenants, from different units and cultures, attempted to shuffle fresh troops to the front. But they lacked the training and discipline and, most importantly, the cohesion between units of the Republic's Legion.

"The stone wall doesn't look that high," commented Senior Tribune Claudius. "In the dark from the swamp, it seemed to be a formidable obstacle."

"It's big enough, sir. If we came at it across an open field, they'd have archers and spears ready," explained Senior Centurion Valerian. "We'd have lost a lot of Legionaries taking that wall. But with their troops on this side, the flow of fighting will carry us over it."

Fighting along the assault line approached the stone wall. Five paces from the structure, the Senior Centurion called out.

"Third maniple to the front," Valerian ordered. Holding up two fingers, he turned his head and instructed. "Bring up two."

**

A work detail removed stones from the wall and the Senior Tribune and Senior Centurion rode through side by side. Their runners and the junior Tribunes followed. The work detail continued to dismantle the wall to allow passage of the Legion's support wagons and mules. In the distance, Claudius and Valerian saw Qart Hadasht wagons and columns of soldiers fleeing from their assault line.

"The field is yours, Senior Tribune," commented Valerian as he pointed at the retreating Empire army. "Orders, sir?"

"What do you think, Senior Centurion?" Gaius asked. "Should we let them go and set defensive positions or pursue them?"

"Senior Tribune, I'm just the mule driver," Valerian answered. "It's the Legion battle commander who dictates the route."

The comment rocked Gaius Claudius. Pericles Requiem was the oversized Legion's commander. All morning, runners kept the Colonel and the General informed of their progress. Not once had Requiem replied with orders or even suggestions for Claudius at the front. Last month, when the Senior Tribune crossed to Messina with the advance units, it had been with twelve Centuries under his command. Looking around, he peered at almost four thousand heavy infantrymen, over eight hundred light infantrymen, plus Doctors and Medics and over two hundred support personnel.

"Orders, sir?" asked Valerian.

"Tell me, Senior Centurion, what is the state of our men?" Claudius inquired as he thought about the hard fighting from yesterday.

"Good question, sir. There are basically two kinds of canes," replied Valerian. "Hunting dogs and guard dogs."

"And what are these?" asked Claudius indicating the Legionaries surrounding them.

"*Canes venandi*," the senior line officer assured him.

"Then turn them loose, Senior Centurion," ordered Senior Tribune Claudius. "And let them hunt."

***

The narrow spit of land broadened and, at midday, the fleeing Qart Hadasht army divided into companies. Once separated from the wagons and support mules, they began forming fighting units. Empire cavalry, which had been absent on the narrows, appeared and rode to flanking positions.

165

"It appears the fox has grown fangs and found his courage," ventured Valerian. After that pronouncement, he sat on his horse staring at Gaius.

"You really aren't going to give me advice, are you?" remarked the Tribune.

"Not unless you order something inspired by Coalemus, sir," replied the senior line officer.

"If I say something stupid, I would hope you would," Gaius agreed. "They have horsemen and we don't. Split our Velites and give them three Centuries of heavy infantry on both sides. That should hold the Qart Hadasht cavalry. We'll go at their center without skirmishers."

Gaius watched the Senior Centurion for any objections or signs of disapproval.

"Yes, sir," Valerian responded. Then he turned to his runners and began issuing orders.

While the senior line officer ordered the adjustments for the fighting part of the Legion, Gaius began sending his Tribunes to the support elements. Supply wagons, the Centuries' mules, and the Medical wagons were directed to stop and set up areas to protect the livestock. Five Centuries were sent back to help arrange and guard the camp.

"They don't seem to be in any hurry," Gaius observed once the crush of runners and Tribunes dispersed. He glanced across the front of the Qart Hadasht's army as their units scurried into defensive formations.

"Our assault detachment disturbed their breakfast. They're probably hungry as well as demoralized from the rude awakening," commented Valerian. "Should we ruin the rest of their day, sir?"

***

General Caudex and Colonel Requiem, surrounded by First Century Headquarters, rode through the wide gap in the stone wall.

"You were correct, Colonel," observed Caudex. "Senior Tribune Claudius is ready for his own Legion."

"I'm glad you agree, General. The Republic needs experienced battle commanders," Requiem replied as he and the General reined their horses around a line of dead Qart Hadasht soldiers. "He'll need backing from the Senate when the next Legion is formed."

"Hopefully, we won't need to field any Legions for a while," Caudex pondered. "But, I'm here and out of touch with the politics of the Republic. With my term as Consul growing short, I'll soon resume my place in the Senate. You have my word that Gaius Claudius will receive my backing."

"You've proven to be a victorious General," commented Requiem. "History will treat you with honor."

"We've fought two armies in two days," General Caudex mentioned. "How many have died to secure a harbor that's redundant, considering Rhégion is just across the Strait?"

"Messina is critical to preventing an invasion of the Republic's southern region," Colonel Requiem reminded him while pointing at three wagons and fifteen men trailing behind. "As far as how decisive were your victories, we'll have a count by the end of the day, General."

Among the detachment following the Colonel and General, three Greek slaves with big scrolls made notes as other men ran to strip the soldiers of their armor, helmets, weapons and personal items. As each finished salvaging, he carried the equipment to one of the wagons and reported to a Greek. A careful accounting kept track of the presumed value of the equipment, jewelry, coins and, added the Qart Hadasht soldier to the body count. While Legionaries bodies and equipment would be returned to their Century, the soldier's equipment would be sold and added to the General's treasury.

***

"Valerian. I'm going to order our flanking units five quick paces ahead and three advances," Tribune Gaius Claudius informed his Senior Centurion.

"What are you thinking, sir?" inquired the senior line officer.

"I'm watching messengers travel back and forth between their command staff and their cavalry. But there's not much communication with their infantry," explained Gaius. "I believe the Qart Hadasht General plans a flanking charge to break through the ends of our lines."

"Bless your eyesight, Senior Tribune," Valerian said acknowledging the gift from Theia and the military instincts of the acting battle commander. "Our flanks moving forward will throw off their coordination. You'll order advances by our infantry to maintain our lines after the flanks move?"

"Of course," Gaius said to the wily Centurion who didn't give advice to staff officers. "Runners, Tribunes. Flanks to advance on my signal. Heavy infantry to follow on my command. Go, alert your Centurions."

Gaius finished sending off the messengers and looked up for Valerian. All morning the Senior Centurion had ridden beside him soliciting orders and pointing out the movement of individual Centuries. Now with the Legion online and about to go into combat across a wide front, the senior line officer vanished.

Two squads broke from a section of a maniple and sprinted towards Gaius. As they approached, one squad wrapped around to his front while the other ten Legionaries completed a circle by running around behind him.

"What's the meaning of this?" demanded Gaius.

"Sir. We have the honor of being the battle commander's bodyguard detachment," a Lance Corporal replied. Then to the twenty Legionaries, he ordered. "Spread out, give the commander room to operate."

As the members of the squads stepped away to create lanes, two young Tribunes raced up. One had his gladius out as if he was a historic warrior prepared to win the battle by himself. The other trotted passed the Legionaries but, the armed Tribune's horse jerked to a stop when two infantry shields slammed into the animal's chest. Not only was he halted, two javelin tips floated in the air a couple hands distance from the young nobleman's face.

"Tribune. Put the weapon away in the presence of the battle commander," a Lance Corporal stated.

As the young man complied and sheathed his gladius, Gaius asked, "Is that necessary?"

"Sir. Senior Centurion Valerian said if he sees a bare blade anywhere near you, we will be on latrine duty for a year after we get off the punishment post," one of the squad leaders informed the Senior Tribune. "The most important unit of a Legion in contact, sir, is you. So, yes battle commander, that was necessary."

"I understand," Gaius said as he waved the frightened Tribune forward. Then, he inquired. "Where is the Senior Centurion?"

"Sir, at his post," the Lance Corporal responded while pointing at the center of the three maniples.

Stationed behind the combat line of Legionaries, Valerian sat on his horse shouting orders and sending runners to specific Centurions. Then, the Senior Centurion twisted around and saluted Gaius. He hadn't realized it during the running fight to reach the open plain because it felt like a running skirmish. But now, with the Legion in maniples, tensed and waiting, Gaius Claudius understood. Responsibility for this massive engine of war had just been handed to him. At his command, men would fight and die.

He felt the weight on his shoulders and uttered a silent prayer to Mars. Then he raised his arms shoulder height, pointed his fingers at the sky, and thrust his arms out to the sides. Valerian mimicked the action, releasing the Legion and letting the fates decide the outcome.

***

The horses of the Empire's cavalry pawed the earth. The nervousness and anticipation of their riders transferred to the mounts and the animals fidgeted knowing a hard ride was ahead. Further back than their infantry's lines and located on the flanks, the cavalry waited for orders.

Without warning, the mixed force of heavy and light infantry of the Legion stomped forward calling out, "One, two, three." The counting stopped as they threw javelins at the cavalrymen while maintaining the forward movement.

Already jumpy in anticipation, when their riders fell from the heavy iron tips or jerked sideways dodging javelins, the horses panicked. Rearing back and spinning, their fear infected the adjacent mounts and the first two lines of the Qart Hadasht cavalry became a milling and smashing jumble of man and horse. Then, the Legion infantrymen hit the front rank of the massed cavalry.

The Legionaries stabbed, horsemen fell and more horses panicked. In a cavalry charge, the horsemen sweep down on isolated infantrymen. But, when infantrymen stomp up to horses, screaming loudly, horses bolt. The well-ordered cavalry of the Empire broke down as horsemen raced away to avoid the mess and to calm their horses.

At the ends of the Qart Hadasht infantry lines, the soldiers watched as the horsemen guarding their flanks raced away. In their place, and actually behind their lines, were Legionaries. To protect their flanks, the end soldiers folded back, then the man next to him also folded back and, then another.

Senior Centurion Valerian looked back nervously. His Legionaries at the ends stood exposed behind enemy lines with the cavalry already beginning to reform. If the Legion's third

170

maniple of infantry didn't move soon, his exposed units would be slaughtered. But Senior Tribune Claudius sat his horse calmly staring off to his left while Junior Tribunes rode towards the ends of the lines. Valerian glanced in that direction but the lines of Legionaries and the dust kicked up by the retreating cavalry horses limited his view. Quickly, he twisted back around and stared at the seemingly distracted battle commander.

With his heart racing, Valerian looked to his right. The Qart Hadasht cavalry lined up and began walking towards his flanking unit which stood out in the open. Gaius Claudius' hands came up but the palms were flat as if to signal for him to wait. Senior Centurion Valerian hadn't disobeyed an order since he was a young, impulsive line officer. But he was tempted.

Then, the battle commander shot his arms out wide and pointed forward.

"Advance. Advance," screamed the Senior Centurion. Seven times he cried out while waving his arms madly as if, by physical force, he could quicken the Legion assault.

A strange thing happened before Valerian's eyes. The Centuries at the ends of his maniples broke off from the attack line and joined the exposed units to meet the cavalry. Meanwhile, the remainder of his maniples folded the line in a u-shape. Glancing back, he watched as the Senior Tribune held his arms out as if carrying a large barrel. Slowly, the arms closed as if crushing the barrel. Looking back towards the fighting, he saw his Legion envelope the Qart Hadasht infantry.

Far off, the Empire's General spun his horse and, with his command staff following, he trotted away from his army and the Legion. Soon the cavalry broke off and galloped away as well. Then long lines of soldiers and mercenaries joined the flight away from the infantry shields and the thrusts of javelins and gladii.

"I'm sorry about the delay," Gaius Claudius said as he, his Tribunes and, his bodyguards moved up beside the Senior Centurion. "The ends of the Qart Hadasht infantry folded back. At first just a few, but there must have been confusion because whole companies came off the line and formed sides. Once we moved, I signaled for the envelope maneuver and two Centuries on each end to help with the cavalry."

"No need to apologize, battle commander," admitted Valerian. "And congratulation on the victory. Orders, sir?"

"This time there is no question about it," Gaius stated. "Hunt them down and kill as many as we can. I want the Empire to think twice before challenging the Republic again."

"Century formations, we are pursuing," Valerian instructed his runners. After listing the Centuries assigned to chase down the army, he looked to the rear where the Legion wagons were setting up the camp. "Senior Tribune. I believe the General would like you to join him and Colonel Requiem."

Gaius reined his horse around and trotted off to join the command staff. Valerian saluted before turning back to the two squads assigned to guarding the Senior Tribune during the battle.

"Get back to your Century and get some blood on your blades," he ordered.

"Yes, Senior Centurion," the squad leaders responded.

***

Later, once the General's tent had gone up, Colonel Requiem and Senior Tribune Claudius marched in together.

"Gentlemen, have some refreshments," Caudex offered. "We're waiting for preliminary numbers."

In a corner of the tent, the three Greeks huddled around their scrolls. They had just returned from guiding their wagons through the battlefield collecting the recent body count.

"Two days and two victories," Caudex exclaimed while lifting a mug of wine. "And I did it with two months still in my

172

tenure as a Co-Consul of the Republic. It will be good to get back to my Villa and the Capital."

"Congratulations, General," Colonel Requiem said as he and Claudius raised their mugs.

"General. We have a count for you," one of the Greeks said. "These are rough but I believe the ratio will hold."

"Speak up, man," urged General Caudex.

"General. In two days of fighting, we estimate that your Legions killed six thousand enemy soldiers," the Greek reported as he read off a scroll. "And lost only one thousand three hundred Legionaries."

"Considering we began by being outnumbered four to one," Caudex boasted. "Those are fantastic numbers."

Pericles Requiem and Gaius Claudius knew the real numbers were closer to twelve thousand soldiers against their nine thousand heavy and light Legion infantrymen, but no one corrected the General. It wasn't a good idea to challenge a powerful man's memory or contest his assumed status as a great war leader.

"Again, congratulations on your victories, General Caudex," Requiem said while raising his mug. "It's a pleasure serving under you, sir."

"I'll gladly add my voice to the accolade," chimed in Gaius Claudius as they toasted Appease Caudex.

***

Centurion Sanctus Carnifex and his assault detachment took their time getting back to Messina. The sun shone midafternoon when they reached the Medical tent and dropped the stretchers.

"These men are dead," complained a Medic as he checked the first three. "They should have been taken to graves registration to await their Tesserarius."

He moved to the other stretchers. After a quick inspection of the wounded, he directed the blood splattered Legionaries.

"Bring them inside for treatment," he instructed. "And take those three away."

"Medic. These men and I have been surrounded by Qart Hadasht soldiers since before dawn," Carnifex informed the Medic. "We'll move them to any area you wish. But, we will not carry them five blocks to registration. Now, where do you want them?"

"Take the deceased to the awning area in the back," advised the Medic. "Graves can pick them up later."

"We can do that," the Centurion assured him. "Let's go people."

The stretchers were lifted and carried towards the rear of the Medical tent. As the exhausted Legionaries neared the back corner, a coarse voice chanting softly reached them.

Reach out for my brother
His light fades as do others
Ease his struggle to survive
As his strength wanes
Pacing steadily to his demise
Grip his hand in yours
Take him from this plain
Free his soul
Cease his pain
Goddess of Death
Reach out for my brother

Sanctus Carnifex led the way and, as he reached the awning, he saw a man in a dirty tunic kneeling beside a wounded Legionary. As he chanted, the priest, Sanctus guessed, washed an injured man's face with gentle strokes.

Nenia Dea
You hover just out of sight
But death is called
To claim his life

With gentle hands so light
Take him with care
As is a worthy man's right
Goddess of Death, Nenia Dea
Hear our plight
As you hover just out of sight

After scanning the area and realizing there were no Medics or slaves in attendance, he pointed at the kneeling man.

"Priest. Where do you want the dead?" he asked indicating the three stretchers.

To the Centurion's surprise, Lance Corporal Alerio Sisera glanced up from where he chanted and washed the pale face. Without breaking his rhythm, what little there was in his rough rendition of the death chant, Alerio pointed to an empty place at the edge of the awning.

Allow him to pass bravely
His comrades call his elegy
We sing Memento Mori
For this man's end
remembering we will all die
Release this Legionary
This son of man
This best of friend
Grant him an end
Goddess of Death
Allow him to pass bravely

Centurion Sanctus Carnifex puzzled by the actions of the Lance Corporal, whom he knew to be a fine weapons instructor and not a saintly priest, pointed out the area to the stretcher bearers. They sat the dead down and stood with Carnifex staring at the kneeling man. Without looking at them, Alerio shifted the bucket of water. Pain showed on his face as he

175

crawled on his hands and knees to the three dead. The rag dipped into the bucket and he began to wash the dirt and blood off the first corpse.

"Sweet Butcher," a voice whispered from behind Sanctus Carnifex. "Leave Death Caller alone. He's been here two days singing and calling for the Goddess Nenia for our dying."

First Sergeant Gerontius of the Southern Legion detachment stood a respectful distance from the awning. He motioned for Carnifex and the stretcher bearers to come to him and away from the critically wounded and the dead.

"Death Caller?" inquired Sanctus.

"What else would you call a Legionary with a record of heroic fighting and killing enemies of the Republic, sir?" explained Gerontius. "Who, even though deeply wounded and in pain, cares for our men in their last moments. Everyone assumes he has the blessing of Nenia and a relationship with the Goddess of Death. For a young man, Sisera has certainly kept her busy."

"You are correct, First Sergeant," Centurion Sanctus Carnifex agreed as he turned and walked away from the area reserved for the dying and the dead. Then a shiver ran through the tough, veteran Legion weapons instructor and, he mumbled. "Death Caller. It's a fitting name."

Act 5

Chapter 18 – Before the March

Centurion Sanctus Carnifex searched for Alerio during the three-day festival ordered by General Caudex. The Lance Corporal failed to make an appearance at any of the sacrifices or the feasts that followed. Nor did he join the Southern Legion formation or attend any of the games. Sanctus was beginning to suspect Nenia had taken Sisera as punishment for the number of times he called out to the Goddess of Death.

On day four, rain poured from the sky and most of the Legionaries hunkered down nursing hangovers or staying in their area repairing equipment. Tomorrow, the Legions would emerge and begin training again. Sanctus Carnifex, as Legion weapons instructor, would be at the forefront of the shield and gladii drills. In preparation, he rose in the dark, weathering the storm, and ran five miles through the deluge. He planned to end his run near the center of Messina where he had training posts set up. As he rounded the final corner and his hobnailed boots pounded and splashed, the faint sounds of practice gladii beating a rhythm on the posts reached him. Pleased at the initiative of a squad rising early to get in extra practice, he strained his eyes to see through the rain. Lightning flashed and he caught a glimpse of a single Legionary running drills with a pair of heavy, wooden practice swords.

"Lance Corporal Sisera. I feared you dead," Sanctus exclaimed as he slowed and walked the last few paces to the training posts.

"The Sons of Mars put me in a steam room and placed seaweed on my wounds," Alerio explained as his hands crossed and uncrossed to keep the hammering on the post at an equal measure. Rainwater ran down his face and off his shoulders causing the tunic to cling to his body. "I remember them waking me and forcing me to drink water tainted with salt. So much water that I never stopped sweating. And they changed the seaweed wrap four times a day. After two days, I threatened to cut the next person who brought me saltwater and, murder anyone who dared pour water on the hot stones."

"That accounts for two days. Where were you yesterday?" inquired Sanctus. "You missed the feasting and games."

"After a meal of meat and wine, I slept for a full day," Alerio informed him. "I woke early and decided to get a workout in, Centurion."

"I'm a little surprised to find you here," admitted Sanctus. "I thought the Legion lost you to the priesthood."

"Not in my nature, sir," Alerio informed the Legion weapons instructor. He increased the pace of his strikes. Rainwater flew off the wooden swords as they blurred from the speed and the wet post vibrated from the heavy impacts. "But I learned something behind the Medical tent. Plus, I made two vows."

"What did you learn?" inquired Sanctus. "And what did you pledge, Lance Corporal Sisera?"

"That the spirit is stronger than the body," Alerio stated as he slowed his pace. "I will train my Legionaries harder than before to toughen their bodies and, do all I can to keep them from the Goddess Nenia."

"You said two vows?" Sanctus reminded him. "What's the second?"

"If I live, I will go to Nenia's temple in the Capital and leave a hefty donation," Alerio said as he stopped and rested the swords on his shoulders. "Aren't you going to run drills, sir?"

"Not yet, Death Caller," Sanctus replied. "Put those away and let's find a pub and breakfast. I have a few things I want to talk to you about."

178

"Death Caller, sir?" Alerio asked at the mention of the strange name.

"It's what the Legionaries have named you, Lance Corporal," explained Sanctus. "Somewhere between your battles with the Syracusan Hoplites and your tender care for the dying, they decided you call to death. And if there aren't enough around, you create dead for the Goddess. That's a heady reputation, Death Caller."

"But sir, I'm a simple heavy infantry Lance Corporal," protested Alerio.

"That's another thing I wanted to talk about," Sanctus responded while pointing at the shed where the wooden swords were stored. "But first food. I'm starved."

***

The cookfire was cold and the innkeeper barely awake when Carnifex banged on the door.

"Not open yet," he protested. Outside the partially opened door, a broad-shouldered man stood in the rain and, behind him another whose features were lost in the sheets of rain. "We open at mid-morning."

"Just looking for a mug of wine and a dry place to talk," the Centurion advised the innkeeper.

"Sorry. We are closed," the man insisted.

Alerio stepped forward out of the rain and the proprietor recognized him.

"Captain Sisera. I didn't see you," he exclaimed. "You and your guest come in out of the rain. I'll light a fire but I've nothing hot to serve."

"Wine and yesterday's bread will be fine," Alerio assured the man as he and Sanctus crossed over the threshold. "But a fire's warmth would be appreciated."

As the innkeeper stacked kindling in the hearth, Alerio and Sanctus took seats at a nearby table.

"Captain Sisera?" inquired the Centurion.

"It's an honorary title from the Sons of Mars," Alerio replied. "I had to have a title when I trained their crews before the Legion arrived. They fought and, most of the crew members survived contact with the Hoplites. The innkeeper has four lads on Sons of Mars' ships. He feels that he owes me for their lives."

A fire blazed and the proprietor vanished into a back room. Warmth reached the two Legionaries and their tunics began to dry.

"You trained oarsmen to fight against Greek Hoplites?" questioned Sanctus in disbelief. "A herd against trained soldiers. It should have been a massacre."

"It almost was. I armed the biggest rowers with long poles and they kept the Greeks off our front rank," described Alerio. "At least until the Qart Hadasht garrison rowed off and the Legionaries got free. Once they arrived, the fight was definitely ours."

The innkeeper returned to the table with two mugs of wine, a loaf of bread, a wedge of cheese and a bowl of olives.

"It's poor fare for a Captain," suggested the innkeeper.

"It's fine for our needs," Alerio assured him.

"Then you trained the Legionaries preparing to defend against King Hiero," ventured the Centurion as the innkeeper walked away.

"That training was to keep the Syracusans from guessing our real numbers," explained Alerio. "The drills had to be convincing. I felt sorry for the Centuries before my time chanting for the death Goddess."

"And now?" inquired Sanctus as he cut a slice of cheese and ripped off a chunk of bread.

"Now? I wish I'd trained them harder," Alerio responded. "Too many joined me under the awning, suffering and waiting for Nenia."

"The Southern Legion detachment is staying in Messina when the Legions march south," Sanctus advised him. "I assume you plan to stay with your Centuries. But I have an offer for you."

"An offer, Centurion?" questioned Alerio as he popped two olives in his mouth.

"Stay with Caudex Legion, help me train the men and, serve as my Tesserarius," Sanctus suggested.

"But a Tesserarius is…" Alerio looked closely at the Legion weapons instructor.

"Yes Alerio, it's a Corporal's position," Sanctus said finishing Alerio's sentence.

The two drank and ate in silence as Alerio thought about the promotion. As a squad leader in the Southern Legion and an asset for the old spymaster, his future was assured. If he stayed with Caudex Legion, after the campaign, he'd be an unassigned Legionary NCO with no command, no responsibilities, and no pay. Nothing, until a Legion was raised for another crisis and then, he'd need to be recruited.

Alerio closed his eyes. A vision of critically wounded Legionaries spread out around him appeared. Their bodies cut to the bone and their faces caked with dirt and dried blood. A Goddess floated above the injured calling to them. Then, one by one their spirits broke free of the ruined flesh and, the Goddess turned her face towards Alerio. Her image began to fade and, as she became as transparent as smoke, she mouthed the words, Death Caller.

"Sisera. Sisera?" Sanctus' voice spoke his name from far away. "Are you alright?"

Opening his eyes, Alerio felt the table top on his cheek and saw the side of the olive bowl. Raising up, he blinked and found Sanctus and the innkeeper hovering over him.

"You closed your eyes for so long, I worried you'd fallen asleep sitting up," explained Sanctus. "Suddenly, you fell forward onto the table."

"I must have overdone it this morning," Alerio explained.

"You do seem a little pale," Sanctus observed. "We can continue this conversation when you're feeling better."

"Sweet Butcher," Alerio said using Centurion Carnifex's nickname. "You've just hired yourself a Tesserarius."

***

The sun rose in a clear sky and the morning's warmth dried the tents at the Legion campsites.

"In both battles, this Century lagged behind the line," explained Sanctus Carnifex. "If it hadn't been for the first maniple, they might have broken and run."

"Fear in the third maniple spreads faster than a rumor," offered Alerio. "Their inexperience can easily overcome their training."

They passed five squares of tents and stopped at a sixth.

"If that was the case, I'd simply drill them until they were too tired to stand. And continue with the Century running shield drills on their knees," responded Sanctus. Then, he faced the square of tents, lifted his chin and bellowed. "Caudex Legion, Requiem Division, Second Maniple, Sixth Century, on the road for inspection."

The announcement shocked Alerio. The second maniple was composed of experienced Legionaries. Those too old for the first and aggressive men who moved up from the third were there to make the Second combat line a steady presence during a battle. To have a Century in the Second falter meant something was very wrong.

"Sanctus. We aren't scheduled for training," a middle-aged Centurion exclaimed as he crossed between tents while strapping on his gladius. A big red-faced Sergeant and an old Corporal followed their officer.

"Optio. Turn out your Century," Carnifex ordered the Sergeant.

"Requiem Division, Second Maniple, Sixth Century, on the road," the Sergeant called out. As close to thunder as the human

182

voice can get, his shook the tents and even rattled a few cooking pots and utensils.

Sanctus glanced at Alerio with a quizzical look before turning to the line officer.

"Centurion, bring your Optio and Tesserarius and come with me," Carnifex instructed before announcing. "Weapons instructor, Corporal Sisera, the Century is yours."

"Yes, Centurion, the Century is mine," Alerio responded. As the Centurions and NCOs marched away, the new Corporal scanned the eighty Legionaries standing in ranks. "Sixth Century, standby."

The stomp was more of a scuff on the dirt and the standing-by-Corporal almost mumbled. Ignoring the disrespect, Alerio marched them from the camp, out the south gate, past the defensive mounds and the trench to an open section of ground.

"Century halt," he ordered. Holding out his arms, Alerio indicated four positions that formed a semicircle. "Two squads to my right, two and two in the center and two on my left. Let's be sure everyone can watch me embarrass myself."

This brought chuckles from the younger Legionaries and snickers from the older infantrymen. One group liked the idea of a friendly weapons instructor while the other held disdain for a weak instructor.

"This Century held up the assault line," Alerio said as he turned from the Century. A few paces away he removed his helmet, set it on the ground and leaned his shield against it. Still, with his back to the infantrymen, he unstrapped his armor. "We are here this fine morning so I can understand why."

Corporal Alerio turned back to face the Century.

"Oh, merda, it's Death Caller," a few men in the ranks swore.

"Who?" questioned a few others.

"The blessed of Nenia," those recognizing the Corporal replied. "Someone will die today."

Alerio heard but, dismissed the comments. It never hurt to have the attention of your students.

"Who is your strongest shield?" Alerio asked.

Heads turned to glance across the ranks until they settled on a man in the second rank. A stout man, he easily shoved aside the Legionaries in front of him and marched to the center of the half circle.

Alerio studied the wide shoulders and noted the man held the shield up and to the front. Most men carried their shields a little off to the side allowing it to hang and take some of the stress off their arm.

"You are going to attack me. Draw," Alerio ordered. Once the man's gladius was free. "Stand by. Advance."

It might have been the lack of armor. The weapons instructor wore only a red tunic, his armored skirt, and a gladius belt, or it might have been the surprise order to kill. In any case, the stout infantryman hesitated. When the shield finally moved, so did Corporal Sisera.

During the thrust out, Alerio jumped behind the shield and into the crook of the Legionary's arm. While driving with his legs, the weapons instructor reached out a hand and clamped onto the gladius arm. The stout Legionary attempted to dislodge the Corporal by backing up. Between his steps to the rear and the Corporal's driving legs, the best shield in the Sixth Century tripped and fell hard onto his back.

"Why did you pause?" Alerio questioned as he jumped up and away from any revenge strikes by the embarrassed man. "Was I not clear? Let me see, attack me, draw, standby, advance. Which of those did you miss?"

The Legionary climbed to his feet and glared at the weapons instructor. Alerio ignored the silent threat and peered at the faces in the semicircle.

"Is there anyone else in the Sixth who is deaf?" he inquired.

A yell alerted Sisera as the Legionary charged at him. Shield to the side and his blade extended, the infantryman closed with the intention of murdering the weapons instructor. Alerio rolled away from the blade, grabbed the shield and felt the strength of the best shield in the Century. As if he'd taken hold of a stone wall, the shield was solid on the man's arm. While a stone wall wasn't mobile, a man was. Alerio dug in his heels and swung the Legionary around.

Like the images of a hammer thrower in Greek frescoes depicting athletic games, the weapons instructor swung the Legionary by his own shield. Three times they spun before the infantryman stumbled, fell, and rolled over in the dirt.

Alerio kicked him onto his back and sat on the man's chest. He rested the palm of one hand on the edge of the helmet's face opening and placed his thumb on the man's eye. With the other hand, he pointed at the seventy-nine standing infantrymen.

"Should I take the eye for his disrespect?" Alerio asked. He felt a shudder go through the downed Legionary. Maimed in battle was one thing, but the threat of losing an eye purposely while training was horrifying. "Well, I'm waiting for an answer."

"No," a Legionary from the man's squad stated.

"What? Are you not Sixth Century, Second Maniple?" demanded Alerio. "Are you not a battle unit trained to move as one, instantly upon command?"

"Yes," a few replied.

"What? Yes! I should take his eye for stupidity," asked Alerio.

"No!" roared back the entire Century.

Alerio reached into the helmet and trapped the infantryman's nose between his knuckles.

"Am I going to have more trouble with you?" he inquired as he wiggled the man's nose.

"No. Weapons instructor," the man promised. "I've learned my lesson."

As they stood and separated, the Legionary walked back to his rank and Alerio announced to the Century.

"That Legionary is a powerful man and I would be honored to stand beside him in an assault line," he stated. Men in the Legionary's squad pounded the shield man's shoulders as a sign of agreement at the compliment. "One shield is not a defensive line. If he had shields next to him the Gods themselves couldn't move him or his squad. But hesitation and uneven shields will get you killed. Today we are..."

"Nice trick, taking an unprepared man off his feet," a voice from the right challenged. "I'd like to see you do that in a fair fight."

Half the Century groaned as if they were accustomed to the insolent tone and defiant words.

Alerio acted as if he hadn't heard the man. But he began unstrapping his gladius belt and armored skirt. After placing the gear beside his shield, he turned and held up his arms to show he was unarmed.

"Step forward, son of Algea," offered Alerio.

A stinted laugh ran through the Century at the prospect of the defiant Legionary being related to the Goddess of pain. Unfortunately, a little truth lies in every joke and the man who stepped forward was more fighter than jester. He began to take off his armor. As each piece came free and was dropped to the ground, knife scars were revealed.

Once the Legionary stood without his armor, he paused before pulling off his tunic. Then he flexed the lean, well-defined muscles of his chest and arms. Knife scars covered him from shoulder to shoulder, down his arms and across his chest. He flexed again making the scars seem to dance on his skin.

"What's your weapon of choice, daughter of Deimos?" inquired Alerio.

186

This time none of the Legionaries could stifle their laughter. It was one thing to call a man a Goddess' son while mocking him. But to call him a woman and the daughter of terror was too much to resist.

"I choose my sica," the Legionary said while reaching behind his back. Hidden in his cloth mentula supporter must have been a sheath. He pulled a knife and the almost foot long, curved blade reflected the sunlight along its razor-sharp edge. "What's your weapon, Death Caller?"

"I'm a Legionary. A proud heavy infantryman and my weapons are on the ground behind me," Alerio commented while indicating his stacked equipment. The words touched the Century and they identified with the Corporal. A few of them started to step forward to defend the weapons instructor, but Alerio ordered. "Stay in your ranks."

"Then how can we have a fair fight," the knife wieldier asked.

"I guess, Honey Cakes, it'll be these against your pretty dinner knife," Alerio replied as he pulled off his tunic and held up his bare hands. "But first, let's compare our trophies."

"Vindictam," the Legionary corrected him.

"My apologies, Honey Cakes Vindictam," Alerio said with a grin.

While the knife fighter's skin displayed slashes from knife blades, the weapons instructor had a different category of scars. Puckered wounds from arrows, gladius scars, long cuts from close in fighting and a crescent-shaped scar on top of his head. Then, the Corporal turned around showing the still pink lines from the whip where they formed an X on his back. Also, a scar ran down the back of his left arm.

"Honey Cakes, do you know the difference between war and street fighting?" Alerio asked as he walked towards the knife man.

"It doesn't matter, weapons instructor. People fight and someone dies," sneered Vindictam as he moved one foot to the rear and dropped into a stance.

"But there is Honey Cakes," Alerio assured him as he strolled to within range of the sica.

The blades slashed out at Alerio's midsection. Rather than jumping back, the weapons instructor sucked in his stomach allowing the curved tip to flash by. Then, Alerio shuffled forward.

A wicked smile graced Vindictam's face as he brought the blade back across…But Alerio's wrist touched the knife hand. The pressure from the wrist drove the blade up and it circled, passing harmlessly between the combatants. Vindictam drew back his left arm and shot a fist at the weapons instructor's chin. It never reached the intended target. Alerio's other wrist snapped up and guided the punch off to the side.

"Ah, Honey Cakes. Is something wrong?" Alerio teased as Vindictam drew both arms down to his sides. The Corporal's palm remained against the knife hand.

"Shut up with the Honey Cakes. My name is Vindictam," the knifeman screamed. "You will respect me or I will cut you."

"Hasn't worked so far," Alerio commented.

Vindictam's knife shot out in a straight line towards the weapons instructor's chest. Again, the wrist shoved it off to the side. Honey Cakes rotated the sica out, down and up from below trying to bury it in Corporal Sisera's solar plexus. But the wrist became the flat of a hand that shoved the knife's hilt towards Vindictam's chest while carrying it to the top of a circle. At the highest point, Alerio locked the knife arm in a painful hold. The elbow bent awkwardly placing the knife blade over Vindictam's shoulder.

Honey Cakes kicked out, trying to get Alerio off him. A swivel of the hips let the foot pass by and, instead of removing the weapons instructor, it created an opening for Alerio.

Stepping in close, he twisted the bent knife arm further back over the shoulder. Human limbs don't flex like that and Vindictam rotated in the direction trying to relieve the pressure. Taking advantage of the positioning, Alerio jerked his head back and smashed Vindictam's nose with his forehead.

As Vindictam crumpled, gushing blood from his nostrils, Alerio, still controlling the knife arm, stepped over his shoulder and wrenched the arm hard. The sica fell into the dirt.

"Honey Cakes. You seem to have lost your weapon of choice," Alerio said. He kicked the knife away and threw Vindictam to the ground.

"Alright, I've learned my lesson," Vindictam stated as he struggled to his feet while pinching his nose.

"No, Honey Cakes. This is a lesson you personally requested," Alerio informed him. Walking to Vindictam's gear, he pulled the gladius and inspected it. "Private Honey Cakes, your Legion gladius is pitted and dirty. Let me see. There is no blood on it. Not a drop of Syracusan or Qart Hadasht blood. Why is it that in two days of fighting, you didn't cut our enemies, not once?"

Alerio picked up Vindictam's shield and, tossed it and the gladius to the Private.

"What's this?" questioned Vindictam.

"You asked about my choice of weapons," Alerio replied as he strolled to his equipment. "I explained to you that I am an infantryman. These are my choice of weapons. Pick up yours."

As Alerio walked back to Vindictam, he fitted the shield to his arm and twirled the gladius.

"Private Honey Cakes. I asked if you knew the difference between street and war fighting," Alerio reminded him. When Vindictam didn't say anything, he continued. "A street fighter can run because he is on his own. A Legionary is a professional warrior. He can't run or his squad mates die."

The Century watched as the weapons instructor walked around Vindictam. All the while the gladius twirled faster and faster. When he returned to his original spot, a change came over Corporal Sisera. Where he had been relaxed and off-handed, now the veins in the Corporal's neck throbbed and his eyes blazed with intensity.

"Who is the squad leader for this sorry excuse of a Legionary?" demanded Alerio. A slender Lance Corporal stepped from the ranks. "And his Right and Left Pivots. All three of you stand with him."

The three Legionaries lined up and Vindictam, suddenly getting courage from the support, reached down and picked up his gladius and shield.

"I am going to bleed Private Vindictam," Alerio announced. The gladius stopped twirling and steadied with the blade pointing directly at the Private's face. "Who are the last three men to be cut by him?"

After some jostling and talk, three men were shoved out of ranks.

"You three stand off to the side. At some point, I'll ask you if he has bled enough," Alerio instructed. Then he looked at the Pivots, squad leader, and Vindictam. "I am Death Caller. The Goddess speaks to me. And she wants death!"

Alerio ran screaming at the four Legionaries. Just before reaching the line of heavy infantry shields, Private Vindictam backed out of line and ran. After a few paces, he realized the weapons instructor wasn't chasing him.

"Pivots. Bring Private Honey Cakes back here," instructed Alerio. "Squad leader, get the rest of your squad."

Nine Legionaries stood facing Private Vindictam. His three victims were off to the side watching Corporal Sisera.

"A coward who hides his true self behind a knife is useless to the Legion," Alerio declared. "While the people he cut observe, the ones who would die because of him must drive him out or break and remake him. Decide."

The nine Legionaries of Vindictam's squad huddled together. A short while later, the squad leader stepped away from the group.

"Weapons instructor. Private Vindictam is one of us," announced the Lance Corporal. "We believe we can salvage and motivate him."

"Then it's up to the squad to show him the way," Alerio offered. "If I walk over there, my anger will get the better of me and he will die."

The nine infantrymen rushed Vindictam knocking him to the ground and beating him with fists and feet. Alerio watched until the coward couldn't defend himself against the blows and kicks. Looking over at the men Vindictam had cut, he waited. When all three nodded, Alerio called a halt to the punishment.

"Enough. Pick up your gear and Private Honey Cakes. Get back into ranks," Alerio instructed. "We will be running shield and gladius maneuvers. No one falls back, especially Private Vindictam. You wanted him, so keep him up and moving with the squad."

At midday, Centurion Carnifex, the line officer, and the Corporal marched across the field towards the Century. Far behind, the Sergeant limped painfully after them.

"Weapons instructor Sisera. Give me a report on the fitness of Sixth Century, Second Maniple," ordered Carnifex. The Centurion looked over the dusty, sweaty and obviously exhausted squads. For a heartbeat, he paused when he noticed one Private wobbling in place and being held up by two Legionaries.

"Legion weapons instructor Carnifex. Sixth Century, Second Maniple is trained and responsive," Alerio announced. "Sir, they are Legionaries ready to take their place in the assault line."

The Sergeant finally arrived and Alerio could see bruises on his legs and swelling on his face. He also noticed a number of smiles on the faces of the infantrymen.

"Centurion. The Century is your," Carnifex informed the line officer. Then before turning away. "Corporal Sisera, on me."

"Yes sir," Alerio responded.

Once out of earshot of the Century, Carnifex looked at Alerio.

"Want to explain the meat bag?" he inquired.

"Private Honey Cakes is a renowned knife fighter, sir," Alerio answered.

"He must be the one the Optio was bragging about," Carnifex suggested. "I'll check in on them occasionally to be sure the lessons hold."

***

While the Legionaries trained, metal workers fired up their forge and smelting fires. The spoils, salvaged from the six thousand dead soldiers, was distributed and the iron, steel, copper, silver, and gold were reworked or melted into bars. Armor, good swords, and helmets were sorted. Merchants from Messina and traders from the Sons of Mars began paying coins for items they could resell at different ports.

The Greek accountants kept track of the exchanges, meticulously counting and logging every transaction. One thing confused them, the Sons of Mars trade representatives outbid the professional merchants for the best weapons and bars of silver and copper.

Late in the afternoon three days later, a messenger arrived at the Citadel with a parchment for Senior Tribune Gaius Claudius. After reading the message, he ordered the formation of a unit consisting of four Legionary guards, one Greek accountant, and a two-wheeled cart with a porter. The Tribune marched his small formation from the Citadel, down the hill and headed towards Messina harbor.

"Tribune Claudius. It's a beautiful afternoon," Captain Ferox Creon greeted Gaius. "I've so been looking forward to this. It's much better than a funeral."

"I can't argue about the funeral but the rest is debatable," Gaius responded as the cart was positioned on the dock beside a tee shaped structure. "Take off your sandals, your weapons belt, and the helmet."

"But this is my normal uniform," pleaded the Sons of Mars captain.

"If you wore that heavy iron helmet and fell overboard, you'd be greeting Neptune before you could get it off, Pirate," Gaius complained. "I said a quarter of your weight, not the weight of anything you could hang off your body."

"I happen to agree, Tribune. I am sick of cheese so let's get this over with," Creon urged while rubbing his belly.

"Greek. Check the scales," Gaius instructed the accountant.

A beam anchored securely to the dock supported a cross beam. From the cross beam, ropes hung down holding reinforced barrel tops on both sides. The Greek reached up and studied a stick protruding from the joint of the beams. After shifting the stick so it reflected one-quarter of the angle, he pulled on one side and then the other.

"Senior Tribune Claudius. The scales appear to be balanced and free," the Greek announced.

"Captain Ferox Creon, please have a seat," Gaius instructed. Once the Pirate was seated on one side of the scales, he looked at the Greek. "Begin."

Pouches of coins and a gold bar were placed on the opposite side of the scale. When another pouch was added, Ferox's side lifted from the dock. Another pouch dropped on the pile caused him to rise higher. Then the Greek reached into a pouch and dropped individual coins on the scale.

Around them, Sons of Mars crewmen cheered as each coin hit the scale and Ferox's barrel top crept higher.

"Captain Frigian. Check to be sure the Legionary officer isn't cheating us," Creon ordered Milon while winking at Gaius.

"I'd say it needs to move at least five more coins worth," Frigian announced after peering at the stick. "Gold coins would be best."

"You'll get copper," Gaius stated nodding at the Greek to add the weight. "Even though I believe you're cheating me."

"Tribune Claudius. Would the Sons of Mars cheat a valuable partner?" Creon asked as the additional coins dropped onto the scale.

"Of that, I have no doubt," Gaius replied. Turning away from the scales, he indicated the alleyway leading off the dock and back into Messina. As the Greek, the porter with the cart and the guards marched off, Gaius glanced at the Pirate. "That concludes our business, Captain Creon."

"If you need the Sons to save the Legion again, you know where to find us," Creon replied. Laughing, the Pirate stood slowly letting the other side of the scales settle on the dock. Then holding out his arms, he addressed the crews gathered to watch the payment. "Tomorrow, I'm taking a turn at the oars. And if I ask for cheese, make me swim behind the boat."

Chapter 19 – A Split in the Road

At sunrise the next morning, advance units of cavalry rode out to patrol the Legion's route. Nicephrus Division led off the march. General Caudex and his staff settled in the middle of the heavy infantry. At the rear, their supply wagons and mules plodded along with the rear security Centuries.

"Colonel Nicephrus. At this pace, it'll take us weeks to reach Syracuse," complained Caudex. "Can't we pick it up?"

"General, the infantry can cover the distance to Catania comfortably in under three days," the Colonel replied. "But we'll out march our supplies. It's better to arrive and be able to sustain the Centuries rather than have the infantry foraging or stealing food from a city."

"When you put it like that, I can see the advantage of not making an enemy of a city to our rear," Caudex agreed.

Requiem Division stepped off next and despite the steady march, it was late midmorning before the wagons and mules moved and the rear-guard Centuries left Messina.

As men do when trudging along on a long march, they sang.

> *Be aware the Legion is over the rise*
> *Give us your grain and your pledge*
> *Give us leeway on the roads ahead*
> *Give us your blade and we'll oblige*
> *With a sharp gladius in your side*
> *Through Sicilia, we stomp and march*
> *Prepare for us a triumphant arch*
> *Stifle your hews and pitiful cries*
> *The Legion is coming over the rise*
>
> *We faced King Hiero and his hoplites*
> *After tasting the strength of our infantry*
> *In moonlit, they crept into the trees*
> *Then we turned on the Empire's might*
> *We flexed but our center held tight*
> *Flung his mercenaries across the region*
> *The Empire learned to fear our Legion*
> *Our arms and hearts know the fight*
> *It's our enemy who panics at our sight*
>
> *Be aware the Legion is over the rise*
> *Give us your grain and your pledge*
> *Give us leeway on the roads ahead*
> *Give us your blade and we'll oblige*
> *With a sharp gladius in your side*

Through Sicilia, we stomp and march
Prepare for us a triumphant arch
Stifle your hews and pitiful cries
The Legion is coming over the rise

Naxos on the shore gone in decay
Ancient ruins with spirits and ghosts
only come out at night, they boast
Holy men, crazies, and priest swear
But we kept an eye out if they dare
We've iron javelins to pierce their souls
In case the spirits come out to stroll
Even the shades know Legion's blades
Stay in their graves during our days

Five days of marching brought the advance units into view of a city on the Strait of Messina. The ancient trading center of Catania smartly sent emissaries to speak with General Caudex. A tent was erected with one side left open facing the road. If the representatives from Catania had any idea of resisting or not offering a fair price on supplies, the long lines of infantrymen marching passed quickly quelled the thought.

Waters of the Strait on our hip
Peaks of Mount Etna on the right
And we watch for Vulcan's light
Down through Sicilia between
Hoping his bellows stay clean
Cool is the forge on Montebello
God resting like a hearty fellow
If it flares we dive over the cliff
Armor too heavy for a deep dip

Be aware the Legion is over the rise
Give us your grain and your pledge

Give us leeway on the roads ahead
Give us your blade and we'll oblige
With a sharp gladius in your side
Through Sicilia, we stomp and march
Prepare for us a triumphant arch
Stifle your hews and pitiful cries
The Legion is coming over the rise

We'll bring Syracuse to her knees
Teach King Hiero the Republic way
We'll reduce his walls to wet clay
Red from his soldiers if he resists
Paint courtesy of the Legion's best
Behind your walls, you cannot hide
Stone by stone a hole we'll pry
We'll come in any way we please
Keep your pleas and your keys

The two Legions reached the split in the road south of Catania and created separate camps. Wagons from both emptied their loads and returned to the city for the purchased supplies.

Headquarters First Century set their ring around the General's tent while Nicephrus Division Legionaries dug a broad trench around their camp. Sentries walked the perimeter and, as they reached the area adjacent to the Requiem camp, they waved across the distance at the other sentries.

***

"Corporal Sisera. Senior Tribune Claudius wants you at the command tent, immediately," a runner informed Alerio.

He stopped pounding in the stake for Centurion Carnifex's tent to reply to the runner, "Inform Tribune Claudius, I'll be there as soon as I get cleaned and dressed."

"No, Corporal. You're wanted at the General's tent," the runner stated while pointing at the other Legion camp. "Colonel Requiem and Senior Tribune Claudius are already there."

Alerio handed the mallet off to a Private, picked up a bucket of water and poured it over his head. With his tunic damp and dirty from the day's march, he pulled on his armor, stuck the helmet under his arm and jogged towards the trench.

***

Access to the General's staff tent was, by necessity, restricted. As he approached the First Century's sentries, Alerio prepared himself for the harassment everyone below Centurion received.

"Corporal Sisera. I've been ordered to report to Senior Tribune Gaius Claudius," Alerio reported to the hard-looking sentry.

"You are cleared to pass, Death Caller," the Legionary informed him.

Confused by the easy passage, Alerio pondered whether it was the nickname or his promotion and position as a weapons instructor. When he pushed into the tent, he discovered it was neither.

"Corporal Sisera. Stand behind Senior Tribune Claudius," Senior Centurion Valerian ordered.

Alerio eased through the tent navigating between Tribunes and Centurions until he reached the Senior Tribune. Claudius glanced back, nodded at him then returned his attention to the map table.

"Corporal Alerio Sisera is here because Gaius requested him as his personal bodyguard," announced Senior Centurion Valerian. "For those of you who don't know the Corporal, have a good look at him. For the rest of this mission, where Tribune Claudius goes you'll find the Corporal."

Because of the Legion training, most of the staff and line officers knew Alerio on sight. A few didn't and their eyes quickly passed over him. Two additional line officers entered and the Senior Centurion acknowledged them before turning to where Colonel Nicephrus and Colonel Requiem stood talking with General Caudex.

"Colonel Requiem. Everyone is here," Valerian informed the battle commander.

Pericles Requiem whispered a few words to the General before facing the room.

"Gentlemen, from this split in the road, we head south to Syracuse," Requiem explained. "The other split heads southwest towards the mountains and a city named Echetla. From our reports, we know Echetla is a thriving community with large garrisons and field units to suppress bandits. This is a concern. When we engage King Hiero's forces at the walls of Syracuse, the General doesn't want Echetla troops coming up on our rear or cutting our supply lines."

"Sir. A garrison and a few marshals who chase bandits?" inquired a cavalry officer. "Why bother?"

"Because Centurion, Echetla's soldiers garrison the mountain pass from the west. They are there to stop a Qart Hadasht invasion," the Colonel informed him. "That means they have enough experienced soldiers to rotate from the mountains to the city. Half of their forces will be in Echetla at any given time to defend against an attack from Syracuse. It's a strong enemy and a valuable potential ally. For those reasons, Senior Tribune Claudius will take a detachment and negotiate with the leadership at Echetla."

A murmur ran through the tent before the Colonel held up a hand to quiet them down.

"Claudius Detachment needs to move fast," Requiem instructed. "It's about the same distance from here to Syracuse as it is to Echetla. But to the west, the hills begin while to the south, the road is flat. We need Senior Tribune Claudius sitting and talking with them before any messengers from Hiero reach Echetla."

"I'd recommend a cavalry detachment," the Centurion of horse suggested.

"We discussed that but decided we wanted a small show of force," offered Requiem. "Six Centuries of heavy infantry, one of Velites and twenty horse. It's a military presence but not enough to be perceived as a threat to Echetla. We prefer talking to fighting. Now, for supplies…"

Alerio tuned out the logistics as he pondered how under six hundred Legionaries could be a show of force to the defenders of a major city. And why would the Senior Tribune require a personal bodyguard? Then a lad's voice spoke up and Alerio refocused on the discussion.

"I would like to accompany Senior Tribune Claudius," volunteered Junior Tribune Castor Ireneus. While staring at the filthy garment under Alerio's armor, he added. "Gaius will need a second set of educated ears to negotiate with Echetla's governing council. My studies of oration and elocution make me the best choice."

"This is an important mission, young Castor," Requiem responded. "I don't…"

"Just a moment, Colonel," interrupted General Caudex. "I understand the hesitation. The mission is important to us as well as dangerous. However, Tribune Ireneus will be in no more peril in Echetla than with the Legions assaulting the walls of Syracuse. I dare say, he will be safer with Senior Tribune Claudius. And no doubt, an asset during the deliberations."

Colonel Requiem's face reddened and, for a moment, he almost objected. But politics triumphed over caution and he nodded his head in agreement.

"As always General, your counsel, and your logic are flawless," Requiem exclaimed. "Junior Tribune Castor Ireneus, you are assigned to Claudius Detachment."

"It's the wisest choice," Castor Ireneus assured the Colonel while smirking at the Tribunes and Centurions in the tent as if he'd won some kind of debate against his tutor.

Chapter 20 – Mules and Grain

Before dawn, five mounted Legionaries trotted away from Requiem Division. Shortly after, a half Century of Velites trotted out of the camp following the cavalry.

"Here, take the reins for my pack horse," instructed Castor.

Alerio shifted in the light armor. His horse shied away from the young Tribune as the animal picked up his rider's agitation at the request.

"I can't do that, sir," Alerio replied.

"I gave you an order, Corporal Sisera. Take the lead," Castor insisted. "Or would you rather have another session on the punishment post?"

For a heartbeat, Alerio wondered if he could knock Castor off his horse and hide the body before the detachment rode out. He was saved from the evil thought when Senior Tribune Claudius and Colonel Requiem emerged from the Colonel's tent.

"The Legions will take about six days to reach Syracuse," Requiem explained. "You have to be in Echetla and making an agreement before King Hiero has time to send them an offer."

"I understand, sir. If it's at all possible, I'll keep Echetla out of the fight," Gaius assured the Colonel as he climbed on his horse. A servant standing on the ground handed the Tribune the reins for a pack horse. Then, to the moonlit shadows of infantrymen, Claudius ordered. "Centurions. Take them out."

"Centuries, standby," shouted the most experienced Centurion. He was from the Seventh Century, First Maniple,

Requiem Division and would act as the detachment's Senior Centurion.

Four hundred and ninety-two Legionaries and their NCOs stomped their right foot and replied, "Standing by, Centurion."

"Detachment, forward march," ordered the Senior Centurion before he fell in step with his Century.

At the front, the Fourth and Third Centuries of the Third Maniple marched over the short bridge spanning the defensive trench. Next over was the Eight Century of the First Maniple.

"Shall we join the march?" Gaius suggested as he kneed his horse away from the Colonels' tent. He and Alerio rode easily to a position behind the Eighth. Castor Ireneus lagged when he jerked the pack horse too hard and the animal backed away almost pulling the young Tribune from his horse. "Tribune Ireneus. Keep up."

Behind Gaius' almost nonexistent command staff, eight mules, a wagon with a team of four horses, and five cavalry mounts pressed into pack duty followed. Behind the baggage, the Seventh of the First Maniple crossed the bridge.

The other half of the skirmisher Century spread out and took up flank security. Behind them, the Seventh of the First marched across the bridge followed by the remaining fifteen cavalrymen. Last over the rough bridge was the Fifth and Sixth Centuries of the Second Maniple.

Once the predawn disturbance of the detachment's departure ended, the bridge planks were pulled back and Requiem Division settled down. The off-duty Legionaries went back to sleep and those on guard duty continued walking their posts.

***

On the road to Echetla, the detachment began to spread out. It wasn't the darkness or the ability of the Legionaries to maintain the stride. The issue was caused by the mules. Heavily loaded, the stubborn but sturdy pack animals set their own pace. As the sun rose, a separation became apparent. Almost as if two separate units, the detachment became divided at the center.

"Mules and grain," Alerio mumbled looking back.

"What's that?" inquired Gaius.

"Mules and grain rule the march, sir," Alerio explained. "When I was a lad on my father's farm, every year a Centurion and Sergeant came to work the harvest. They taught me weapons and military tactics. And a few sayings I didn't appreciate until we left Messina."

"That Corporal Sisera, is rubbish," announced Tribune Ireneus. "It's the command staff who rules the march."

"If you say so, sir," Alerio responded.

When the morning sun was high in the sky, three mules stopped in their tracks. Despite savage tugs from their handlers, the animals refused to budge. Soon, all the mules stopped, refusing to move.

Tribune Claudius looked back at the sounds of men cursing. He took a long look at the pack animals and mumbled under his breath.

"Mules and grain," the Tribune said, then loudly. "Centurions. Rest your Centuries and post guards."

Gaius' orders were passed up and down the line of march. Soon both men and mules were munching on grain. The pack animals on the raw stalks and seeds and, the Legionaries on biscuits made from water, salt, and stoneground grain.

***

Three days later as the sun dropped low in the sky, the road topped a hill and the walls of Echetla came into view. Gaius and Castor rode to the front of the detachment and sat on their horses gazing at the city's defenses. A granite stone ribbon appeared from between trees, wrapped around the sides and face of a steep grade before vanishing into the forest on the other side. The tops of buildings were visible over the wall.

"That would be an ugly assault," Senior Tribune Claudius observed. "I'm glad we're here to talk."

"We can push on and get to the city by nightfall," announced Castor.

"Corporal Sisera, your thoughts?" inquired Gaius looking over his shoulder to where Alerio had been since they left the Legions.

"Sir, a tall pedestal requires a stout base, just as a Legion needs a strong base of operations," Alerio replied. "If you are to put on a show of force, shouldn't it be from the ranks to the rear, sir?"

"You're suggesting we build a fortified camp within sight of the city walls," scowled Castor. "Your uncouth idea will only cause suspicion and create mistrust in Echetla's leadership."

"I believe the Centuries would be more impressive if they were rested and cleaned up," commented Gaius. "Especially if the citizens of the city could see our formation. We will not approach tonight but in the daylight. Centurion, mark us a camp further into the flat."

The cavalry officer gave a cross chest salute and kneed his horse away from the formation. Six horsemen followed him until he sent one off towards a line of trees. Then he indicated an area and the five remaining cavalrymen dismounted. They stood back to back before pacing outward.

"Where is the lone rider going?" inquired Castor.

"To locate a water source, among other things," Gaius informed the young nobleman.

"But we carry water," insisted Castor. Then he nudged his horse forward as if to ride off. "The cavalrymen are marking off too large an area. We should stop them and have them start over."

"That's the extent of our defensive trench," Gaius explained. "With enough room for a picket wall of spears around our tents."

"But, I thought we decided not to build a fortified camp," insisted Castor. "So, we don't offend our hosts."

"Junior Tribune Ireneus. Let me remind you that I make the decisions concerning this mission and this detachment," Gaius informed the young man. "I elicit advice but, in the end, it is my choice. Why? Because the success of the mission and the lives of the men, including your life, are my responsibilities. Do you understand?"

"Yes, Senior Tribune Claudius," Castor admitted but he glared at Gaius as if he wanted to add another thought or maybe argue.

Unfortunately, Gaius either didn't see him or he chose to ignore the insolent stare. Alerio noticed it but, no Corporal alive ever got between quarreling staff officers and kept his career intact.

By nightfall, the trench was completed, the animals hobbled and the tents set up in neat Legion squares. Then, every Legionary not at a cooking fire or on guard duty or off on a water run walked to the perimeter and picked up three or more long poles. With knives or their gladius, they hacked points in one end of all the sticks.

"Set pickets," instructed a Centurion on one side of the camp.

The Legionaries on that section of the trench lined up the sticks and pounded the point into the embankment of earth. As the poles were set, the line officer moved to direct the placement on the adjoining section. Once the Centurion finished circling the camp, it was ringed by solid, evenly spaced but blunt poles.

"Sharpen them," the Centurion directed. All the Legionaries leaned out and began hacking at the tips. Soon the camp bristled with a picket line of sharp points.

Claudius Detachment settled in to eat and rest. Tomorrow, the small number of Centuries would attempt to show the might of the Republic to the leadership of Echetla.

Act 6

Chapter 21 - The Walls of Echetla

Alerio rose before daylight and scrubbed Senior Tribune Claudius' helmet and armor. After the outerwear was cleaned, he drew the gladius and Legion dagger and polished both. He had ground them last night and the blades were already sharp.

"Sisera. Hand me my armor and pass the word to the Centurions," Gaius Claudius called through the tent flap. "Officers' meeting at daybreak."

"Yes sir," Alerio replied as he stood and put the blades in their sheaths. After handing the equipment into the tent, he walked backward, passing five tents, until he reached one for a line officer. "Centurion. Senior Tribune Claudius wants an officers' meeting at daybreak."

"I'll pass the word, Sisera," a voice from the tent responded.

Having delivered the message, Alerio walked back to the Senior Tribune's tent. He'd never taken his eyes off the structure.

"Out wandering around, are you?" accused Castor Ireneus as he and Alerio converged at the campfire outside the Senior Tribune's quarters. "Probably off gambling and gossiping with other lowlifes. I warned Gaius you couldn't be trusted. Maris Eutropius, before he died, said you were a slacker and not fit to be a Legionary."

"Sir, I can't help what people think or say about me," replied Alerio as he circled the Senior Tribune's tent.

Castor Ireneus followed him, bending over and peering at the tent sides as if checking and questioning the thoroughness of the Corporal's inspection. They completed the circuit and returned to the campfire.

"Castor. Is that you?" Claudius inquired from inside.

"Yes, Senior Tribune," Ireneus responded.

"Get in here and help me get dressed," ordered Gaius.

The Junior Tribune gave Alerio a triumphant look, marched to the tent's entrance and vanished inside. Puzzled, Corporal Sisera began another circuit, wondering why Gaius Claudius would need help getting dressed. It never occurred to Alerio that it was the same reason for his assignment as a bodyguard.

***

As Claudius wanted, the heavy infantry marched from their reinforced camp in full daylight. They proceeded in two columns until the detachment reached just over a bowshot from the gates of Echetla.

"Parade formation," the Senior Tribune commanded.

"Lead Centuries, by maniple," Centurions ordered. "Column left, March."

In sync, the first Legionaries at the head of each maniple made sharp left turns. Behind them, the rest of the men in those Centuries marched to the turning point and made a left face. From two long columns, the six Centuries of heavy infantrymen formed three broadly spaced lines. Their Centurions and NCOs marched to positions behind each rank.

The field was broad and four hundred and eighty Legionaries occupied only a small portion. But, their approach hadn't gone unnoticed. Heads appeared over the wall and people watched the Legion detachment's precise maneuvers.

"Rest them," instructed the Centurions. The Legionaries lowered their heavy shields allowing the bottom edge to rest on the ground as well as the ends of their javelins.

"Senior Tribune. The detachment is ready for inspection," the Senior Centurion announced.

Gaius Claudius in his dress armor rode stately to the last rank looking carefully down the lines of Legionaries. Once at the back, he rode between the ranks. After completing a ride-by of the last rank, he trotted to the next and inspected the second maniple. At the front, he rode down the line before trotting back to the front center of the formation. Junior Tribune Castor Ireneus reined in beside Gaius while Corporal Alerio Sisera stopped his horse just behind Claudius. The three sat on their mounts silently watching the gates of Echetla.

Far behind the heavy infantry formation, the Velites spread out around the Legion camp. The skirmishers stood at their posts so they were visible from the walls of Echetla. Outside the Legion camp, eight cavalrymen sat in pairs on either side of the approach to the camp while the other twelve rode out patrolling the surrounding area.

Gaius Claudius had his show of force from ranks to rear. Now it was up to Echetla's leadership to send someone out to inquire why the Republic was at their gates.

***

Standing in formation was boring but the Optios and Tesserarii cautioned the infantrymen about fidgeting, slouching or breaking ranks. They were under the eyes of Echetla soldiers, and being judged, they warned. At any moment, hordes of Greeks could swarm through the gates and the Legionaries would be fighting for their lives. Their only chance of survival was the solid shields of their maniple.

Junior Tribune Ireneus heard the admonishments, glanced around at his exposed position and his stomach knotted. In his head, the gates slammed open and a wave of blades came right at the young nobleman's face. Then, the gates did open. Realizing his worst fears had come true, Castor jerked his horse around and, as he kneed the mount away from the enemy, he screamed, "Attack. It's an attack."

He reached the first maniple and the laughter of the veterans brought him out of his nightmare. Dragging the horse to a stop, he looked over his shoulder to see two armored Hoplites finish shoving open the gates. Three lines of armed Greeks marched through the opening. Not far from the gates, they turned to the right and formed three lines. When they were parallel with the detachment's formation, the Hoplites did a left face.

Castor rode back to rejoin the Senior Tribune. Each line he passed brought another chorus of laughter. Shamed and humiliated, Junior Tribune Ireneus fell in beside the Senior Tribune.

"How do they look?" asked Gaius.

"Look? I don't. Do you mean the Greeks?" stammered Castor.

"I assumed you went back to check on the readiness of our Legionaries," Gaius suggested. "How do they look?"

"Online and steady, Senior Tribune," Ireneus reported. But, a quiver in his voice revealed his terror at the situation. Sneaking a glance over his shoulder, Castor noted that Corporal Sisera had eased his horse closer to Gaius's mount. The tight set of his shoulders and the shifting of the bodyguard's eyes showed that he, as well, was afraid. Boasting to cover for his true feelings, Ireneus announced. "Stand easy. We have this under control. Remember, we're here to talk."

The Echetla soldiers in their Greek armor marched forward closing the distance between the opposing forces. Then they stopped, dropped the butt end of their spears on the ground, and stood perfectly still.

"Corporal Sisera. What do you make of their formation?" Gaius inquired without looking back.

"Sir, they have matched your formation exactly," observed Alerio. "Although their NCOs don't seem to know what to do with themselves. Is it possible they don't use Sergeants or Corporals?"

Gaius didn't respond to Alerio's question. Instead, he spoke to Castor.

"Tribune Ireneus. What do you make of their formation?" he asked, again, without looking away from the enemy.

"Anybody can see they've matched our formation," blurted out Castor.

"They have," agreed Gaius. "Not only the formation but, the number of infantrymen, line officers, and NCOs. Except for one position."

"They have no battle commander," ventured Alerio. "Sir, you have no opposing number."

"Which tells me, when he arrives, we'll begin negotiations," explained Gaius.

A silence fell over the field. It was broken when one of the two men at the front of the Echetla formation shouted a command. Their soldiers hoisted their spears and held their shields higher.

"Get them up," Claudius commanded.

The orders were passed back through the ranks and the shields and javelins lifted from the ground.

A large man on a stallion galloped through the gates. Slowing to a trot, he, like Gaius did earlier, rode between the ranks inspecting his men.

"He is mocking us," accused Castor.

"Or he is showing his presence to his soldiers," suggested Claudius. "Keep quiet, let me do the talking. Do you understand Junior Tribune Ireneus?"

"If I remain silent, how can I advise you?" demanded Castor.

"Listen now. Advise me later," urged Gaius.

The Echetla officer finished his inspection and rode to where two men waited at the head of his formation. Together, the three came forward.

"Do you lay siege to my city with so few?" the officer asked as he pulled up two spear-lengths from Gaius.

"I am Senior Tribune Gaius Claudius, representative of Consul, General Appease Clodus Caudex of the Republic," Gaius stated. "I carry an offer of trade and friendship between the citizens of my Republic and the City State of Echetla."

"I am Sub Commander Ezio," the officer said. "I was hoping for a fight. How disappointing you mentioned trade and friendship. You'll need to speak with Magistrate Basil and the other members of the council about those things. Follow me, Senior Tribune Gaius Claudius. And bring your Lieutenants."

"He's not an officer," Castor protested while pointing at Alerio.

Ezio had started to turn his horse but stopped.

"You mean Alerio isn't a Lieutenant," Gaius spoke quickly to shut the young nobleman up. "Of course, Captain Sisera will join us. Sub Commander, please lead the way."

The six riders reached the gates and Gaius glanced back at the steep slope, the broad plain and his small detachment of infantrymen. As he suspected, a fight up to the walls would be difficult for an entire Legion and impossible for his small number of Legionaries.

Gaius raised an arm and signaled for the Centuries to go back to their camp. Ezio, seeing the motion, addressed one of the men riding beside him.

"Once the Legionaries are safely tucked in their pen," he explained. "Pull our troops back."

"Yes sir," the Lieutenant replied as he reined his horse around and trotted back to the field.

Then they rode through the gates and into the city of Echetla.

Chapter 22 – Words of Deceit

Alerio peered at the one and two-story buildings. Echetla was a maze. Haphazardly built, it lacked the uniformed and ordered streets of the Capital. Also, the city had more wood construction than stone or brick and fewer finished roads. Yet the streets, both narrow and wide, bustled with citizens and tradesmen rushing about their business. One feature stood out. There seemed to be a lot of soldiers. Then he recognized the same group of soldiers a couple of blocks from when he first sighted them. He appreciated the ruse and would mention it to Tribune Claudius when he had the chance.

The group of riders took side streets, doubled back and crossed the city several times. More tricks, Alerio thought. A building with a high, steeped roof deep in the city seemed to be getting closer no matter where they traveled. Eventually, Sub Commander Ezio guided them to the main road with stone pavers and they headed for the tall building.

As they approached, Alerio noted the distance separating the commercial buildings across wide streets from the large building. And while the façade of the structure was open and accessible, high walls started at the sides and wrapped around, enclosing a large rear area. Although he couldn't see, Alerio was sure there would be barracks, storehouses, and stables behind it. It might be a public building out front but the construction showed the back to be a defensive stronghold in the center of the city.

Five stone steps and a porch spanned the front of the building. On the veranda, men in robes and tunics lounged in groups. They paid little attention when grooms took the horses as the five armored men dismounted. A few on the porch greeted Ezio but he didn't stop to chat. His Lieutenant opened a door and ushered Ezio, Gaius, Castor, and Alerio into a large meeting room with wooden columns.

One side of the room had four highbacked chairs along the wall and a desk off to the side. Three of the chairs were occupied by men talking with a group in tunics and robes. At the desk, a clerk scribbled furiously as the men talked. Beside the desk were stacks of scrolls and piles of parchment.

"Sub Commander. Please escort Tribune Claudius and his Legionaries to the feasting table," one of the three called out. "We will join you shortly."

Alerio eased up beside the Senior Tribune.

"Sir, how did he know your name?" Alerio whispered as they followed Ezio towards the other side of the room.

"Obviously, they sent a runner ahead," scolded Castor. "Don't get above your station, Captain or Corporal or whatever you are."

"The Sub Commander never sent a runner," insisted Alerio.

Ezio turned and inquired, "Is something wrong?"

"No, Sub Commander," Gaius assured him. "Just a matter of a relief room for Captain Sisera. Something he ate is disagreeing with his stomach."

"Down the hallway, through the back door and to your right," Ezio directed as he stopped at a long table. "We'll be here when you get back."

While Gaius and Castor took seats facing the entrance to the building, Alerio strolled down the hallway. The interior walls were wood planks broken by flimsy doors. Halfway down the hallway, he reached a set of open, massive doors anchored to stone. Beyond the stone partition, the floor changed from wood to stone. And, the entrances to side rooms changed to thick, heavy doors with big brackets for loosely securing the doors.

It seemed the exterior defensive wall extended through the large building separating the public section from the military compound of the structure. At the rear door, he pushed it open and stepped into a military facility complete with a parade ground. As Alerio suspected, this was a defensive position. He located the latrine shed, pushed aside a curtain and walked in.

After relieving his bladder, Alerio stepped on the raised seat and peered through a crack in the rough boards. Soldiers wandered between buildings, some armored and some not. It was a typical day at a military post and, despite the Legion encampment outside their gates, no one seemed to be in a rush. He was about to climb down when the figure of a man standing in a doorway caught his eye. Although the man had his back to the Corporal and stood out of the sunlight, there was something familiar about him. When the shape moved deeper into the room and out of view, Alerio stepped down. Outside he found a water barrel and washed his hands. Then, he entered the building and walked down the hallway to the great room and the long table.

***

Roasted bull ribs on platters had been delivered along with bread, bowls of fruit and olives. It seemed the leadership wanted to prove how prosperous Echetla was to their guests.

"I am Basil, Magistrate of Echetla," said a man whose short body carried layers of fat. "We've been expecting you, Tribune Claudius."

"Me, sir?" inquired Gaius.

"Well, not you specifically," Basil replied. "Just someone of importance from the Republic's Legion."

Alerio heard the exchange as he approached the table but his mind was on the shadowy figure in the doorway. Automatically, he walked up and stood a respectful distance behind the Senior Tribune's chair.

"Captain Sisera. Are you still unwell?" Ezio questioned.

214

"I'm better, Sub Commander," Alerio said realizing he had assumed his bodyguard position. Quickly, he moved to take a seat on the other side of Gaius from Castor. "Thank you for asking."

Two of the other men from the highbacked chairs arrived and as they took seats, they introduced themselves.

"Tektōn Adrian, I'm the commerce advisor to the Magistrate," one exclaimed as he sat and picked up a long meaty rib bone. "How does a military presence concern trade?"

"The Republic is keen on opening trade routes with valuable partners," Gaius assured Adrian. "Castor Ireneus and I are from trading families. While currently serving in the Legion, our hearts and purses are always concerned with business."

"My kind of men," Adrian said as he took a bite of the meat.

"I am Demagogue Nicos, advisor for the citizens of Echetla," Nicos explained. "How could a partnership with the Republic serve the people of Echetla?"

"Beyond the goods and services, we can discuss travel to the Republic," Gaius stated. "Safe passage and the security of having a strong neighbor."

Castor grew bored with the diplomatic chatter and, as all growing lads do when idle, he wolfed down an enormous number of ribs. The bones were stacking up quickly beside his plate.

"Strong neighbors?" Ezio injected. "We have strong neighbors. And it's why we have so many men under arms. How is the Republic's Legion any different than the threat we face from Syracuse or Qart Hadasht?"

"The Republic maintains a strong home guard," Gaius informed the Sub Commander. "Our presence on Sicilia was forced on us when Qart Hadasht forces moved into Messina. We couldn't allow a hostile base just across the Strait from our territory. As far as I know, we have no designs on expanding the Republic."

"Then how do you explain the attack on Syracuse?" demanded Basil.

Everyone at the table tensed at the obvious challenge. From simple questions, the conversation had shifted to hard reality.

"We have issues with King Hiero blockading our ships," Gaius began when a loud burp from Castor broke his chain of thought.

In the momentary silence, the Junior Tribune threw down a rib bone and blurted out his own thoughts.

"Enough of this idle chatter," Castor announced. "Come on Gaius. Simply bribe these cūlus hill folks and let's get back to the Legion and the fighting. General Caudex can come back for them later."

"And the true nature of your visit is revealed," Magistrate Basil declared. "Ezio, if you would?"

"Guards," the Sub Commander shouted and spearmen came through the front doors and down the hallway. "Finally, I was afraid we would never get to the fighting."

Alerio dropped a hand to his gladius and started to stand. But Gaius rested a hand on his arm to still the bodyguard.

"Too many to fight, Sisera," the Senior Tribune warned. "Let's see how this plays out."

Spear tips aimed at the Legionaries' heads allowed no room to set up a counterattack, so the Corporal did as he was instructed. Then a familiar voice, gloating and sneering from behind, reach the table.

"Wise move and a good choice, Magistrate," Macario Hicetus said as he swaggered around the table. "Senior Tribune Claudius, we meet again. Under different circumstances."

"You're looking fit, Lieutenant Hicetus," Gaius greeted the Syracusan. "I take it King Hiero's advisers devised this side trip to keep you away from the King."

"Not at all, Tribune. I was honored to be chosen to lead a delegation to our allies," Macario said with a bow in Basil's direction. "And who better to warn the council about the treachery and greed of the Republic than from someone who has suffered under your boot's heel."

The Senior Tribune studied the council members and the armed men.

"Now that we know your game," Gaius inquired. "What's going to happen to my advisers and me?"

"I'm buying you from Echetla. Because noblemen can be ransomed, if they live," Macario explained while looking at Castor Ireneus. Then a huge smile crossed Macario's face when he saw Alerio. "Lance Corporal Sisera?"

"Lieutenant Hicetus. Good to see you again, sir," Alerio said nicely because his mother had taught him there was always time for good manners. Although she couldn't have imagined being nice to someone who had murder in their eyes.

"And for those with no value, I'll still pay," Macario announced. "How are you feeling Sisera? Have you healed from the lashes?"

"I still suffer from back spasms, Lieutenant," Alerio lied. "But I manage to get around. Is it a long journey to Syracuse?"

"Not to worry, Lance Corporal Sisera," exclaimed Macario. "The Tribunes will make the trip in relative comfort. You will not be coming with us. My soldiers burn for revenge after Messina. Legionary blood is just the tonic they need."

"What about the men in my encampment?" asked Gaius. Macario looked at Ezio and smiled.

"Sub Commander, I have placed my men and me under your command," he stated. "I defer to your judgment."

217

"Very good, Lieutenant. In the morning, Tribune Claudius, the forces of Echetla and Syracuse will sweep your Legionaries from our plain," described Ezio. "It'll be a good fight."

"Hopefully, enough will live, Sub Commander," Tektōn Adrian added. "We are in need of replacement slaves for our silver and copper mines."

"We'll do the best we can," promised Ezio. "But in the heat of battle, who really knows."

"We need to interview Tribunes Claudius and Ireneus to establish their worth," announced Magistrate Basil. "What do you want to do with Sisera, Lieutenant Hicetus?"

"Unfortunately, most of my troop are off scouting the Legion's backtrail," Macario replied. "I wouldn't want to deprive them of participating in the execution. Have you a holding room where I can keep him until the morning?"

"The doors near the end of the hallway are solid," Ezio answered. "And can be barred from the outside."

"Lance Corporal Sisera. Kindly place your blades on the table before you stand," Macario instructed.

"Yes, sir," Alerio replied. He eased his gladius out of the scabbard and placed it on the table. Then, he reached across his body to pulled a Legion dagger from the other hip. As he twisted, he gave a yelp of pain. "I apologize for the outburst."

"The Lance Corporal recently ran afoul of the regulations and was severely whipped," explained Macario cheerily. "Come Sisera. Perhaps stretching out on a hard, stone floor will ease the pain."

Alerio slowly pushed out of the chair. Before he could stand erect, he doubled over in pain. His legs gave out and he fell against Gaius' back. Stumbling further, Alerio dropped to his knees between the two Tribunes. His elbows, obviously the only thing supporting his weight, rested on the tabletop.

"I've failed you, sir," he mumbled to Gaius.

Resting a hand on the Legionaries back, Gaius bent over Alerio and replied, "No Corporal Sisera. It is I who have failed you."

"How touching?" commented Macario. "Can someone please get him out of here so we can get on with this?"

Two soldiers grabbed Alerio's arms and pulled him off the table. With his heels dragging on the floor, they carried him down the hall. Still doubled over and groaning.

Chapter 23 - The Bones of a Plan

As the two soldiers pulled Alerio towards the empty storage room, he moaned, twitched, let his urine leave a trail on the floor and spit run freely down his chin. None of these were signs of a back injury but, they were symptoms of some illness.

His escorts didn't know what was wrong with him. Rather than deal with a sick man, any more than was necessary, they dropped the Legionary on the stone floor and fled the room. They were so disgusted, the soldiers left him in his leather cavalry armor and riding boots. Once the pole rattled in the brackets securing the door, Alerio uncurled his body.

Clutched in his fists were the treasures he appropriated from beside Castor's plate: two bovine ribs about the size of Legion daggers. And to his delight, Tribune Ireneus had left meat on the bones.

Alerio started to sit up, but something under the right shoulder of his armor poked him in the neck. Reaching up, he located the source and extracted it. Senior Tribune Claudius had stuffed a third rib under the armor as they talked. Alerio wasn't sure if the Tribune was attempting to arm him or feed him, because this rib was heavy with meat. Alerio scooted back against the rock wall. Then, he began chewing the meat and gnawing the gristle from the thick bones.

As he dined, he studied the sturdy door. Constructed of thick planks, it fit snuggly on the sides. At the top, a large gap provided weak illumination to the room and space to remove the door. The gap allowed the pins on the door to be set in the pintle hinges attached to the frame. If he could shift the door up and dislodge the pole from across the brackets, before the guard hacked off his hand, he could get out. However, only a finger's width gap ran along the bottom of the door.

After thoroughly cleaning the bones and licking his fingers, Alerio held one bone in each hand. Reaching back to the rough stone wall, he began scraping sharp points out of the ends.

Dinner and daggers, he thought. Now all he had to do was get through the door, overcome the guards, locate the Tribunes, spirit them out of a strange city and warn the detachment before daylight. He would prefer anchoring a shield wall against a hoard of murderous barbarians.

***

Based on the fading light, the sun was setting. Hearing noises outside his cell, Alerio crawled to the door and listened through the gap.

"A room with a bed would be preferable," Castor Ireneus explained. "We discussed my value to my father. It should rate me a bed."

"Sorry Lad, I don't have the manpower to guard you," Macario Hicetus replied. "And I'm not going to chase you around Echetla if you decide to go gallivanting about the city. Get in the storage room. You, as well, Senior Tribune."

"What have you done with Corporal Sisera?" Gaius demanded. "Get your hands off the lad."

Claudius grunted, his boots scraped on the stone floor before the sound of his body armor hitting the stone floor reached Alerio. Placing his cheek on the stones, the Corporal attempted to see under the door and into the other storage

220

room. His view was limited to a hand's width of the hallway. The rattle of a pole dropping into the wide brackets told him Macario had barred the Tribunes' cell door.

Alerio shoved back from the gap and relaxed a little. At least he knew where the Tribunes were being held. They were across the hall but that meant the guard or guards would be stationed right outside his door. Rolling over on his back, Alerio closed his eyes and visualized all the things that could go wrong with his plan.

***

The natural light had faded. But flickering candlelight cast a narrow bright strip under Alerio's cell door. Then voices carried to the Corporal.

"I'm taking the troop into the city for the festival," Macario Hicetus' voice floated into the cell from the hallway. "Your only job is to be sure no one opens either door. Those two in there are valuable. The other one, well, we'll be using him for spear practice in the morning."

"I thought we were joining the Echetla companies for the attack in the morning, Lieutenant," a gruff voice ventured.

"Sub Commander Ezio is hot to take on the Legionaries," explained Macario. "We'll let his men cross the trench and break down the pickets. After his soldiers are hacked up, we'll march in and save the day."

"He really doesn't have a clue about them," offered the guard. "Shouldn't you warn the Sub Commander. We learned a lot at Messina."

"One day, we may need to march on Echetla," explained the Syracusan cavalry officer. "If the Republic removes some of Echetla's veterans, who am I to complain. So, relax. In the morning, you'll be the only sober soldier on the field."

"That's what I'm afraid of Lieutenant," the guard replied. "But, you can count on me, sir. Your prisoners will be here in the morning."

"Good man," Macario exclaimed as the sound of his boots on the stone floor faded.

***

The rear door slammed shut and the guard exhaled. Grunting as he lowered himself to the floor, he leaned against the wall settling in for a long night. He closed his eyes and began snoring softly.

"If I had some water," a grating voice sang from inside the condemned man's cell.

"You in there, shut up," the Syracusan soldier growled.

There were a few moments of silence and the guard settled back. Then the caustic voice started up again. His voice coming clearly through the gap near the floor.

If I had some water

Goats milk, you would serve me?
I would churn butter
Make cheese from curd and whey
The kid's milk stolen from a doe

Red wine, you would serve me?
I would feel better
Drink it to waste away the day
The vino from a grape grotto

But, if I had some water
I'd cool my neck
Clean my clothes
Wash my toes
Sprinkle a rose
And quench my thirst
If I had some water

"I told you to shut up," ordered the guard. "I'm not getting you water. Now go to sleep and leave me in peace."

But, if I had some water
I'd cool my neck
Clean my clothes
Wash my toes
Sprinkle a rose
And quench my thirst
If I had some water

The soldier scowled at the gap then spit. A glob hit the door, dripped down and plopped onto the stone.

Olive oil, you would serve me?
I would grease a wheel
Dip and soak it up with bread
The rich oil from an olive pressed

Honey, you would serve me?
I would add it to a meal
Eat the comb's delicious spread
The sweet of the honeybees' nest

But, if I had some water
I'd cool my neck
Clean my clothes
Wash my toes
Sprinkle a rose
And quench my thirst
If I had some water

Gritting his teeth, the soldier climbed to his feet and drew his sword. Bending down, he judged where the voice was behind the door and rammed the length of the blade through the gap. What difference would it make if the Legionary was injured? He could die as easily hurt as being thirsty.

***

Bent double so his voice projected under the door, Alerio held the ends of his gladius belt. On the floor, the looped end lay flat on the stone. When the soldier's blade poked through the gap, he jerked the belt, trapping the blade. Using two hands, he pulled up hard. A slight bend held the sword against the bottom of the door and, with the upward pressure, the door lifted. Both pins in the pintle hinges separated from their bases, leaving the door hanging by the slack pole in the outside brackets.

Alerio dropped the belt, grasped the edge and opened the door as far as it would go. With the third bovine rib held between the fingers of his right hand, he reached out and knocked the pole free from one bracket. The end of the pole fell to the floor allowing the door to open a little wider.

At this point, Alerio's mind screamed at him to stop. The plan was flawed. The soldier stood on the other side of the door ready to hack into his wrist and remove his hand. But he was slated for an agonizing death in the morning anyway. At least he wouldn't live long enough to miss the hand. Besides, the Tribunes needed to escape and warn the Legionaries. Biting the inside of his lip, Alerio shoved his arm through the crack in the door and grabbed the pole.

His arm shot straight up to the top of the doorframe. A jolt took the pole from Alerio's hand as the guard's blade chopped into the wood. With the door free, the Corporal pulled it back, released the weight and it thumped against the stone floor of his cell. Then, he stepped to the side and stood in the darkness. What light there was in the hallway barely penetrated the storage room.

"Cute trick. That took some cōleī," the soldier admitted. "But you're still in the room and you'll need to get by my sword to get out."

"Why don't you come in and get me?" asked Alerio. "Better yet, go get some help."

"I'm not going anywhere and neither are you," the guard advised. "Let's make this easy. Show yourself and I won't hurt you too much."

Alerio shuffled from the dark. His right hand behind his back and the left cocked in what appeared to be an awkwardly held fist.

"Do you participate in Apollo's sport?" the Legionary inquired. "I'm just learning. It's wonderful exercise."

"Apollo is a God and you're not," replied the guard. "You want to box against a sword? Step right up."

Alerio shuffled from side to side while jabbing slowly with his left hand. He looked at his own feet. To the guard, he resembled a person who had watched people box and was mimicking a few of the fundamentals.

Olive oil, you would serve me?
I would grease a wheel
Dip and soak it up with bread
The rich oil from an olive pressed

He sang while lumbering forward. Before he came close to the tip of the Syracusan's blade, he scooted back, still looking down and jabbing in slow motion with the left fist.

Honey, you would serve me?
I would add it to a meal

Suddenly, the Legionary sprang at the guard. His left fist rotated up revealing a sharpened rib bone. The bone smacked the blade shoving it aside. As Alerio pushed the blade, his right arm came around. From an inept boxer, the soldier faced a man holding two sharp objects. One pointing up and the other down.

Eat the comb's delicious spread

225

The sweet of the honeybees' nest

Alerio sang as he got his hip past the tip of the sword and swiped at the guard's face. Ducking back, the Syracusan tried to disengage by putting distance between himself and the prisoner.

But, if I had some water

I'd cool my neck

The soldier stomped backward and the Legionary crowded each step. The sword rising, lowering and swinging to the left and right. But every attack was stopped from reaching the Legionary by bone knives pressed against both sides of Syracusan's blade.

Clean my clothes

Wash my toes

Alerio rotated his wrists juggling and countering the movement of the sword. Bent to the side, he imagined himself rowing a canoe and badly mishandling the paddle. In one breath the bones were over and under the blade and, in the next breath, they caught the sides of the blade. Then the soldier drew back his sword arm while throwing a punch at Alerio's face with his left fist.

Sprinkle a rose

And quench my thirst

The Legionary stabbed the sword hand while spinning away from the fist. As he completed the circle, Alerio raised the bone knife and backhand, sank it into the soldier's neck. As the guard fell to his knees, he grabbed for the rib bone with both hands. Alerio finished the song.

"If I had some water," he sang as he reached down and picked up the sword. "I'd quench my thirst."

Chapter 24 – A Celebration of Sterculius

"Senior Tribune Claudius?" Alerio called into the storage room.

"What was that noise?" Castor asked in a sleepy voice. "It sounded like lost souls from Hades crying out in agony."

"I don't know, Tribune Ireneus," Alerio replied. "We can discuss your nightmare later. Right now, we need to vacate this area."

"Corporal Sisera. How are you? Did they injure you?" inquired Gaius as he crawled to the entrance and used the doorframe to climb to his feet. Then he stepped out of the storage room and into the light of three candles.

"I'm fine, sir. But we need to move," insisted Alerio.

Gaius glanced at the dead guard with the rib bone sticking out of his neck and the missing door on the storage room across the hall.

"I slipped you the rib so you could eat," Gaius explained. "I never considered it would be used as a weapon."

"It was delicious, sir," Alerio assured the Tribune. He pulled the guard into his cell, reset and closed the door. Then, he dropped the poles across both storage rooms. Heading up the hallway towards the front of the building, he called back. "This way."

"We need to slip out the back," Castor exclaimed. He marched in the direction of the rear door.

"Sir, that's a military compound full of Echetla soldiers," described Alerio. Castor stopped in the candlelight, glared at the Corporal and shook his head. He pointed at the rear, insisting they go that way. "Tribune Claudius. I'm trying to get you out of the city safely. However, it's impossible if Tribune Ireneus questions my directions. And it leaves me with split loyalties."

"How dare you, Corporal Sisera," challenged Castor.

"Let him finish, Junior Tribune," ordered Gaius. "Please explain, Corporal Sisera."

"Tribune Claudius, we have Legionaries, your detachment, who will be wiped out in the morning," Alerio replied. "I may be able to get you and Tribune Ireneus out of the city in time to warn them. Or, I can leave you on your own and definitely alert the camp."

"You'd leave us here?" asked Castor.

"Not willingly," admitted Alerio.

"Corporal Sisera. We'll follow your lead without question," promised Gaius. He began to walk up the dark hallway. "Get me out of the city."

"What about me?" asked Castor.

Alerio didn't say anything. Picking up a candle, he handed it to the Senior Tribune and guided him towards the meeting room. Then Alerio felt along the walls for the heavy doors. Once he located them, he began pulling them to close off the hallway. Castor brushed by him and joined the Senior Tribune.

"You can't lock them," Gaius exclaimed, noticing the brackets were on the other side of the closing doors.

With only the single candle for light, it was dark and Gaius didn't see Alerio pull out the sharpened bones and jam them under the defensive doors. It wouldn't prevent the doors from being pushed or pulled open but, the wedges held the doors firmly, offering some resistance.

"Move to the front of the room and wait by the entrance where we came in," instructed Alerio.

While they crossed the meeting room, he walked to the far side and located the four high backed council chairs. Selecting a chair, he lifted it and upended it in front of an entrance. Then he moved the other chairs and placed them as obstacles at three other entrances. Before rejoining the Tribunes, he selected two chairs from the feasting table and placed them at a wooden column. Between the sword and his foot, the two chairs were soon splintered and heaps of wood.

"I don't understand," questioned Castor when Corporal Sisera appeared behind him. "I thought we were sneaking out of the city."

"Hand me the candle, sir," instructed Alerio. Taking it, he went back to the column and lit pieces of the shattered chairs.

The interior of the meeting room went from darkness to shifting shadows in the growing flames. Slowly, the fire began to climb the column.

"We need to get out of here," Castor asserted. He took a step towards the entrance.

Placing a restraining hand on the young nobleman's shoulder, Gaius ordered, "You will wait for instructions."

"We're trapped in a burning building, in a city filled with hostile soldiers," Castor protested. "And you want to wait for a mad Legionary who is touched by Furor?"

"Right now, I'll take crazy over rash," Gaius informed Castor. Then looking at Alerio who was at the entrance watching the porch and street. "Corporal Sisera. I don't mean to question your tactics, but is there a method to your insanity?"

Turning from the entrance, Alerio's face glowed in the light from the flames and he did appear to be touched by the God of Madness.

"The Echetla Council has declared a feast. Probably to honor Ares and ask his blessings for ferocity tomorrow," Alerio explained. "If our escape is discovered, every soldier will stop drinking and begin searching for us."

"It won't be difficult to find us," commented Castor as he coughed on the smoke. "We're standing in a burning building."

"I'm hoping the citizens and soldiers get busy fighting the fire," Alerio offered as he turned back to watch the porch. "I'm hoping it will delay them in setting up their search grids."

"You'll sacrifice two noblemen to save a bunch of common Legionaries," shouted Castor.

"Tribune Ireneus. Life in the Legion isn't for everybody," Alerio suggested. Then he added. "Excuse me, Senior Tribune."

Two figures broke through the entrance on the far side of the meeting room. Alerio sprinted towards them and arrived as they tripped over the highbacked chair. With the flat of his blade, he beat the two unconscious and stripped them of their robes. Clutching the garments in his arms, he raced back to the Tribunes.

"Put these on," Alerio ordered. "It's time to go."

"You were waiting for clothing?" Castor asked as he wrapped the garment around his shoulders.

"How did you know the first ones in would have robes?" inquired Gaius as he settled the cloth over his ornate armor.

"Only a wealthy man would run into a burning building to save contracts and deeds, before shouting for help," offered Alerio. "To them, the stacks of scrolls and parchment were more valuable than anyone's life. When we leave, shout and point back at the burning building."

Alerio stepped onto the porch and immediately cried out. Waving his arms frantically at the gathering crowd, he guided the Tribunes down the steps and away from the smoke and flames consuming Echetla's administration building. Once across the street, they ducked into an alleyway to avoid mobs of soldiers and citizens rushing towards the fire.

***

Three streets from the blazing building, the three Legionaries changed direction and headed towards the wall. After a few blocks, the buildings went from residences to commercial buildings then tradesmen compounds and warehouses.

"The gates and the wall facing our camp are that way," Castor said pointing to his left.

"Yes, sir. And that's where Sub Commander Ezio will have staged the most troops," Alerio pointed out as they crossed a dark street. "We'll need to go over where they least expect us."

"And where would that be, Corporal?" inquired Gaius.

"When we rode in, I noticed the stockyards near the wall," Alerio advised the Tribunes.

"We're going to climb the wall with animals whinnying, neighing and pawing the ground?" ventured Castor. "Don't you think the stockyard guards will hear and come to investigate?"

"Not the stockyards," Alerio corrected. "We're going to worship Sterculius."

"Because no one wants to loiter at the dung piles," Gaius guessed. Then he had to catch his breath before continuing. "For this mission, the God of manure should be invoked. Or he has been involved the whole time. And, I'm just now realizing it."

The usually robust Senior Tribune appeared to be exhausted. Not wanting to drag a youth who couldn't keep silent or a man who might collapse from exhaustion, Alerio decided to leave them.

"Wait here, sirs," instructed Alerio as he gently shoved the Tribunes in a space between two warehouses. "I need to find some supplies."

"How do we locate the manure piles in the dark?" inquired Castor.

"Sniff the air, sir. You'll detect the location by the time I get back," Alerio answered before slipping away in the dark.

***

In a port city like the Capital, Messina, Syracuse or Catania, the place to find hemp rope and hooks were the shipbuilder's compound. In an inland city, the craftsman with the widest selection of ropes and hooks was a stonemason. Alerio's problem. He had no idea where to find the compound in Echetla. Doubling back the way the three had come, the Corporal jogged until he located a group of civilians. Rushing to the torch-carrying men, he slid to a stop.

"I'm with Lieutenant Hicetus' company from Syracuse," he lied while stepping into the torchlight. "I was told to report to a position near the stonemason's compound. But I got turned around. Can you point me in the right direction?"

231

"The quarryman is located near the wall in that direction," a man replied. Luckily, he indicated a quadrant of the city not far from the stockyards. As Alerio ran off, the man spoke to his companions. "Why would they station troops at Xander's compound?"

Alerio missed the comment as he jogged down twisting and winding streets. The buildings became widely spaced until he located empty lots across from warehouses. Dividing the vacant areas were short walls around tradesmen compounds. A tanner and a soap maker were close together. One scraped fat from hide and the other rendered the fat and mixed it with wet ash to make soap. And, both used urine in the process. Even in the still of the night, the sharp aroma of ammonia was overpowering. Wisely, the compounds were located near the city's defensive wall so as not to offend their neighbors.

Staying next to the warehouses, Alerio stuck to the shadows. Once he avoided a patrol marching up the street and hid several times from night watchmen carrying lanterns. In all the cases, there was no immediacy to their steps. It appeared the Legionaries' escape had gone unnoticed.

Beyond the soap maker, Alerio saw the outlines of large blocks of stone. In the midst of the blocks sat a large house and stable. On the side of the house was a spacious covered work area. Alerio left the warehouse, crossed the street and moved between the stones. He detected no movement as he approached the awning. Squatting down, Alerio listened for snoring or similar noises made by sleeping men. Once satisfied the work area was deserted, the Legionary crept onto the stone flooring.

He located hemp rope and pulled two lengths off a pile. With the ropes over one shoulder, he sorted through tools. Small hammers, large mallets of wood and steel, various sized chisels and wedges, were arranged on benches. As he approached the far end of a bench, his hand identified oversized iron hooks with eyelets at one end. To move heavy pieces of stone, the stonemason placed these hooks under the blocks so they could be hoisted. Strong and built to lift stones, the weight of one or two men on a hook posed no problem. Then, the door to the house opened and a man, whose shoulders crowded the doorframe, limped into the work area. Holding a kettle sized lantern in one hand and a spear with a broadhead tip in the other, he peered around checking for shadows in the dark beyond the light.

"Put my equipment back where you found it," the massive man instructed once his eyes settled on Alerio. When the Legionary hesitated, the man sat the lantern on a workbench. In a blur, the spear spun. Passing the rotating shaft over his head, the man continued spinning it with the other hand and warned. "Run and you'll never make it off the patio."

"I was only borrowing the ropes and hooks," Alerio explained as he placed the climbing gear on the stone floor.

"Borrowing is usually a two-party agreement," observed the man. "When the taking is one-sided, it's called stealing."

Holding out a hand to show he needed a moment, Alerio reached under his leather armor and pulled out a coin pouch.

"How about a lease?" Alerio asked as he tossed the pouch to the man.

"I catch you stealing and now you want to buy the rope and hooks?" inquired the man after snatching the purse out of the air.

"Not buy. I want to rent them," explained Alerio.

"So, we've gone from theft to a gentleman's agreement," teased the man while pointing the spear's tip at Alerio. "What's your name lad?"

"Corporal Alerio Sisera of Caudex Legion," Alerio responded figuring that if one of them was killed, his name and affiliation wouldn't matter. "And your name Master Stonemason. Or should I call you Lochagos based on your expertise with the spear?"

"I was never a Captain," he replied. "Lochias Xander, a descendant of The Sacred Band of Thebes."

"I thought Thebes was destroyed by Philip II of Macedonia, Sergeant Xander?" questioned Alerio. "About seventy-one years ago, if my history lessons and memory hold true. You have aged well."

"A few years after they defeated The Sacred Band, Philip II and his son Alexander destroyed my ancestral home," Xander admitted. "I was a baby when my father and uncles spirited our families away. Growing up with shield and spear, I learned about my celebrated heritage. As a young man, I hired out to Syracuse as a mercenary dreaming of glory and riches. When a sword hacked my knee, I learned glory was a fevered dream and loyalty as fleeting as my usefulness. After limping around Sicilia, I arrived at Echetla and found work protecting several merchants from a gang of thugs. One of the merchants was a stone craftsman. By night, I speared two-legged rats and, by day, apprenticed with the stonemason. And here we are, a thief and a Master Stonemason."

"And masters at arms," Alerio added. He slowly drew his sword and began twirling it. When it whirled fast enough to buzz, the Corporal released the hilt. Soaring up, the tumbling blade almost touched the roof before it arched over and, still revolving, fell to his other side. After catching it by the hilt, Alerio brought the blade to his forehead and bowed to the former Greek Sergeant.

"One of us dies tonight leaving the other crippled or waiting for death," Zander ventured.

"Or, we can make a gentlemen's agreement and, you rent me the ropes and hooks," offered Alerio.

"The sword thing? Can you catch it every time?" the stonemason inquired.

"Since I was twelve years old," Alerio assured him. "Before that, I dropped it a lot."

"As I dropped the spear when I was learning," Zander admitted. He bounced the coin purse in the palm of his hand before saying. "You have the agreement. When will you return my property?"

"I won't be returning the gear, personally," Alerio informed the stonemason. "However, I will tell you where you can recover the items."

Alerio only told him about being hunted by Syracuse forces, the messy death sentence, and where the stonemason could pick up his rope and hooks.

"I should have gutted you at first sight," Zander complained, then added. "But a deal has been struck. Go, before I have time to question our agreement."

***

Castor jumped and almost cried out when a voice from behind him spoke his name. Before he embarrassed himself, the young nobleman recognized Corporal Sisera's shape coming from between the warehouses.

"Tribune Ireneus. Have you located our escape route?" Alerio asked.

The Corporal pushed by the Tribunes without waiting for an answer and peered up and down the street. Then he sniffed and announced, "Follow me."

Alerio guided the Tribunes onto the street and led them around the corner. Constantly pivoting their heads watching for patrols or night watchmen, the three angled across the road. Two blocks from the alleyway, when their noses twitched and stomachs revolted, they left the road.

The major features of the isolated lot were the city's defensive wall and mounds of black matter piled in front of it. Almost immediately after leaving the road, their boots began squishing in slush. Flies rose in sheets to clog their mouths, requiring them to breathe through their noses. And, the insects' bit at their exposed skin, adding to the horror of the city's merda dump.

Castor and Alerio struggled as the sticky dung closed in around their ankles. The further off the road they got, the deeper they sank in the soft mush. Flies crawled in their ears, across their eyes and settled in mass on their necks biting into their flesh. Castor swiped at the insects trying to dislodge them. Alerio, holding the ropes and hooks, had to settle for swinging his head back and forth. The movement offered little relief from the biting flies.

With knees dragging in the wet slush, Castor and Alerio high stepped to the top of the mound and arrived at the wall. Then, from behind them, they heard whispered curses of frustration. Glancing back, they saw Senior Tribune Claudius sprawled out with his legs vanishing into the soft merda and his chest resting in the manure. Both of his arms were in ruts from where he attempted to claw his way out of the slimy muck.

"Leave him," Castor demanded as he panned the street searching for patrols. "That's an order, Corporal Sisera."

Alerio twisted his mouth into a sneer that the Junior Tribune couldn't see.

"Fine with me. Hold these," Alerio urged while dumping one length of rope and a hook into Castor's arms.

After fixing one end of the rope to the hook, Alerio whirled it around four times and released the iron. It sailed up and caught on the stone wall.

"Give me the other rope," Alerio instructed.

"I'm going first," Castor announced.

"I need to place the other rope," Alerio informed him as he reached for the rope and hook. "Unless you want to jump off the other side."

"No. You'll leave me," Castor accused, holding the rope tightly as Alerio attempted to take it. "You said you would."

"The rope is there," Alerio pointed out. "I'm going to hang the other one. You can come up right after me."

With a final jerk, Castor released the rope and hook. Alerio tied the rope to the hook and coiled the line around his body and hung the hook over his shoulder. Then he climbed to the top of the wall. Castor followed on his heels. Once the other rope hung down the far side, Alerio placed Caster's hands on the rope.

"Climb down and make for our camp," he instructed. "Watch for patrols. Send back the cavalry with two spare horses."

"You need to guide and protect me," insisted Castor. "I can't make it alone."

"Of course, you can, Tribune Ireneus," Alerio assured him while placing a hand on Castor's hip. Then he shoved it and the young nobleman rolled off the wall. Hanging by the rope, Castor heard the Corporal. "When I get Tribune Claudius over this wall, if Legion cavalry isn't waiting for us, I'll hunt you down. Then, I'll call the Goddess Nenia for you. Do you understand me?"

"Yes, Death Caller," answered Castor. He had no choice but to climb down as Alerio placed a hand on his head and forced the descent.

With the Junior Tribune on his way, Alerio swung his legs over the wall and dropped back into the merda to retrieve the Senior Tribune.

***

Gaius felt trapped and alone. After hearing Castor order him left behind, the fight went from his heart and his exhausted body refused to move. With the negotiations crashing before they started, his unsuspecting Legionaries soon to be attacked and, his mission a monumental failure, the once proud nobleman rested the side of his face on the night soil. He waited to be discovered even as he anticipated the shame when he faced the smirking Lieutenant Hicetus.

"I'm going to raise you upright, sir," Alerio told Claudius. "Once you're up, step with one leg and I'll support you. Ready?"

"Sisera? I thought you left?" Gaius mumbled in surprise.

"Sir, the detachment needs you. Plus, it's my duty to guard you. Even if it includes pulling you out of merda," Alerio responded as he grabbed the Tribune's armor and lifted. Amazingly, the weight of the man and armor were far heavier than expected. At first, Alerio assumed the chest piece and the Tribune's arms were caught in suction. But the weight remained steady as he pulled the Tribune up. "You may need to back off the bread, cheese and un-watered wine, sir."

"That's not exactly the problem," countered Gaius. He pulled and, one leg came free. Using Alerio for balance, he managed to pull the second leg from the sucking dung. Together they sank, stepped and sank again until they reached the rope. Gaius reached out and tugged, then he admitted. "I'm not sure I can climb it."

"Get your legs up, sir," directed Alerio. He stepped under the Tribune and placed Gaius' feet on his shoulders. With a firm grip on the rope, he hoisted the Tribune up and Gaius reached higher and lifted his overweight body.

Each time they rose, the Tribune's boots smeared Alerio's cheeks with dung. On the third hand-over-hand ascent, the caked boots closed and pushed merda into Alerio's ears. Deaf, struggling, and trying to ignore the filth, Corporal Sisera boosted Claudius to the top of the wall.

"Hum, hum…"

"I can't hear you, sir," admitted Alerio. "We'll go down the same way."

There was one advantage to having your face and ears covered in poop, Alerio thought as he dropped over the wall.

The flies can't reach your skin. Once Gaius' boots were firmly on Alerio's shoulders, they climbed down.

"Blessings from Sterculius," Gaius announced as he used the stone wall for support. "We crossed the manure unobserved."

Alerio used his little fingers to dig the merda from his ears. Glancing around at the deep shadow of the wall, the bodyguard realized they weren't safe.

"The tree line, sir. Can you walk?" Alerio asked.

"Flat ground is fine as long as I don't have to run," Gaius informed him while pushing off the stone wall.

***

They were halfway to a crop of trees when the sounds of hooves reached them. At first, Alerio thought they were Legion cavalry. But the jingle of weapons as the riders drew closer, came from along the wall.

"It's an Echetla patrol," warned Alerio.

Taking the Tribune by the arm, he attempted to rush Gaius. Their slow progress and the approaching patrol put the Legionnaires on a converging path with the mounted soldiers. They stumbled into a depression and Alerio stopped the Tribune.

"Get down, sir," he instructed. After helping Gaius to the grass, Alerio drew his sword and stretched out on the ground beside him.

Hooves beat the earth as the cavalry troop bore down on the Tribune and the Corporal. Alerio raised his head and saw the outline of the riders. He tightened his grip on the sword and braced himself, preparing to defend Claudius. Then two of the horses snorted as if attempting to clear a stench from their nostrils. When the animals danced sideways to avoid the odor, the riders, after catching the scent, allowed their mounts to dance away from the offensive smell.

"Something died there," a soldier stated as he guided the patrol around Alerio and Gaius.

"Smells like one of yours, Urion," another voice called out.

"Mine smell like freshly baked bread," a soldier responded.

"Maybe to you," replied another as the patrol moved beyond the Legionaries.

Alerio tugged Gaius to his feet, again marveling at the weight of the Senior Tribune.

"Blessings of Sterculius," proclaimed Alerio as he guided Gaius towards the trees.

The God of merda had been very kind to the escaping Legionary and the Tribune on both sides of the wall.

***

They edged along the tree line putting distance between themselves and any patrols near the wall. Gaius, using tree trunks, moved quickly as if the ability to support his upper body negated the exhaustion. Occasionally, they caught a glimpse of the Legion camp but Alerio insisted they continue. His plan was to cross the open field and approach it from the side. Hopefully avoiding any Echetla forces stationed between the gates and their camp.

"Senior Tribune Claudius?" a voice asked as shapes separated from the deep shadows.

Alerio raised his sword and stepped in front of Gaius.

"Stand down, Death Caller. We're Second Squad, Velites Century," the man informed him.

"How did you find me in the dark?" inquired Gaius.

The Legionary sniffed the air and started to say something. After a pause, he changed his mind and informed the Tribune. "Fieldcraft, sir. Just good scouting."

"The Tribune requires a horse," Alerio explained.

"We have two mounts hidden a short distance from here," the skirmisher Lance Corporal assured him. "Squad. Fall into a protective formation but give the Senior Tribune room to move."

Considering the stench, Alerio knew the order to give the Tribune space was unnecessary. With Velites surrounding them, although at a distance, the tension in Alerio's shoulders eased. If they were attacked, it wouldn't be his single blade defending the Senior Tribune.

At a clearing, he gave Gaius a hand up, then mounted the other horse. Leaning over, the Tribune whispered to Alerio.

"Corporal Sisera. I'd appreciate if you never mentioned your Senior Tribune being face down in wet merda," instructed Gaius.

"Sir, I have no idea what you are talking about," Alerio assured him.

"Good. Let's get to camp and find buckets of water," suggested Gaius. "And soap, then more water."

"An excellent plan, sir," Alerio replied.

They nudged their horses out of the clearing and onto the open plain. Together, they raced towards the temporary safety of the reinforced camp.

Act 7

Chapter 25 – Retreat from Echetla

"Centurion. Send men on water and firewood runs," Gaius ordered as he slid off the horse.

"Sir, we have plenty of water for you and Corporal Sisera to wash," the line officer from the First Maniple, Eighth Century exclaimed.

"I understand. But I want every water vessel, pouch and wineskin filled," insisted Gaius as a bucket was dumped over his head. "And every fire stacked with extra wood. We are marching out and it's going to be fast."

"I'll order a breakdown of the tents," the confused Centurion announced.

Another bucket emptied. Gaius scrubbed his scalp, face, neck, and arms with soap and motioned for another bucket. "No. The camp stays. I want all officers and Tesserarii in my tent. I'll explain then. Come with me, Corporal Sisera."

Alerio, unlike the Tribune who still wore his armor, was naked and thoroughly washing his body.

"Sir, I'm not dressed," he protested.

"I've got a tunic you can use," advised Gaius as he marched to his tent. The Corporal grabbed the Syracusan sword and raced to catch up. He entered the big command tent right behind the Tribune. "Help me get this armor off."

"Sir, you'll soil your tent," commented Alerio as his fingers reached under a shoulder piece and started to unstrap the armor.

"Good. It'll give Sub Commander Ezio a memento of my visit," Gaius said as the shoulder sections came off. When the chest and back sections were removed, the Senior Tribune wasn't naked or just wearing an under tunic. Wrapped around his chest, stomach and back was a leather garment with pouches. "You'll find a tunic in my bags. I can't have my bodyguard standing around naked. The line officers might start measuring mentula instead of listening to me. But first, help me get this off."

Standing behind the Tribune, Alerio ran his hands under the shoulder straps and lifted. The mystery of why the Tribune appeared so heavy was solved.

"Put it on my campaign table and get dressed," Gaius instructed as he ducked down and away from the garment.

"Yes, sir," Alerio said as placed the heavy vest on the table. Then he went to a satchel, pulled out a tunic and dropped it over his head. "What's in those pouches and why have you been wearing that rig?"

"It's why Colonel Requiem assigned me a bodyguard," Gaius explained. He took a dagger from another satchel and began slitting the pouches. Finally, he lifted out a palm size bar of gold. "Gold intended to bribe the Council of Echetla."

As he talked, Gaius placed the small bars of gold beside the table. When he had two tall stacks, he indicated a box on the table. "There are writing utensils in the box. You are my acting Tesserarius. Write down the distribution."

"To whom, sir?" Alerio asked.

Before Gaius could reply, three Centurions and their Corporals came through the tent flap. They looked confused seeing Corporal Sisera sitting at the Tribune's desk dressed in a gold-trimmed tunic. His hand held a quill positioned over a blank piece of parchment. Or, the reactions might be from seeing stacks of mini gold bars beside the desk.

"Sir, you passed the word to get the Centuries on the road for a march," one Centurion questioned. "But not to break down the camp. Are we attacking Echetla?"

243

"We are not attacking. Bear with me," offered Gaius as he turned to Alerio. "Tesserarius. Get a count and I'll initial your total."

As Alerio counted and marked down the number of bars, the remaining Centurions and their Corporal's entered and stared at the fortune in precious metal. Gaius took the quill, wrote Alerio Sisera and the number three beside Alerio's name. Next, he signed the document Gaius Claudius and handed the quill back to a shocked Alerio. Then the Senior Tribune faced the officers and their NCOs.

"In the morning, a combined force of Syracuse and Echetla soldiers are coming to kill or enslave us," Gaius announced. Mumbling ran through the assembled Legionaries. The Senior Tribune waited for it to die down. "We are leaving Echetla. And we are leaving anything that will slow us down. I want them to see fires, clothing on lines, and tents when their commanders look over the wall while releasing their morning urinae."

"Sir. We can carry all of our gear," a Corporal assured the Tribune.

"Not this time. Food, water, and weapons," Gaius listed. "Nothing else. We have to make the crossroads near Catania, then do the same distance to reach the Legions at Syracuse. It's over a week of hard marching. And I don't think our enemies will simply let us dance away on the morning dew."

A couple of the Centurions protested but Gaius silenced them.

"I realize it will be a financial loss for the Centuries," Tribune Claudius acknowledged. "That's why Corporal Sisera is going to distribute gold to your Tesserarii. While they collect for your Centuries, I need you organizing the march. Centurion of Cavalry, a word, the rest of you are dismissed."

While the line officers filed out, the eight NCO's in charge of their Century's finances crowded around Alerio.

The first Tesserarii to receive and sign off for his share raised the gold bars over his head and jokingly called out, "Fortune reigns."

In the rear of the tent and away from the noisy distribution, Gaius and the cavalry officer talked.

"What happened with Tribune Ireneus?" Gaius asked the cavalry officer.

"A skirmisher watching post found him stumbling around in the dark," the Centurion reported. "At first we couldn't get him to talk. But after washing, he seemed to revive. That's when he told us about you and Death Caller being trapped in the city."

"He never described where he crossed the wall?" questioned Gaius. "Where I would cross the wall?"

"No, sir. Tribune Ireneus went to his tent to sleep, we thought," the horseman related. "Before anyone could stop him, he jumped on his horse and galloped away."

"Did you send riders after him?" Gaius asked.

"No, sir. There are Echetla patrols out and it's too dark to safely go after him," the officer replied. "We did send skirmishers and two horses to the woods in case you got out. I am sorry about not retrieving Tribune Ireneus."

"You made the correct decision. We can't spare men to chase down a deserter," Gaius informed the cavalry officer. "Right now, we have bigger issues. Here's what I need from your mounted Legionaries…"

***

Before the sky lightened, Lieutenant Macario Hicetus and Sub Commander Ezio stood on a platform looking over the wall.

"Have you found your Tribunes?" Ezio inquired.

"No. But they'll turn up," Macario assured him. "We have men searching the city. The Legionaries are probably holding up in a dark corner. Come sunrise, the light will reveal their whereabouts."

245

"It appears the Legionaries are getting a good night's sleep," the Sub Commander said as he pointed in the direction of the Legion camp. Far off, cookfires burned and, although tiny, he could make out the silhouettes of men passing in front of the flames. "They do keep an orderly guard throughout the night. You've got to admire their discipline."

"You can tell the survivors of your admiration when they're in your slave pens," suggested Macario. "Do we allow them breakfast?"

"Never fight on an empty stomach," the Sub Commander counseled him. "Let them eat. We'll dine before crushing them."

"I like your confidence, Sub Commander," commented Macario.

"If you like my confidence, Lieutenant Hicetus," boasted Ezio. "Wait till you see the size of the breakfast my staff lays out. Come, we dine then we fight and kill Legionaries."

"I can think of no better way to start my day," Macario responded as he followed the Sub Commander down the ladder.

For the Syracusan cavalryman, to be awake this early and sober was a new experience. But since he'd received the acclaim from King Hiero II and the royal proclamation honoring his family and his mother, he felt revitalized.

***

The sun had cleared the mountain tops to the east and the Legion camp seemed peaceful. It remained calm as fifteen hundred soldiers marched through the gates and spread out in lines across the plain. Following the footmen, nine hundred horsemen trotted through the gates.

Sub Commander Ezio expected to see a panicked flurry of activity. Instead, the Legionaries slept and their cookfires smoked as the flames died.

"Advance the lines," the Sub Commander shouted to his Lieutenants. Then he commented to Macario, who rode beside him. "I take it back. Their discipline is not something I admire after all."

"You'll have to change that when they're working your mines," ventured Macario.

The lines of soldiers drew close to the pickets and still there was no response from the Legion camp.

"Attack the lines," Ezio commanded.

Soldiers jumped into the trench, climbed to the sharpened picket poles, yanked them out and ran screaming into the camp. Some tents were hacked to shreds while burning embers were kicked into other tents. Despite the fire and shouting, no one came out to do battle. When the large command tent collapsed, the Sub Commander realized the Legion detachment had fled.

***

Before daylight, twenty-five Velites jogged along the trail. Their food pouches and packs left on horses so the Legionaries traveled light. Spying a campfire flickering in the distance, they slowed and angled for the flame.

Five Syracusan cavalrymen lounged around the fire, their horses tied on long leads to a lone tree. While their mounts nibbled on grass, the men gnawed on hard bread and cheese.

"We'll need to get an early start back to Echetla," the cavalry Sergeant suggested. "I want one of those Legion short swords."

"Lochias, do you think the foot soldiers will let you have any spoils?" inquired another cavalryman.

"I didn't say I was willing to fight for one," the Sergeant responded which elicited laughter from his troops. "I'll buy one from a soldier."

"That's a fine idea. And a lot safer," another offered. "After Messina, I don't want to…"

A rustling of grass around them stopped the conversation. The five Syracusans grabbed their spears and jumped to their feet. They tightened into a circle forming a ring of iron tips

247

around their cookfire. Whoever emerged for the night was about to be gutted by the cavalry patrol.

Rather than bandits, ten Velites stood up, drew back their arms and threw. Javelins flashed into the firelight and iron tips pierced the Syracusan's leather armor. The five cavalrymen fell back into the fire with shafts hanging from their chests.

"Why do they always circle the campfire," complained a skirmisher as he grabbed the boots of a dead cavalryman. Pulling the body from the ash and burning logs, he added. "It ruins the fire."

"What do you care?" inquired another of the Velites. He picked up a wedge of cheese and a heel of bread. After brushing off the dirt, he added. "We're not staying long enough to warm our hands."

"I know but I like fires," the first advised his companion as he picked up a wineskin. Waving the vino around, he proclaimed. "The smell of wood smoke, a good days hunting behind you, the stars overhead…"

"You two poets knock off the chatter and retrieve the javelins," their Optio ordered as he came out of the dark. "Lance Corporal, you and the remainder of Third Squad take the horses back to the column. The rest of you, rebuild the fire. Make it quick, we're running out of dark."

The fire was stoked as a marker for the column and, the food and drink divided among the skirmishers. As the twenty Velites jogged off, hunting for more patrols along the detachment's line of march, the five members of Third Squad mounted the horses.

"Take it slow," recommended the squad leader. "Senior Tribune Claudius wants the horses healthy."

"It's all right if we run in the dark but not the horses?" a Private grumbled.

"You aren't running now," the Lance Corporal pointed out. "You are riding. If you prefer, I can have someone lead the horse and you can run and catch up with the Optio."

"Riding is good," the Private announced.

The five mounted Velites nudged the horses forward and they headed back to the column.

***

All night, the Legion cavalrymen placed wood on campfires, paced back and forth in front of the flames before moving to the next campfire and repeating the tasks. Almost one hundred fires blazed throughout the night and the guard posts appeared to be occupied, thanks to twenty cavalrymen. Long before dawn, all of them received a visit from their officer.

"Burn your wood," the Centurion ordered each man as he arrived at their cluster of fires. "Filter out in pairs and walk your horses. Don't mount until you reach the Optio."

"How far out is the Sergeant?" asked one of the horsemen.

"Far enough so the Echetla soldiers on guard duty don't hear your clumsy cūlus stomping around," offered the officer. "Stoke your fires and get moving."

The order was repeated eighteen more times before the Centurion tossed wood on his fires and untied his mount. He guided the horse through the opening in the picket line and away from the detachment's camp. Far from the fires and abandoned tents, a voice spoke to him.

"All accounted for and on their way, sir," his Sergeant reported.

"Then we better catch up," the officer responded as he mounted. "How far is the column?"

"No idea, sir," the Optio answered as he mounted. "But we have to get over two hills before the sun catches us or all this subterfuge will be for naught."

They gently kneed their horses, letting the animals pick their way over the dark ground. With their exit, the last of the

Legionaries had left the plain of Echetla. But the detachment was a long way from the crossroads and the safety of the Legion.

Chapter 26 – Give me a Day

The sun came up on the detachment and everybody was fatigued, footsore and hungry. Except for short breaks, Senior Tribune Claudius had kept them marching ahead of the Syracuse and Echetla foot soldiers. Even the enemy cavalry maintained a respectful distance.

Once, the nine hundred horsemen had done an all-out charge. They discovered the Legion detachment could assemble in two lines of two hundred eighty-five Legionaries rapidly and effectively launch five hundred and seventy javelins before the first horse reached the shield wall.

The uninjured cavalrymen from Syracuse and Echetla settled for stalking the Legionaries. Far behind them, their soldiers were never close enough to be a threat.

***

Alerio shifted his shoulders under the infantry armor and repositioned the big shield on his back.

"Troubles, weapons instructor?" Private Vindictam inquired.

"It's not the three days of marching, Honey Cakes," Alerio replied. "It's the mismatched armor."

"It's all they had in the supply wagon," the squad leader informed him. "You could have stayed with the Senior Tribune."

"He has no use for a bodyguard and I was sick of riding," Alerio explained. "I'm an infantryman, not a Tribune."

"No offense Corporal, but you are a little crazy to refuse a mount," Vindictam offered.

The Legionaries of the Second Maniple, Sixth Century all agreed. Most were too exhausted to actually vocalize their support.

***

"We'll reach the crossroads sometime during the night," Gaius informed the line officers at one of the infrequent breaks. "The land is open so I want a Century and our cavalry dedicated to the rear in case their horsemen decide to come around us."

"Sir, could we use one of the old Legion camps?" inquired a Centurion.

"If we stop, their horses and foot soldiers would surround us," Gaius informed him. "It wouldn't take long to whittle us down to nothing. Our best hope is reaching the Legions at Syracuse. It's another four days of hard marching. But, then we'll have the numbers to face them."

"Sir. The Sixth Century will take the rear guard," Centurion Geraldus offered. "Besides, we have a secret weapon."

"Death Caller?" another officer asked.

"I prefer weapons instructor Sisera," Geraldus informed him.

"How is the Corporal holding up?" Gaius inquired. He already had an idea as he could see most of the detachment during the march. He hoped the other Centurions would pick up a little motivation from a good story.

"When we marched out of camp, the squads got mixed up and couldn't tell who was marching with them," Geraldus related. "In the daylight, they recognized Corporal Sisera and the men avoided him. I didn't know if it was his reputation as Death Caller or his training techniques. In any case, on the second morning, one of my Privates twisted an ankle. Sisera was the first to reach him. After wrapping the ankle, he took the injured man's helmet, pack, javelins and shield. The Century watched as he struggled under the load of equipment while pacing along with the limping Legionary. Finally, someone called out, 'Let's see some fancy weapons instructions now.'

A few of the Centurions chuckled as their Centuries had suffered through Corporal Sisera's training sessions.

"He could only see half a length in front of him through the equipment," Centurion Geraldus continued describing Alerio's reaction. "I can't see, I'm overloaded and a little busy. But, come over here. So, the Legionary came up behind the weapons instructor and mimicked walking with an armload. He added a waddle to the effect and the Century roared in amusement. Suddenly, Corporal Sisera spun around as if confused. His armload of equipment smacked the comedian. Apologizing and asking for forgiveness, he swung the load back and knocked the Legionary off his feet. Then while facing off to the side, Sisera tripped over the downed man and kneed him in the face. After standing, still holding all the gear, he went back to the limping man and announced, a trained Legionary is deadly. Even when he is doing his laundry."

"What does laundry have to do with this?" one of the line officers asked.

"It's a euphemism for being ready no matter what you're doing," Geraldus answered. "After that, Private Honey Cakes, excuse me, I meant Private Vindictam took the extra shield. And my best shield, Private Hermanus took the pack. Other men took the rest of the gear. Then, weapons instructor Sisera allowed the injured man to lean on his shoulder so he could keep pace. Tribune Claudius, the Legionaries of Second Maniple, Sixth Century will defend your rear, sir."

"Yes, you will and successfully, I have no doubt," Gaius exclaimed. "Gentlemen. If there are no other stories, get them on their feet and marching."

***

The sunlight faded and the detachment tightened the columns. Marching when you could see the man in front and at your side gave you comfort. In the dark, his voices or reaching out was the only way to assure yourself they were in position.

A horseman came out of the dark and approached the forward element.

"Halt!" ordered the Velites walking far ahead of the columns.

After a few words, the cavalryman was allowed to pass. Hearing the commotion and wanting to know what brought the man, Senior Tribune Claudius kneed his horse and met the rider at the head of the columns.

"Sir. There's trouble at the crossroads," the rider informed Gaius. "We sent a few scouts ahead to check the way. Tribune Claudius, there are Legion units on the road."

"That doesn't sound like trouble," Gaius ventured. "In fact, it's good news."

"No, sir. The units are the guards for the supply wagons and the mules. Plus, there are walking wounded and more critical in medical wagons," the messenger explained. "Colonel Requiem ordered them away from Syracuse. The infantry is trying to disengage and retreat. But, sir, they have been in contact for two days and nights."

Senior Tribune Gaius Claudius' stomach knotted, and his breath caught in his throat. For three and a half days his detachment had stayed ahead of a large enemy force. Now, he had to stop running and fight to protect supplies and wounded Legionaries. He lifted his face to the night air, inhaled and dropped his chin.

"Take all of our mounted Legionaries to the crossroads," Gaius ordered. "Requiem Division's old camp is closest to the crossroads. Have the wagons and mules circle up there and start rebuilding the defenses. We'll get there as soon as possible."

"Yes, sir," he replied. The cavalry officer trotted away and vanished in the dark.

Claudius twisted around and yelled.

"Centurion Geraldus, gather your NCOs and Corporal Sisera, I'm coming to see you," Gaius called out as he reined his horse about and walked the animal towards the rear of the columns.

His request was passed back through the ranks. As the horse clopped along, Gaius was troubled. His next order would send Legionaries to their death. But, he had no choice. Sliding off his horse, he stood waiting for the leaders of Sixth Century to arrive along with the detachment's weapons instructor.

***

"Legionaries, we have used misdirection, subterfuge, stealth and intestinal fortitude to stay ahead of a superior force," explained Gaius to Sixth's Century's command staff. "But we have come to the end of Minerva's blessings. We are forced to cast away military strategy and the tactics of evasion. The Legions at Syracuse are in distress. It falls to our detachment to prepare a strong point for them to fall back to while protecting their wounded. However, it will take an entire day to prepare our defenses."

"What do you need from the Sixth, sir?" asked Centurion Geraldus.

"The enemy cavalry delayed for at least a day," answered Gaius. "I need them hurt so badly, they can't ride on us in force."

"We can use a fighting square," Geraldus offered. "We'll march into their camp and fight until their numbers are reduced. Then, we'll do a fighting retreat to your position."

"Very noble, Centurion," Gaius commented knowing that most of Sixth Century would fall during the constant fighting. "Do any of the NCOs have thoughts?"

No one replied for a few heartbeats until Alerio spoke.

"Sir, a fighting square will be a stationary position allowing the cavalrymen to back away," he described. "It'll

254

require them to come to us. I don't believe they will willingly throw themselves on our gladii."

"You're recommending an assault line," ventured Gaius.

"They can circle around our line or even punch through and get behind us," Centurion Geraldus pointed out. "We'll be devastated before we do any real harm."

"Yes sir, that's correct," acknowledged Alerio. "However, in training sessions, I work the men in three-on-three drills. If we attack in widely spaced trios, we can move through their camp, turn around and come back through. It'll require less coordination and do more damage."

"If the soldiers attack from behind as you make your pass," Gaius observed. "None of the small units will live to make a second pass."

"They will if we put two shields at the threesomes' backs," explained Geraldus seeing the value in Alerio's idea. "We can field sixteen units. Seventeen if one is only three shields."

"I'd recommend fourteen five-man units," Alerio proposed. "We'll need the Centurion, Sergeant, and Corporal with Legionaries online to gather the survivors and organize the retreat. Plus, we'll need the services of fourteen Velites."

"You want to take light infantrymen into a close quarter's fight?" inquired Gaius.

"No, sir. We need them to steal twenty-eight horses while we attack," Alerio stated. "The horses are for our retreat. To carry the wounded and to drag us to your position, sir."

"Centurion Geraldus, are you in agreement with this plan?" question Gaius.

"It'll deliver maximum damage on the enemy and minimum casualties on us," Geraldus confirmed. "Senior Tribune Claudius, Sixth Century will deliver your day."

"I know and it's appreciated," Gaius acknowledged. "Go. And may the blessing of Mars be with you all."

Chapter 27 – Pull Us Out

"Whose Coalemus inspired plan was this?" Private Hermanus asked.

"That would be the slightly stupid weapons instructor on your right," Private Vindictam answered.

"Just keep it tight," Alerio urged while ignoring the insult. "And remember to take it slow so our rear can keep close."

"My rear is puckered and as closed as you can get," commented Vindictam.

"Honey Cakes, we're here to keep your rear from getting chopped off," one of the two Legionaries at their backs advised Vindictam. "Walk slow and you'll have it when we get back."

In the distance, they could see rows of fires in the cavalry camp. Centurion Geraldus' shape separated from the darkness as well as ten Legionaries crowding around him.

"We step off on the count of fifty," the line officer instructed. "Runners. One, two, three, go. Four, five, six."

Five of the Legionaries acting as runners went to the left and the others moved right. They whispered the count as they walked. By the count of twenty-five, the Sergeant on one side and the Corporal on the other plus all fourteen assault units were counting in sync. Some of the runners stayed with the NCOs and others returned to the Centurion at the center of the formation. They would act as a defensive line and gather the assault units when they returned from the attack.

"Forty-eight," Alerio counted.

"Forty-nine," Hermanus continued.

"Fifty," announced Honey Cakes. "Forward."

From the deep night, fourteen teams of Legionaries marched towards the sleeping cavalry camp. With the space between the units, not all the sentries were taken out. A cry of alarm went up, but the cavalrymen were exhausted from days of riding and sleeping on the ground. A few rose and ran to the perimeter to check on the alarm. They died first.

***

Alerio's view over the infantry shield and under the brim of his helmet showed them approaching the edge of a group of sleeping men. Hermanus shifted his line of march. Alerio on his right and Honey Cakes on his left adjusted to maintain alignment with the center shield. Then they were jabbing cavalrymen and stomping bodies as they moved through the center of the campsite.

The screams and shouts awakened the camp and men rose clutching spears and swords. But there wasn't a solid line of enemy forces to attack. Looking around, each group of defenders was limited to shapes in the dark. Some caught a glimpse of a packed Legionary unit. They ran at the Legionaries. Rear shields deflected the spears and javelins stabbed out, leaving even more Syracusan and Echetla horsemen dying on the ground.

Another campfire glowed but this one had seven Syracusans standing side by side with spears. An iron tip clipped the top of the Legion shield and scraped the side of Alerio's helmet. Catching the soldier leaning in for the jab, Corporal Sisera sliced across his face and poked the man next to him in the eye. Then, Hermanus powered into the soldiers bullying them over and knocking three of them to the ground. The five Legionaries stomped the soldiers as they moved towards the next campfire.

Cries of attack, attack roared across the cavalry camp. The survivors behind the Legionaries tracked the paths of each assault unit by the trail of dead and suffering. They followed the line of scattered campfires and attacked.

Alerio raised his head and saw only four more wood fires. Behind him, he heard the smack of swords and sharp reports of spears on the rear shields.

"Hermanus. Stay with Honey Cakes," he shouted. "We're going back. I'll take the center shield."

Hermanus' shield pushed Alerio's, allowing the Corporal to step back, spin around and shove his shield between the Legionaries in the rear.

"Forward," Alerio shouted when the two locked in with his shield.

The Echetla and Syracuse soldiers had been dashing in and striking the receding shields. After following for half the camp, they had bunched up and fallen into a rotation. They would dash in from different quadrants, beat on the rear guards and take a partial step back to safety. It made sense as a shield wall wasn't a cavalrymen's preferred type of fighting. When a third shield appeared and the assault unit suddenly came at them, the horsemen backed into each other.

"Push," Alerio ordered. They broke into the wall of stumbling bodies. "Push."

Stomping and stabbing, they moved towards another group of cavalrymen.

All the javelin tips were out of alignment and cracks appeared in the shafts. While a devastating weapon, when thrown or plunged into a foe, the iron and wood had limits. And the assault across the camp and now over halfway back caused some to shatter while putting others on the verge of breaking. Alerio kept his javelin as it let him reach out and keep the soldiers back from his shield.

Not all the cavalrymen were caught up in trying to reach the Legionaries. Some stood back, raised spears and, chucked them over their fellow riders and into the assault units.

Legionaries practiced blocking spear tips, sword blades, battle axes, and long knives with the big infantry shields. It became second nature, a reflex and, they were good at it. But a shaft angling down from a dark sky was practically invisible.

The Legionary to Alerio's left fell to his knees and his shield began to fall forward. To prevent it from opening a section of the unit's defenses, Alerio hooked the shield with his foot and jerked it and the falling man back. That's when he saw the spear shaft protruding from the Legionary's neck. The iron tip had found the narrow gap between the helmet, the shield and the top of his chest armor.

"Brace," instructed Alerio as he threw his splintering javelin. Bending down and reaching behind his shield, he pulled the dead Legionary's gladius. Then he ordered. "Advance, advance, advance."

Alerio and the other Legionary shoved with their shields and followed up with stabs. Soldiers fell and were stomped as the assault unit broke through the human wall. Behind him, Alerio heard Vindictam and Hermanus grunting as the wall of cavalrymen closed in and attacked the retreating unit. Briefly, a space opened in front of him and Alerio resisted the urge to move faster. It wasn't possible. His rear guard walked backward as they fought off spears and swords.

The moon rose and cast a weak light over the battleground that had been the bivouac location for the Syracuse and Echetla cavalry. In the illumination, groups of horsemen ran to help the wounded or raced off to check on their horses. But most ran to engage the Legionaries.

Off to his left, Alerio caught a glimpse of another Legion assault unit, then a hoard of soldiers closed in and he was blocking and stabbing as he shuffled forward.

Alerio's shield pressed solidly against the adjacent shield. Then the even pressure changed. The bottom of the Legionary's shield rested on the ground and the man stood bent over his bleeding right arm.

"Honey Cakes, wrap his arm," directed Alerio as he began to slash frantically at the cavalrymen. His attempt to do the work of two and the ferocity of the attack backed the horsemen up. With his head half turned, Alerio called back. "Hermanus, we've overstayed our welcome."

"How do we exit gracefully?" the Legionary asked between hacks and stabs with his gladius.

"He's good for now," Vindictam reported the condition of the wounded Legionary. Then he added. "He can hold his shield but not much else."

"Hermanus, when I give the word, move to the front," Alerio instructed. "Honey Cakes, shields only. Help him keep up."

"Are you going to pull a weapons instructor trick out of your helmet?" Hermanus inquired.

"Just the opposite," admitted Alerio as his borrowed gladius bashed aside an Echetla knife. "If I caught a Legionary doing this, I'd beat him to his knees."

"This should be interesting," Honey Cakes ventured.

"Hermanus, step up here," instructed Alerio as he threw his shield at the cavalrymen and drew his gladius.

With the best shield in Sixth Century and a slightly insane Corporal, brandishing two gladii, the assault unit waded into the cavalrymen.

***

Hermanus' shield smashed forward, tilted, and hooked a spear tip. From side to side, it moved in jerks, hammering cavalrymen, assaulting those to the Legionary's front and protecting Corporal Sisera's right side.

Alerio's wrists crossed briefly before the gladii sickled outward hacking spears, deflecting swords and cutting cavalry armor and flesh. Then, each gladius wove a figure eight pattern and the Echetla soldiers leaned back. While they could see the Legionaries and helmets in the moonlight and their own spears and swords, the speed of the two Legion blades caused them to blur.

An opening appeared and a cavalryman thrust his blade forward. Alerio's left wrist made small circular movements and his gladius deflected the blade but it didn't knock it aside. Rather, the Legion blade circled the sword trapping it in a cone of spinning steel. Then, Alerio tightened the cone and, with a flick of his writs, he sent the sword flying from the soldier's hand. It twirled into another cavalryman. The unarmed soldier and the man who was hit by the dislodged blade eased around the Legion assault unit and walked away from the fighting.

While the left gladius disarmed the man, Alerio's right gladius hacked downward cleaving a horseman from forehead to chin. Blood spewed and coated the men on either side. Whirling blades that seemed to be everywhere, a shield pounding at them and splatters of warm blood, proved too much for the soldiers who usually fought from horseback. Panic ran through their ranks and they scrambled over one another to escape the assault of Alerio's terrible blades and Hermanus' punishing shield.

"Honey Cakes, you still with us?" Alerio shouted as the last of the cavalrymen ran, leaving an open path from the camp to the dark field where the Centurion and blocking force waited.

"We're here, weapons instructor," Vindictam assured him. "That two-gladius-thing is one trick I don't care to learn."

"My shield is in need of repairs," Hermanus announced. He shook his left arm. The splintered edges and separated sections of his ravished infantry shield rattled and a couple pieces fell off. "Nope. I need a new shield."

Alerio raised up and looked back at the camp. Officers were organizing the cavalrymen into an attack line.

"Let's move it," suggested Alerio. "We've stirred up a hornet's nest."

They moved quickly through the night being wary of an ambush. It never came and, soon, they were stopped by Geraldus' voice.

"Fall back to the horses," the Centurion directed as he grasped Alerio by the shoulders and pointed him in the correct direction.

On either side, voices came from the dark instructing assault units where to rally. With no need for stealth, the blocking force and the NCOs shouted out searching for lost units. Some units were down to one, two or three Legionaries. The survivors were pushed towards the rally point. Some assault units, however, would never respond to the calls.

***

Alerio, Hermanus, Vindictam and the wounded Legionary, easily found the rally point. Horses stomped and Velites pulled the returning men to separate areas. One grabbed the wounded Legionary, tossed him over a horse's back and handed lines to Alerio, Hermanus, and Vindictam.

"Hang on to these," the Skirmisher directed. He gathered three more Legionaries and handed them the ends of ropes. "Fall and you'll be left behind. Hold on."

The skirmisher vaulted onto a second horse's back and nudged the animal into motion. Behind him, the lead line to the second horse tightened. At a steady gait, the horses moved out of the rally point. As they progressed, the slack was taken up in the six dangling lines. Before his rope tightened, Alerio began to jog. Soon all six Legionaries were running behind the horses. Their pace sustained by the ropes attached to the powerful animals.

Legionaries ran. They sprinted in battle, ran for exercise and competed in footraces. But the remaining members of Sixth Century were exhausted. If given the order to run, they would for a short distance before collapsing. With the tow lines pulling them, they were able to stumble along in a daze without thinking, simply moving their legs.

The hint of a sunrise went unnoticed. Focusing on their clutching hands, they ignored everything except the ropes and the burning sensation in their legs. Far from the cavalrymen's camp, the skirmisher slowed the horses giving the Legionaries some relief from the punishing pace.

***

Alerio barely noticed when the horses passed between the picket spikes and slowed to a stop. With the sun in his eyes, he walked forward almost bumping into the rear-end of the horse. Someone offered him a wineskin but his hands were frozen on the rope.

"Sixth Century," Centurion Geraldus commanded in a weak, drained voice. "Fall in at the medical tent."

"I'd rather eat," an equally tired voice called back.

"First let the Medics check you out," replied Geraldus. "Then food and rest."

Alerio released the rope and let it dangle in the dirt. Looking around, he saw the rest of Claudius detachment digging trenches or pounding stakes into the embankment. He followed Legionaries to an area near the medical wagon.

"How many made it, sir?" he asked the Centurion.

"A few dropped off the ropes," Geraldus responded. "Hopefully they can walk in before the Echetla cavalry sends out patrols."

"How many, sir?" insisted Alerio.

"Thirty-seven reached the rally point," the Centurion reported.

Sixth Century had lost almost half of the Legionaries who had participated in the assault. The loss of so many infantrymen was awful but not unexpected. The worst part, they had no idea how badly they had hurt the enemy cavalry.

The medic was surprised when he checked Alerio's hands. Except for the weapons instructor, all the left hands of the Century were rubbed raw from the ropes. Legionaries were trained to use only their right hands for the gladius so they were uniform in a shield wall. Alerio practiced gladius drills with

263

both hands and had calluses on his left as well as on his right hand.

"You are good, Death Caller," the medic pronounced. "Go get some stew, eat and rest."

A short while later, Corporal Sisera placed the empty bowl on the ground, stretched out and closed his eyes. He'd just fallen asleep when a cry went up around the Legion camp.

"Riders coming. Centuries form up," Centurions and NCOs ordered.

Legionaries dropped their mallets and shovels and ran for their armor and shields.

Alerio raised up on an elbow and glanced over the trench and the partially constructed picket spikes. Ragged columns of Syracuse and Echetla cavalrymen trotted off the road heading directly for the unfortified camp. Pushing to his feet, the Corporal staggered to the supply wagon in search of an infantry shield.

But a Centurion's call stopped him and the weapons instructor turned around and went back to his place in the shade.

"We are only responding with one heavy infantry Century and two squads of Velites," the line officer announced. "The rest of you get back to work."

The cavalrymen only numbered about one hundred. Alerio figured the rest were burying their dead. Or were dead, he hoped as he closed his eyes and went to sleep.

Chapter 28 – Fear and Superstition

Two days later as the sun rose, columns of Echetla soldiers marched from the road and spread out behind their cavalry.

"Think they'll come right for us?" Vindictam asked.

Sixth Century stood in positions spread out behind the trench. Because of their reduced numbers, another Century covered the back side of the perimeter.

"They look tired," Hermanus commented after studying the dragging feet of the soldiers. "Their officers must have pushed them pretty hard."

"Maybe they need a good long rest," Vindictam ventured as he glanced across the camp and down the road heading south. "Maybe long enough for the Legion to get here."

"Honey Cakes, they will or they won't," Hermanus advised. "And there's not a thing you can do to change our fate. Except to fight."

"I can do that," Vindictam assured his squad mate.

In the field beyond the reinforced camp, fifteen hundred soldiers from Echetla broke into units and began setting up campsites.

"I guess they need to eat first," Hermanus suggested. "What do you think, Death Caller?"

Alerio strolled up from the adjacent position. He was touring the defensives for Centurion Geraldus. This freed the line officer from the duty so he could meet with his Optio and Tesserarius to decide the best approach for reforming the squads.

"I think they should have brought more men," Alerio replied as he pointed and appeared to count the enemy soldiers. "Just as I suspected. It's no more than a three on one drill. Shouldn't be a problem."

"Weapons instructor Sisera, you are so full of merda," Hermanus observed.

"Not for several days," Alerio responded as he walked off to finish the inspection.

Five positions from Hermanus and Honey Cakes and at a different Century, Alerio spotted a familiar figure jogging from the Senior Tribune's tent. The Tribune's tent was back at Echetla so Claudius had taken Colonel Requiem's tent from the supply wagon. This was good for the Senior Tribune but didn't bode well for the Colonel.

Junior Tribune Castor Ireneus reached the sentry post and spoke to the Legionaries. As they talked, all three glanced in Alerio's direction. Then Castor spun quickly and ran back to the big tent. One of the duty Legionaries waved for Alerio.

"What's up?" Alerio inquired as he approached the position.

"The Senior Tribune wants to see you," the Legionary answered. "Or as the snot-nosed brat put it, he requests the pleasure of your company. Don't know why anyone thinks your company is a pleasure, weapons instructor."

Alerio smiled and indicated the field full of soldiers.

"Tell that to me when you don't dip your shield to the left and, let an Echetla sword gut you," Alerio pointed out. It was a fault the Legionary exhibited during a training session. "Why didn't Ireneus tell me himself? And where did he come from?"

"When we marched in, the Junior nobleman was hiding in the medical wagon," the Legionary replied. "As to why he didn't go to you directly? The little general is afraid of you, Death Caller."

"Just once I'd like him to strap on armor and join us for a training session," Alerio said as he walked towards the Senior Tribune's tent.

"I don't like the lad but, I wouldn't wish that on anyone," the Legionary mentioned to his squad mate.

"Keep your shield centered," Alerio reminded the man in a voice loud enough that he didn't have to turn his head to be heard.

***

"Sir, you wanted to see me?" Alerio asked as he performed a cross chest salute.

266

"Corporal Sisera. I'm pressing you back into bodyguard duty," Gaius announced when he looked up from a piece of parchment with a drawing of the camp and the location of the Echetla forces. "We don't have enough Legionaries for me to pull any off our defenses. And I plan to be where I'm needed when they assault us."

"Sir, it'll be my honor," Alerio assured the Senior Tribune.

"Do you think they'll come at us directly from their camp?" inquired Gaius while pointing at the crude map. "Or they could move south and come up the road? It's the smoothest approach."

"Neither, sir. They'll shift left and come at us out of the setting sun," Alerio explained. "If it's a dawn attack, they'll march around us and come from the east."

"They want the sun in our eyes," surmised Gaius. "Go eat and get what you need. I fear once again, you'll earn your rations."

"Sir, no one has harmed you yet and they won't," Alerio promised as he headed for the tent flap. "If you'll excuse me, I have some preparations to make."

Senior Tribune Gaius Claudius waved the Corporal away then stood staring at the entrance for a long time. Before Corporal Sisera came into the tent, he had a feeling of foreboding. Now, for some reason, he was optimistic.

"Why do you listen to him?" asked Castor Ireneus as he slipped in from a back entrance. "And how can you trust him? Or stand to be around him? He's frightening."

"Because he has tactical knowledge beyond most of my line officers," Gaius informed the young nobleman. Then he paused before adding. "These are dangerous times, Castor. Legionaries touched by the Gods, like Corporal Sisera, carry a blessing and a curse. We pray for the benefit while fearing the bane."

"But the Goddess Nenia?" questioned Castor shivering as if from a chill. "Death hangs on him like a custom-made cloak."

"And I will keep Nenia's beloved close," Gaius assured the young noblemen. "Let Death Caller present her with gifts as long as they're someone other than me."

***

"Centuries, prepare javelins, standby," the experienced Centurion shouted.

"Centurion, standing by," four hundred heavy infantrymen responded as they stomped and lifted javelins to their shoulders.

Another one hundred and thirty mixed light and heavy infantrymen were spread around the other side of the camp. They observed Syracuse and Echetla riders rush forward as if the horsemen were going to ride their horse onto the picket stakes. No one believed they would sacrifice their mounts. It proved true when they turned and rode away. On the heavily defended side, the Legionaries squinted at the Echetla soldiers marching out of the bright afternoon sun.

The older Centurion, acting as the field commander, watched the Senior Tribune waiting for a signal. Gaius had his hands cupped over his eyes trying to block the strong rays. He stood so still with his eyelids pressed close together, the line officer feared the Tribune had fallen asleep.

A flight of spears, unseen as the sun ate the shape of the shafts, descended suddenly from the sky. Two infantrymen staggered back with spear tips in their legs.

"You want to move that thing," demanded Gaius. "You're blocking my view."

"Sorry, sir," Alerio replied as he lowered his shield. He had thrown it up to protect the Tribune. With it down, Claudius was exposed to enemy spears. "I'd feel better if you'd step back from the trench."

"Not yet," Gaius said brushing off the advice.

Alerio, Gaius and the Centurion stood on the embankment. The Legionaries waited in ranks behind them marveling at the stupidity of their commander. Secretly, Alerio agreed.

"Now Centurion," Gaius announced as he spun, walked off the mound and strolled between the ranks. With the shield held high and angled to deflect a spear, Alerio followed. "The spears were from a small group that crawled close to us. Sub Commander Ezio wanted us to waste our first volley."

"Centuries, throw," the Centurion shouted.

Four hundred javelins soared up and arched down into the amassed soldiers who appeared on the far side of the trench.

"Third and second maniples to the mound," command the Centurion. "First throw."

Soldiers poured into the trench and their forward elements attempted to bash aside the stakes. But javelins poked down, stabbing them and only a few picket stakes were dislodged. Behind the assault lines, javelins fell among the soldiers waiting to move forward.

Spears thumped against the infantry shields and fell harmlessly into the trench causing soldiers to trip over the free shafts. The center was under control. Then, Sub Commander Ezio sent another force into the fray.

A group of soldiers appeared from the back of his formation. Sprinting to another section of the trench, twenty of them bounded through the trench, shoved a hole in the stakes and burst into the Legion camp.

"First maniple, plug that hole," the Centurion shouted seeing a new surge by the soldiers rushing forward.

Sergeants and Corporals fell back from the defensive line and moved to engage the ones that made it through the breach. The NCOs smashed into the soldiers. Most turned to face the Legionaries. But four seemed to have a different mission. They headed for the Senior Tribune.

"Stay behind me, sir," instructed Alerio as he swung his shield from side to side.

The movement confused the soldiers. They jogged left then right trying to decide how to get around the obstacle. When the shield cocked to the right, they knew the Legionary defending the detachment's commander was out of place. They had watched and knew Legionaries always fought with swords in their right hands.

Alerio reached behind his shield, switched it to his right arm and extracted a cutoff javelin head. In one motion, he sent the iron tip twirling at the nearest soldier. The heavy object flipped over just before the weight drove the point into the soldier's neck. A second one flew and the next soldier fell as the iron tip penetrated his thigh.

Corporal Sisera drew his gladius with his left hand and ran at the last two soldiers. They moved in, shoulder to shoulder, preparing to bull the lone Legionary out of the way. Just before the three collided, Alerio dropped to a knee and pivoted to his left. Both soldiers had their shoulders down for the impact. They bounced off the shield and stumbled to the side.

Alerio jumped up, ran towards them and hacked the first one in the back of his neck. The second spun, swinging his sword at the Legionary's head. But Alerio went to a full squat while driving the tip of his gladius up into the man's groin.

Gaius watched as his bodyguard rose to full height and calmly walked to the soldier with the wounded thigh. The man looked up, possibly expecting mercy. But Death Caller plunged the gladius into the man's eye socket splitting his face open and killing him instantly.

"Blessed of Nenia," Gaius whispered.

"Senior Tribune, are you injured?" Alerio asked when he saw the blood drain from Gaius' face.

"I'm unhurt," Gaius assured his bodyguard. Recovering quickly, he informed the Corporal. "I'm moving to the defensive line."

"Yes, sir," Alerio acknowledged falling in beside the Senior Tribune.

The Centurion, acting as the field commander, glanced back. Tribune Gaius Claudius strolled towards the ranks with Corporal Sisera a step behind him.

But the bodyguard resembled something mystical. Almost as if he was a mirrored reflection of a victorious warrior. The blood splattered shield on his right arm and not his left. The gladius, dripping blood onto the ground, clutched in his left hand, not his right. And, as Corporal Sisera shadowed the Senior Tribune, his eyes moved rapidly as if searching for another life to take.

"Death Caller," the Centurion whispered.

The sun began to sink behind the mountains allowing the Legionaries to select targets for their javelins. When the Sub Commander lost two of his best Lieutenants, he called for a withdrawal. Horns sounded and the soldiers rushed away from the reinforced camp.

Cries of wounded soldiers and Legionaries filled the void left when the clash of spears and javelins against shields faded. Medics rushed forward to treat the living.

***

"Sixty-seven Legionaries and half our Optios and Tesserarii are dead or severely wounded," reported the experienced Centurion. "Sir, if they come at us in the morning, we may not be able to repel them."

"We don't have much choice," Gaius replied. "I'll be around to see to the men shortly."

"Very good, sir," the Centurion acknowledged before he pushed through the tent flap.

"Corporal Sisera. Any tactics left in your purse?" Gaius asked.

"No sir," Alerio admitted. "The Centurion and Sergeant who trained me said sometimes you can't run so resign yourself to the fates and go down fighting."

"Then that's what we'll do in the morning," Gaius said as he stood from a camp chair. "Let's go and motivate the Legionaries."

After making a round of the hospital tent, and each Century's area, Gaius fell into bed and suffered a tortured nights sleep. His bodyguard dozed in the corner of his sleeping tent.

***

Before dawn, Gaius Claudius was up and walking the perimeter. Talking and encouraging the men on sentry duty, he lifted spirits and offered encouragement. Always close behind, Alerio watched for any signs of discontent from the Legionaries. They all knew the Echetla soldiers outnumbered the detachment and one breach could lead to a total defeat. At a time like this, men's minds turned to self-preservation and a quick way to force negotiations was to assassinate the Commander.

A runner came through the camp asking guards where he could find the Senior Tribune. After checking with a few sentries and getting directions, he raced to the Gaius.

"Sir. The Echetla are moving around the camp," the skirmisher reported.

"An attack from the east," commented Gaius. "It was expected. Thank your Centurion for the information. I have no orders, dismissed."

The light infantryman vanished in the dark and Gaius continued his rounds of the guard positions.

***

The sky showed a line of pink over the eastern mountains. On Sicilia, the land lay in darkness and the morning was still.

272

Beyond the picket stakes, the trench and the rough grasslands beyond, Echetla soldiers stretched out waiting for the call to rise and attack.

Sub Commander Ezio had the bulk of his forces staged to attack from the east. In response to the information from his cavalry, he placed a second force on the west. At daybreak, his soldiers would crush the Legion detachment from two sides.

While dining on a big breakfast, the Sub Commander realized he no longer cared about taking Tribune Gaius Claudius prisoner. Macario Hicetus would get a refund and Ezio would get the pleasure of stabbing Claudius in the heart. This thought filled his mind as he ate his large breakfast.

Light crept over the mountaintop and cast rays on the Legion tents. Ezio peered at the taunt goatskin in the distance of the commander's tent.

"Sound the attack," he ordered as he mounted his horse. "And send a runner to the other force. Have them wait for my word."

Over nine hundred soldiers stood, picked up their shields and spears and began walking towards the Legion camp.

***

"They're staged to the east with a smaller force to the west, Colonel," the light infantryman reported.

"Senior Centurion Valerian. Get them up and moving. Now that we know where they are," Pericles Requiem directed. "Send the cavalry and Velites to the west as a delaying force until our heavy infantry finishes with the main force of soldiers."

"Yes, sir," the Senior Centurion replied as he turned to his runners.

By the time the orange ball of the sun was halfway over the mountains, two thousand heavy infantrymen were running from the depressions south of the reinforced camp. Legionaries ran and by the time the Centuries reached the Echetla soldiers, they were warmed up and ready for a fight.

Chapter 29 – A Promise Fulfilled

Claudius' detachment had no rest. Sub Commander Ezio's forces were in full retreat and Gaius expected the Legions to pursue the soldiers or rest for a few days. Neither happened.

Appease Clodus Caudex's term as Consul and General was drawing to a close. Before he returned to his Senate seat, Caudex wanted to make a final report on the Sicilia operation. And, he was determined to do it as a Co-Consul of the Republic.

Unfortunately, the acclaim he expected for freeing Messina by defeating two armies, vanished at the walls of Syracuse. Too much wall and too many Syracusan troops handed him an ugly defeat and swept away his popularity. His best hope to leave his mark on history was a powerful speech in front of the Senate.

The survivors of Nicephrus and Requiem Divisions along with the men under Gaius Claudius were on the road as soon as the Sub Commander fled. By nightfall, they camped north of Catania. Days later, the Legions limped into Messina to find twenty Republic warships patrolling the Strait and freighters in the harbor. Caudex Legions were on their way from Messina to the Capital where they would be discharged.

***

"Corporal Sisera. I understand why you didn't want to stay with the Southern Legion. But there are other options. Say the word and I can get you a position at any Legion you want," offered Centurion Sanctus Carnifex as he shifted his pack. "Colonel Nicephrus is taking his Division north. They could use you."

"Centurion, there is nothing wrong with the Southern Legion," replied Alerio as the walls of the Capital came into view. "I have something to attend to in the Capital. Then I'm going to my father's farm and help with the harvest."

"Rumor has it the top candidates for Co-Consul this coming year have all made speeches about going back to Silica," Carnifex suggested. "They'll be putting together Legions. If you need a recommendation, let me know."

"What about you, sir?" inquired Alerio. "What will you do?"

"What I always do between Legions," the Centurion responded. "I'm going to my Villa and tend my gardens. Rich earth, no one second guessing my decisions and, no ignorant Legionaries questioning why I'm so hard on them."

"I certainly understand the last part," commented Alerio.

***

The Priestesses went about their rituals quietly. So silent were the devotees, that their footsteps and voices didn't echo around the sanctuary. Braziers burned but, the light barely reached the recesses of the Temple. The flickering flames only served in making the shadows appear to twist and sway. Visitors coming to worship and asking for the Lady's services were usually exhausted and searching for answers. Loved ones lay at home sick, injured or old. No one joyfully or enthusiastically entered the Temple of Nenia. The wealthy paid ancylites to come to their Villas and sing the Naenia, thusly, avoiding the Temple. Those entering, were of humbler means. Despite their status, they all asked for death to take a stricken acquaintance.

Hobnailed boots on the granite floor sent echoes around the Cella with each stride. Priestesses lifted their heads or turned towards the entrance to see who was disturbing the sedate atmosphere. Down the aisle, between the columns, marched a Legionary. His armor polished, a gladius hanging at his side and a helmet tucked under his arm. Halfway through the Temple, he stopped and stared at the statue of Nenia and the marble altar.

"Have you come to request a service and a blessing from Dea Nenia?" a Priestess inquired as she approached the scarred military veteran. "She is always available."

"I'm too familiar with Dea Nenia," Corporal Alerio Sisera informed the young woman. "Where I've just come from, the Goddess was very busy."

From a back room, a choir of female voices began the Naenia. The tones blended creating a warm melody until one voice rose above the others. Everyone within earshot shivered from the sweet notes and perfect pitch as she sang for the Goddess of Death.

The Legionary reached under his armor and pulled out a leather-wrapped package. Taking the Priestess' hand, he gently placed the package in her palm. Then, he about-faced and marched away.

What the Priestess couldn't see was the smile on the Legionary's face or hear him humming the dirge.

She peeled back the leather to find three mini bars of gold. By the time she looked up, the Legionary was gone.

The End

Note from J. Clifton Slater

Thank you for reading Clay Warrior Stories. Fortune Reigns is the 6th book in the series. During Alerio's journey, I have written 18 songs or chants. Each was designed to explore and represent segments of life in the mid Republic era. From dirges and tavern songs, to rowing and military chants, the verses tell tales of things people in that period took as everyday occurrences.

Some readers have said they enjoy the songs and chants. Others read through them quickly so they could get on with the main story. And, a few have chastised me for bad poetry. I thank you all for letting me know your thoughts. Please remember, Alerio likes to sing while he fights.

A few readers have commented on the amount of research I do for these books and how true they are to the times. Hopefully, the research is buried in the narrative. These are adventure books first and historical fiction second. But, I do value the recognition of my efforts.

If you have comments please do not hesitate to e-mail me. Thank you for making Clay Warrior Stories a successful series. Are my readers the best? Ita Vero!

Sincerely,

J. Clifton Slater

To sign up for my newsletter and to read blogs on ancient Rome go to my website.

www.JCliftonSlater.com

If you have comments, please contact me on email.

E-mail: GalacticCouncilRealm@gmail.com

I write military adventure both future and ancient.
Books by J. Clifton Slater

Historical Adventure – 'Clay Warrior Stories' series
#1 Clay Legionary   #2 Spilled Blood
#3 Bloody Water   #4 Reluctant Siege
#5 Brutal Diplomacy   #6 Fortune Reigns
#7 Fatal Obligation   #8 Infinite Courage
#9 Deceptive Valor   #10 Neptune's Fury
#11 Unjust Sacrifice   #12 Muted Implications
#13 Death Caller   #14 Rome's Tribune

Fantasy – 'Terror & Talons' series
#1 Hawks of the Sorcerer Queen
#2 Magic and the Rage of Intent

Military Science Fiction – 'Call Sign Warlock' series
#1 Op File Revenge   #2 Op File Treason
#3 Op File Sanction

Military Science Fiction – 'Galactic Council Realm' series
#1 On Station   #2 On Duty
#3 On Guard   #4 On Point